REQUIEM OF REVENGE

Richard Kurti

SAPERE
BOOKS

REQUIEM OF
REVENGE

Published by Sapere Books.

24 Trafalgar Road, Ilkley, LS29 8HH

saperebooks.com

ISBN: 978-0-85495-243-4

"But what will not ambition and revenge descend to?"
Paradise Lost

ACKNOWLEDGEMENTS

Many thanks to my agent, Roger Field, as well as Amy Durant and the entire team at Sapere Books for their wisdom and creativity. Thanks also to Julia Kreitman for being such an enthusiastic early reader.

Huge thanks to Karen and Hugo for their love and support — it's never easy living with a writer, but somehow they manage it.

And special thanks go to The Society of Authors and the Authors' Foundation. During the deepest days of lockdown, they awarded me a grant to help research this book, which was a precious lifeline in dark times.

PROLOGUE

Bath, England, 1761

It was the stench that first aroused suspicion.

Everyone was used to the pungent faecal aroma at street level in the city of Bath, because although it had been designed as a beacon of culture and elegance, no-one had solved the problem of how to dispose of the vast quantities of excrement. These had increased when the city had become the most fashionable spa resort in England. The only solution was to build upwards. The best townhouses, where the most wealthy and beautiful spent the season, had four floors, so that the genteel classes could lounge in the upper stories, windows open to the stench-free breeze blowing in from the Mendip Hills.

It was therefore strange when one of the most esteemed residents of Bennett Street reported an acrid smell coming through the wall of their upper drawing room. They suspected their neighbours, in number twenty, of being guilty of less than dignified behaviour.

The authorities were alerted.

That evening, a sergeant hammered on the basement door with his fist until a nervous scullery maid opened up.

"This ain't right," she said. "The mistress'll be furious."

"Official business." The sergeant flourished a letter bearing the town clerk's stamp. "No-one else in? Just you?"

"Yes, sir."

"Wait in the kitchens till I'm finished."

The sergeant began his exploration, trying to detect any unusually strong aromas.

In the ground floor dining room were two crockery cabinets, a few old paintings on the walls, an expensive table with gold inlay and matching chairs stretching the length of the room. The sergeant ran his finger across the table — not a speck of dust. This room was clean; the smell wasn't coming from here.

He crossed the hall and entered the drawing room. Again, there was nothing unusual, just the normal superior furniture sitting on a thick, flower-patterned rug.

The sergeant was getting impatient. The Night Watch's business was murder and thievery, not investigating smells, but following orders was how he had achieved his rank, and he wasn't going to change the habit of a lifetime.

He made his way up the stairs to the first floor with its morning-room overlooking the walled garden, and a library at the front. He took a deep breath — the smell of old leather bindings mingled with a faint background miasma drifting in through the sash windows. Again, nothing unusual.

He climbed the next flight of stairs to the bedrooms and dressing rooms … and it was here that the sergeant first heard a muffled groan of anguish.

It sounded animal-like rather than human, and it wasn't coming from this floor, but from above. This was puzzling, because there were no more stairs.

The sergeant scratched his stubbly chin and looked around the landing.

"Hmm…"

He wasn't imagining it; something was definitely above him.

He slid open one of the sash windows and peered into the gloom, where he could just make out the shape of a small window in the tiled roof; there seemed to be another room in

10

the attic. Mystery awoke the bloodhound in the sergeant, and he took out his dagger and started tapping gently on each of the landing walls.

Just as he'd suspected, there was a false wall. The sergeant pushed and prodded until a beautifully crafted panel opened to reveal a narrow service staircase leading up to the roof space.

He peered into the darkness and strained his ears.

"Here…"

It was a man's voice, broken and hoarse, too weak to be a threat, but the sergeant kept his dagger drawn just in case. Slowly he started to pick his way up the stairs.

The moment his bulky foot pressed on a loose step, the house betrayed him with a creak.

The disembodied voice knew someone was coming and took on a desperate urgency. "Help! Please!"

As the sergeant reached the top step the smell hit him, pungent and obscene — filth and rotting flesh. Three doors faced him. He tried each one, but all were locked.

"Mercy … please…" the voice gasped as it heard the door handles rattle.

The sergeant pressed his ear to each of the doors, trying to locate the source of the pitiful moans. Then he stepped back, raised his foot, and kicked. The door juddered on its frame. He aimed the heel of his boot at the brass handle and kicked repeatedly, denting it out of shape until the lock cracked the wood apart and the door flew open.

Immediately the full horror of the stench billowed out. The sergeant recoiled and pressed a scarf to his face, covering his nose and mouth. With his other hand, he held up an oil lamp.

A naked wretch was slumped on the floor, an iron collar chafing round his neck as it dragged on a heavy chain that was bolted to the far wall. His body was filthy, his hair was matted, excrement was smeared across the floor and his sightless eyes were caked in puss.

"Help me!" he cried. A bony hand reached out, flailing in the air, trying to find salvation. "She blinded me! She is the Devil!"

Gasping for breath, the sergeant stumbled backwards and half-fell down the steep steps, the creature's anguished howls ringing in his ears.

A quarter of a mile down the hill, Handel's glorious music soared into the delicate tracery of Bath Abbey's gothic vaulting.

As patron of the concert, Lady Arabella Taylor had her pick of the seats. She chose the front row — all of it, so that she could sit alone and undisturbed by the chattering classes. She had taken off her embroidered silk shoes with their pinched toes and flared heels, and placed them on the pew next to her, so that no discomfort would distract her.

Arabella understood the ins and outs of the elaborate dance of Bath etiquette, but the truth was, she didn't care about people. She was indifferent to their petty desires and ambitions. All that mattered to her was music.

Perhaps that was why she didn't even flinch as the doors to the abbey burst open and the Night Watch thundered in like avenging angels. While the rest of the audience watched in consternation as armed men strode up the nave, swords clanking, Arabella remained focussed on the concert in front of her.

Bravely the choir and orchestra tried to keep going, but in a few moments Handel's psalm setting had crumbled, leaving the conductor flailing.

"There! On the front row."

The Watch surrounded Arabella, weapons drawn, yet she remained still and silent. There were no protestations of innocence, no struggles, no expressions of outrage. Quietly she put on her shoes and stood up. Never has anyone been arrested with such poise.

Even as she was escorted from the abbey, the city's glitterati staring at her with a mixture of shock and scorn, Arabella held onto her dignity.

It was as if she had known all along that this moment was coming.

PART ONE: DOCTOR HARVEY

ONE

This is the best moment of the day.

I get out of my stiff doctor's suit and put on my favourite silk banyan. With a steaming honey and lemon toddy, I retire to my private study where the world of medicine gives way to literature. I pick up a slender volume of Indian love poetry, but just as I leaf through the pages to find my place, there is a loud hammering at the front door. "Dear God. What now?"

"Open up! Open up!" The fists hammer urgently.

"Don't worry, sir," my assistant, Joseph, calls from the hallway. "I will attend to it."

"Unless they're dying, tell them to come back in the morning," I reply.

"Very good, Doctor Harvey." I hear him run to the front door to fend off the needy patient.

Joseph has been with me for nearly two years and has proved to be a most capable young assistant. Yet tonight, even he is outwitted.

There are raised voices as an argument breaks out. Heavy footsteps approach, then the study door flies open and bangs back against the wall as three men of the Night Watch barge in. The sergeant is cradling a skeletal wreck of a man in his arms. "You have to save him!"

"What on earth's happened?" I put down my poetry and stare at the crumpled figure.

"Murder. Attempted murder." The sergeant crouches to lay the victim down, but even from here I can smell the filth on him.

"No! Not on the rug!" I instruct. "Joseph, take them to the consulting room."

Joseph leads them through the house and supervises as the man is laid on a surgical table. Immediately, I can see the patient is caught in some kind of delirium, moaning incoherently, his arms reaching out wildly. He is confused and disorientated.

"Clean him up, Joseph. And try to calm him down."

"Yes, Doctor Harvey."

As I put on my medical overcoat, I take the sergeant aside. "Exactly what happened here?"

"He was being held prisoner, sir. In his own house. It looks like his wife tortured him."

"Here? In Bath?" I can barely believe what I'm hearing.

"She's under arrest. That's all I know."

"And who is he?"

"Chevalier John Taylor."

"Unusual title. Is he French?"

"From the way he's swearing, I'm guessing not."

"Doctor Harvey," Joseph calls over from the table, "you need to see this."

I do up my last buttons, thank the sergeant and ask him to wait in the kitchen. As I return to the table, I see that where Joseph has cleaned off the filth, he has revealed a torso covered in angry bruises and vivid crimson wheals. It is as if the chevalier has been savagely whipped and beaten over many months. "Dear God," I whisper.

"He has abandoned me! God has sent me to Hell!" The chevalier grips my arm and pulls me close. "Who are you?" His hand feels my face, his filthy nails catching my skin.

"My name is Doctor Erasmus Harvey."

"How very pretentious."

I exchange an uneasy look with Joseph. It is never good to get into an argument with patients. "It was not of my choosing," I reply. "You would have to take the matter up with my parents."

"Is it done? Is she in prison?" he demands.

"Your ordeal is over now, sir."

"She is insane, you know! A madwoman! Deluded!"

"Chevalier, you need to rest."

"I need to know she is finished! That she will never torment me again! Never!" A cry of fear and hysteria erupts as he squirms on the table.

I hold him tight and nod to Joseph, who reaches for a bottle of brandy and manages to get a few sips down the chevalier's throat. Despite his strength and youth, Joseph has a tender touch that has always impressed me.

Thankfully, the brandy starts to soothe the chevalier.

"We are going to make everything right, sir. I promise."

"How can you undo the evil she has done?" He reaches up and touches his eyes, red and inflamed. "She has robbed me of my sight! That most precious gift."

I beckon to Joseph to pass a candle, and move it back and forth in front of the chevalier's eyes, trying to detect a flicker of reaction. "Can you see the flame?"

"Are you deaf?" The chevalier lashes out, knocking the candle from my hands. "Everything is black! I am locked in the darkness of Hell!"

"Please, Chevalier, I am trying to help, but I can do nothing unless you remain calm."

"Do not lecture me about medicine." There is a flash of venom in his voice. "I was a genius. You are nothing but a provincial quack."

Immediately Joseph gets some more brandy down the chevalier's throat.

In the calm that follows, I apply dressings to the wounds around the man's neck and ankles where he has been chained. At a guess, I would say he is in his mid-sixties and is malnourished, but even though he has been beaten, no bones are broken. There are no indications of disease or infection; all things considered, the chevalier has survived his ordeal in reasonable condition.

Suddenly his hand reaches up to his chest and he starts to scratch his skin ferociously, as if trying to tear it off. I hold his wrists to stop him. "How long were you held captive, Chevalier?"

"An eternity," he moans. "An eternity." Overcome with self-pity, he starts to sob.

"Why did this happen, sir? Do you have any notion?"

"Because she is the Devil!" His sorrow turns to anger in a split second. "She is the Devil incarnate!"

His hands break free and attack his own skin again, scratching until he draws blood.

I realise that it's a sign of addiction. "This is how she kept him quiet, Joseph. She gave him sedatives to stop him crying out. Laudanum."

Immediately the chevalier's whole demeanour changes. "Give me some. Give it!"

"Laudanum is not the answer, sir."

"Give me the damned laudanum, man!"

Joseph is shocked at the aggression, but I reassure him. "It's the addiction. Just give him a few drops."

Joseph takes a bottle from one of my tall mahogany cabinets, and the chevalier opens his mouth like a starving bird, desperate for relief.

Immediately his body relaxes, his fingers stop tearing at his skin, a pathetic smile plays on his lips and he falls into an incoherent stupor.

"Did you ever encounter such a thing, Doctor Harvey?" Joseph whispers, his face pale with shock.

"Never in all my life."

"God help him."

It is the first time Joseph has seen such depravity; I daresay it won't be the last. It is one thing to see a man tortured in a Shakespeare play, but quite another to witness it in real life.

Suddenly the door to the consulting room is thrown open. "Come along now, Harvey. That's enough fussing," an imperious voice declares.

I turn and see a tall, slim aristocrat standing in the doorway: the marquess of Lansdowne. Although we have never been formally introduced, I know that his word is the ultimate authority in this city. Everyone knows that.

"My lord, I just need to —"

"Put him down! Come with me."

Lansdowne walks away, and I follow like an obedient puppy. As he ushers me through the door, I see that two more aristocrats have made themselves at home in my private study.

"Take a seat, Harvey," Lansdowne smiles. "Do you know Viscount Melville?" He turns to a sharp-faced man whose forehead is too big for his chin. "And the earl of Stratford?" To his left sits a stocky man with small black eyes. Both men seem tetchy at having to share a sofa that is a little too small for them.

"My lords." I take a seat as directed. Although it is humiliating to be treated like this in my own house, I know better than to protest. These men may not be the city's elected officials, but they are the power *behind* those men, the great landowners who have held this country since the Norman Conquest and control it still.

But why are they here? The great families have their own physicians and would never deign to consult a doctor like myself, who cannot boast a knighthood.

"Will he live?" Viscount Melville enquires.

"I believe so, my lord."

"Good." Lansdowne seems to breathe a little easier. "That means we can contain it."

"Do you have any notion why this tragedy has happened?" I ask.

"Lady Arabella Taylor is the cruellest woman I have ever met," Melville says coldly. "Simple as that."

"But has she given a reason?"

"She's not being very co-operative," Lansdowne prevaricates.

"Then you've questioned her in gaol?"

"We tried. But…" Lansdowne reaches for the square decanter and starts to pour three glasses of my finest port.

"What exactly has she said?" I ask. "People don't do this sort of thing for no reason."

"She's refusing to explain." Lansdowne hands two glasses to his friends. "She says everything will come out in court."

"And that is the problem," the earl of Stratford says darkly.

"Then it seems we will have to be patient," I reply. "Let British justice run its course."

Melville glares at me. "We're not interested in 'justice', and we don't care about her motives. All that matters is that she remains silent, so that Bath is not embroiled in an ugly scandal."

I shake my head. "A scandal like this cannot just be swept into a dark corner."

"That's where *you* come in, Harvey." Lansdowne opens his arms in a magnanimous appeal. "You need to think about what is good for this city. Bigger picture, and all that."

"She has the right to a fair trial, my lord."

"Technically, yes."

"And if you deny that right to an aristocrat, you will set a dangerous precedent."

"We really don't want the scandal," the earl of Stratford insists.

"I'm not sure that can be avoided, my lord. I mean, she tortured and imprisoned her own husband."

They glare at me silently, like three birds of prey perched on my giltwood salon furniture.

"Fact is, Harvey, we've been keeping an eye on you," Lansdowne says with a charming smile. "And we rather like what we see."

"I try to keep abreast of the latest developments in medicine, my lord."

"Not that business. We're not interested in your potions." Lansdowne waves his hand dismissively. "Put simply, Lady Arabella wants to go to trial, but we want her committed straight to an asylum. We want you to declare her insane. Then the whole problem will go away. No scandal. Justice served, as only a madwoman would do such a dreadful thing to her husband. Surely you would agree?"

I struggle to hide my disbelief. "My lords, I cannot do that without a compelling cause."

"Cannot? Or will not?" Stratford demands.

"Both. Absolutely."

"No need to get upset," Lansdowne warns.

"It would be unethical. And a breach of professional trust."

"Harvey, I don't think you understand." Melville helps himself to another glass of port. "We need to protect what is ours, and we cannot tolerate this city being corrupted by scandal."

"Fact is, this all comes down to decency." Lansdowne picks up the decanter and refills his glass as well. "Any misdemeanour that remains behind closed doors is not a problem."

"The syphilitic sufferings of betrayed wives are acceptable. Likewise the petty perversions of their husbands," Stratford elaborates, "as long as they remain private."

"Alcohol addiction is tolerated so long as it doesn't bring chaos to the family," Melville concurs.

"Same goes for bastard children, provided they are sent away within the first month," Lansdowne offers as his own example. "So, you see, Harvey, we are reasonable men, modern men, with the city's best interests at heart. But this chevalier and his wife will break the cardinal rule if they go public."

"It lets the side down," Melville mutters.

"Be that as it may, my lords, it is not my fault, and there is no reason to compromise my professional integrity."

Stratford scowls at me. "You need to show more respect, Doctor Harvey."

"I respect my professional oath, my lord."

"In any case, it doesn't really matter what you think. We have made up our minds," Lansdowne pronounces. "You're perfect for this because honour isn't so important to a man like you."

"A man like me?" For a moment I am bewildered.

"Well, you know…" He looks me up and down.

In my guts I feel a flash of anger, old and familiar, but I have long since learnt how to channel it away. So I say nothing.

"Bath has been good to you," Stratford observes pointedly. "We have been pleased to accept you and see you prosper. But it doesn't have to be that way. You could so easily be overlooked, Harvey."

They sip their drinks in silence; no-one thinks to offer me a glass of my own port. That would never occur to men like them.

"So we're all agreed," Lansdowne says cheerily. "You are to go to the prison, examine this Arabella woman, and pronounce her insane. There will be no trial, no fuss and no scandal."

"Your loyalty to us will be duly noted," Melville adds.

TWO

I walk along the cold, dank corridors of the prison to a chorus of jeers and swearing from rowdy pickpockets and diseased streetwalkers who have been arrested over the past week. The city authorities have a policy of pressing harsh punishments on these undesirables in the hope of driving the underclass away from Bath's more elegant streets. Most here will be transported on the prison ships, and if they survive the journey, they will die broken on some harsh land in the colonies. Yet still they come to Bath and try their luck.

The constable leads me up a small flight of steps, and suddenly we are in a quieter part of the prison where the stench is not so rank; Arabella has obviously bribed her way to a half-decent cell.

"She's at the far end," the constable says.

I find myself gripping my leather bag a little tighter; whatever I am about to confront, I feel confident that my neatly ordered instruments will be able to cope.

Finally we arrive at a gnarled oak door that is reinforced with iron straps. The constable unlocks the bolts, then hesitates. "Is it true, doctor? Did she really blind her husband?"

"That's precisely what I am here to find out."

"You want me to stay with you in the cell?"

"I don't think that'll be necessary. But thank you. I'll call when I'm done."

"Very good." He swings open the door and I step inside.

The prison cell is surprisingly large, about the size of my kitchen. A single barred window high up in one of the rough walls casts a pool of light onto the dirty stone floor. But the extra space has also given the prison mould a larger canvas on which to grow, and the musty smell catches in the back of my throat.

Lady Arabella Taylor sits on a simple wooden bench in the middle of the space, her back to the door. She doesn't move or turn her head. She is surprisingly slender, with dark hair dressed down her back. There is nothing threatening about her, yet her silence makes me feel politely unwelcome.

"My name is Doctor Harvey. I am a physician here in Bath. You may have heard of me?"

"I don't believe I have."

Softly spoken, with every syllable precise. There is not a shred of humility in her voice.

"Well," I say, clearing my throat, "the authorities have asked me to make an assessment."

"As you wish."

Arabella turns to face me, and I am struck by how much younger she is than her husband; she is in her late thirties, and has dark eyes, a beautifully carved chin and a clear complexion. The chevalier must have thought himself most fortunate … until she blinded him.

She says nothing as I admire her, then after an uncomfortably long silence, she asks, "Have you seen enough? Have you 'assessed'?"

"Do you understand the gravity of your situation?"

She shrugs. "I wonder, is it to be another hot day outside?"

"Are you seriously intending to discuss the weather?"

"I was just trying to be polite."

"What type of woman are you?"

Arabella Taylor cocks her head as she contemplates the question. "At this moment, I am a contented woman."

"Is it not evil enough that you tortured and humiliated your husband? And now you insist on showing not a shred of remorse!"

"All will be revealed at the trial, Doctor Harvey. Do not judge until you have heard the evidence."

"There can be no defence for what you have done."

"That is for the court to decide."

"What man deserves to be blinded?" My voice trembles with indignation. "Or perhaps you intend to buy your way to freedom with the aid of silver-tongued lawyers?"

"I will walk out of here, of that you can be sure. But it won't cost me a farthing."

I step closer and study her inscrutable face. "You are utterly deluded. The evidence against you is overwhelming."

"What I have done is merely justice in action."

"We are not in the Old Testament now. England is a civilised nation."

"Just because we have fine silks and elegant townhouses, it doesn't mean the Devil has vanished. He has merely found new places to hide."

"He? It seems to me that the Devil may well be a 'she'."

Arabella smiles to herself. "I thought my husband might try that one."

"You sit here and laugh? After what you have done?"

"If you had been in my position, Doctor Harvey, you would have blinded him as well."

"No. I have devoted my life to healing. A code of ethics governs everything I do."

"I am banking on it. Just as I expect British justice to live up to its reputation. My testimony will shake London society and reveal the chattering classes for the fools they are."

Suddenly, my patience drains away. "I am afraid you will be disappointed. There will be no trial."

For the first time there is a flicker of vulnerability in her eyes. "Why?"

"I shall pronounce you insane, and you will be committed straight to an asylum, never to be heard of again."

Now I have her attention.

Arabella presses the tips of her fingers to her eyebrows, partially obscuring her face. "I must have my day in court."

"It's too late. The authorities are moving against you."

"No-one can judge me until they know the truth. No-one." Her voice seems calm, but there is rage simmering beneath her words.

"Then talk to me, Arabella. Explain what you have done."

She lowers her hands and studies me. "I doubt you have the strength to listen."

"I have no fear of words. I am an educated man."

"Which only makes you more vulnerable."

"To you?"

"Once you know the truth, Doctor Harvey, you will open that prison door yourself and let me out. And that will bring ruin on your neatly constructed life."

I laugh at the absurdity of her warning, but she remains serious.

"My husband made the mistake of laughing at me," she says quietly.

"I am done with this." For my own sanity I must get away from her, but as I turn to leave, she reaches out and catches my arm.

"Very well, Doctor Harvey, I *dare* you to listen to my confession."

"If you want to confess, call a priest."

"If God had not abandoned us, perhaps I would." She stands up and locks eyes with me. "But of all the people in this city, I think perhaps you are only one who might understand."

"Because I am a doctor?"

"No. Because you don't quite belong." She scrutinises every button and fold on my coat.

"Meaning what, exactly?" I try not to sound defensive.

"Where are you from, Doctor Harvey?"

"Bath."

"No, I mean originally."

"Bath."

She smiles. "Come now, you know as well as I do that no-one sees quite as clearly as the outsider."

"In what possible way are you an outsider, Lady Arabella?"

"If you want an answer to that, you will need to hear my confession."

"I think you are merely playing for time."

"This is a test of your moral strength, Doctor Harvey. Can you survive the truth?"

She is close enough for me to catch her perfume: a delicate amber top-note masks a deeper musk. I look into her eyes, and she holds my gaze without flinching. A sudden compulsion to feel if her skin is warm or deathly cold overwhelms me. I raise my fingers to her cheek, but she brushes my hand away.

"Do not presume. I have no interest in men. Not anymore."

She sits back down on the bench, fully aware of the strange, silent power that she wields.

I call for the constable. As the door is being unlocked, I can feel her eyes on me. "If you do return, you won't need to bring your little doctor's bag," she advises. "What I have to say is beyond the reach of your clever instruments."

It is a relief to step outside the prison gates and breathe in the fresh June air. The hard sunlight is surprisingly warm on my face. Needing to clear my mind, I decide to walk the long way back to my surgery, along Monmouth Street and up through Queen Square.

Reflecting on everything Arabella has said, I realise why the city authorities are terrified of her. It's not just that she has broken all the rules of marriage and decorum, it's that she shows not a scintilla of remorse. Quite the reverse: she seems proud and defiant. No wonder they want to silence her, banish her to an asylum for the insane. I really do not want any part in their bullying scheme; if Arabella has a defence, she must have her day in court.

And yet, am I prepared to incur the wrath of the Birds of Prey? Should I jeopardise my own career for a woman who treats me with such cool disdain?

She intrigues me. I cannot believe that a woman as intelligent as Arabella would commit such a violent crime without good reason, yet I find it impossible to imagine what that reason could be.

THREE

I arrive home to find the chevalier awake in his room, sitting in a chair facing a window he will never see through. He looks pale from his ordeal, yet still finds the energy to scratch incessantly.

"Joseph wouldn't give me any laudanum," he complains. "He said only you could make that decision."

"Chevalier, you have been given so much, I worry about addiction." I brace myself for another fight, but he just hangs his head in sorrow.

"This is what she has reduced me to. A husk of a man."

"Come now, I am determined to restore your strength."

The chevalier reaches out and gently takes my hand. "I apologise if I spoke harshly to you yesterday, Doctor Harvey. My mind was…"

"Think nothing of it. Please."

"You are a kind man, doctor. You have a heart. Unlike *her*."

"Try not to dwell on it, Chevalier."

"How can I not? This is how she controlled me, through laudanum. It's how she took me out in the wheelchair every Sunday, the one day of the week I was washed, clothed and paraded to perpetuate the deceit. All of Bath marvelled at her patience, while I was merely a drooling invalid. The real torture, and she knew it, was that I could hear everything. I was forced to endure the pain and thirst and hunger she inflicted on me, yet I was unable to cry out or signal to anyone. The laudanum made me a prisoner in my own body."

"It's a terrible thing."

"I know that you will help liberate me from this appalling drug, Doctor Harvey, but please, at this precise moment…" He scratches his chest with a frenzied determination. "For the love of God, give me some."

How can I refuse such an appeal?

As soon as it is administered, the chevalier sits back in his chair and sighs. "So, when will my wife be executed?"

"The investigation has already begun."

"Investigation? Save yourself the time and effort. Send her straight to the gallows."

"I understand your impatience, sir. But procedures must be followed."

"Why is my testimony not enough? Do you not trust me? Does the victim count for nothing anymore?" The chevalier seems genuinely hurt.

"You have clearly been the victim of gross cruelty, but we must be accurate and precise in our response."

"Then start here." The chevalier removes his tinted glasses, revealing painfully swollen, red-raw eyelids. "Did they tell you that I was an eye surgeon? The finest in Europe. Celebrated in all the great capitals, until she turned on me." The chevalier puts his dark glasses back on. "Can you even begin to understand the anguish I have endured? For an eye surgeon to be blinded … and by his own wife."

"It is hard to imagine."

"Do not let her talk, Doctor Harvey, I'm warning you. Do not let her open her mouth."

"She has to be questioned."

"You don't understand." He beckons me closer. I crouch next to him so that he can whisper. "Once she speaks, she will manipulate you. Persuade you. Win you over."

"But there can be no justification for what she has done."

"You are an erudite man. A medical man, much like myself before I was so cruelly abused."

"Come now, you were far more specialised, Chevalier. As a general practitioner, I would never dare go near something as intricate as the eye."

"Quite the opposite," he says modestly. "I only had to worry about one small organ, while you must administer to the whole body. That's quite an achievement." He clasps my hand tightly, like a trusting child. "So hear me now, as one physician to another. When I say Arabella Taylor is the Devil, I am not using a metaphor. She. Is. Evil. And if you don't hang her, then you must burn her at the stake. Like a witch."

Instinctively I recoil. "We are not in the Dark Ages now, sir."

"You have no idea what she is capable of." The chevalier's words are loaded with menace. "She must be crushed, or like Mephistopheles, she will bend you to her terrible will."

There is a dark and twisted lie being spun between the chevalier and Arabella Taylor. One of them is damned, for sure, but which one?

Hoping to find a clue inside the privacy of their home, I walk up Gay Street to King's Circus, then cross the road to arrive at an elegant townhouse on Bennett Street. One servant has been left behind to look after the building until the chevalier is well enough to return, but she lets me in without question.

Immediately I am struck by the sense of calm in this house.

The drawing room is a beautifully light space, with yellow walls that seem to glow in the afternoon sunlight. The damask armchairs have been arranged with a natural gap where the chevalier's wheelchair can be stationed. In the centre of one wall is a grandfather clock with a delicately painted face, and a blushing cherub-like moon that moves through a window on the dial. I notice that the weights are nearly touching the floor, and find a clock key on the mantlepiece to wind the mechanism.

At the back of the house, the dining room is just as one would expect for a dwelling of this size, but when I open the cutlery drawers and crockery cabinets, they are all empty, suggesting that it has been some while since anyone actually dined here.

I climb the stairs to the first floor, where a pleasant morning-room overlooks a walled garden; on the far side of the landing is an impressive library which draws me in. On the right-hand wall, bookcases are filled with the usual collections of classics, along with various medical textbooks and journals, presumably from the chevalier's previous life. But what really strikes me is the opposite wall, where the shelves are crammed with musical scores that have been imported from across Europe. The Birds of Prey told me that Arabella sponsors concerts in the abbey, but this is the collection of an obsessive. Several pieces of music have been gathered on Arabella's writing desk, as if she had been in the middle of planning the next recital when she was arrested.

And then I realise this beautiful writing desk is not so innocent. I have seen one of these under construction in the workshop where my own cabinets are made; this is a desk with secret compartments.

The two drawers at the front open as expected, revealing nothing more than household bills, and leaving the bulk of the internal space unaccounted for. Eagerly I run my hands over the polished cherry wood, feeling for catches or buttons, but the workmanship is too perfect. I press this panel, try to slide that one, but nothing clicks. This desk is a masterpiece that will only yield its secrets to someone who knows exactly where to apply pressure and in which sequence.

What scandals is Arabella concealing to warrant such an elaborate safe-desk?

I climb another flight of stairs to the bedrooms, where the coldness of this household suddenly becomes apparent. Three of the rooms are empty, with no beds or furniture, because no guest ever comes to stay.

Strangest of all is Arabella's room: a single four-poster bed sits in the middle of the floor, a chair is positioned by the window overlooking King's Circus, and a mirror hangs on the wall above a modest washstand. I am reminded of one of those solitary trees you see growing on barren hillsides — self-contained, resilient, and utterly at ease with their loneliness.

There is one framed picture on the wall above the fireplace, but it is a curious object. A sheet of musical manuscript paper has been torn up and painstakingly reassembled like one of the new jigsaw puzzles that are so delighting children. The whole thing has been mounted and secured behind glass.

I study the handwritten flurry of crotchets and semiquavers, trying to work out the melody, then notice the inscription. Written at the top of the aria are the words 'Für Arabella'. At the bottom, it has been signed 'J.S. Bach'.

How can a woman who is so enthralled by beauty commit a crime of such depravity? I make my decision: I need to hear this woman's story.

Despite the chevalier's warning, I am sure that I can listen to Arabella's confession without falling under her spell. I have no intention of conspiring to set her free, for I have spent too much energy building my life to throw it away so carelessly; but I must know the truth.

FOUR

The constable is surprised to see me return so soon. "How long will you be, sir?" he asks.

"Hard to tell. It's a complicated case."

He escorts me to her prison cell, whistling cheerfully, enjoying the echo his rough tune makes in the cold stone corridors.

"What do you make of her, Constable?" I ask as we approach her cell door.

"I think I'm glad she's not my wife, sir."

"Yet she's a very attractive woman."

"Only on the outside." He puts a heavy key in the lock, clunks it open, then slides the bolts back.

I step inside. Arabella smiles at me but says nothing until the cell door is firmly closed and we are alone. Then she points to a wooden stool that has been placed by the wall.

"Please. Take a seat."

"That wasn't here earlier," I observe.

"I knew you'd come back, so I asked for it to be provided."

Is she bluffing? Or did she really see through me at that first meeting?

I sit down and wait for Arabella Taylor to begin.

PART TWO: ARABELLA

FIVE

My entire childhood was spent in the stink of my father's tannery, scraping fat from animal skins and soaking them in faeces. They say each animal has enough brains to tan its own hide, which I now find ironic; but as a seven-year-old girl, forced to spend every waking hour rubbing pig brains into hides to soften them, all I could think about was the smell. The dreadful, pungent smell. It comes to define you.

Many times I would plead with my parents to let me fill one of the metal tubs with hot water so that I could have a bath at the end of a filthy day, but they forbade it.

"Once a month is all you need," my mother would say, her mouth set hard.

"Unhealthy to wash too much," my father nodded. "Dirt is what keeps off the illness."

"Who says?" I would reply.

"Listen to your father!"

"Good enough for me, good enough for you," he declared, and that was the end of the discussion.

As I approached womanhood, I tried in vain to struggle against my fate. In summer I would escape to the river just before sunset to bathe in the cool water until my fingers shrivelled and my mind lost itself. I would rub petals onto my skin and soak herbs in jars of water, a homemade perfume to create the illusion of civility.

But that smell of death ... it follows you around, it leaches into your hair and seeps into your very soul. Like poverty, it clings to you.

I prayed every night; not just for a bath, but that enlightenment might come to my parents, so that they would cast off the stupidity into which they had been born and open their minds. Slowly I realised that far from feeling cursed by their ignorance, my parents embraced it; they rolled around in it and celebrated its stench. They were pig ignorant in every sense of the word.

You see, Doctor Harvey, from the moment I was born, my chances were grim; years of hard toil for a meagre living were the best I could hope for. Either God had abandoned me, or He didn't exist at all.

Which was worse? It didn't really matter.

And yet, just as I was sinking into despair, my prayers were answered in the unlikely form of Josiah Roope, a prominent businessman in Norwich, founder and proud owner of the city's biggest rope factory. For his fiftieth birthday, he had decided to gift himself a grand new saddle, and he summoned my father to present a cartload of leather so that he could choose the very finest skins. I was taken along to help with the sale.

My first glimpse of Josiah Roope was bizarre. He was 'riding the trolley' down the ropewalk in a building that stretched for a quarter of a mile. Half-finished ropes stretched from end to end like an enormous moving cat's cradle; huge iron wheels clattered at speed, twisting hundreds of strands together, and in the middle of it all was the trolley transporting Mr Roope back and forth, like an admiral surveying his fleet.

A stocky and sober man with an earnest brow, Josiah took his work seriously. He took everything seriously. And that came to include me.

The moment he saw us, Josiah stepped off the trolley and bobbed between the moving ropes with well-practised ease.

"That looks like a fine set of hides." He stretched out his hand to greet my father, but his eyes moved towards me.

"All top quality, Mr Roope. Top quality. But best you make the final choice yourself."

"Excellent."

My father started taking more leathers off the cart, describing the merits of each one in turn. Josiah nodded and murmured his approval, yet all the while I could feel his eyes returning to me.

"Is this your daughter?" he asked finally.

"It is, Mr Roope."

"Last time I saw her, she was knee-high." He tried to smile, but it came out awkwardly. Yet it was enough for my father to notice, and to understand.

"Yes, yes. Arabella's a young woman now. Hard-working, very capable."

"You've been keeping her a secret out at that tannery of yours."

"Well, we…" My father struggled to find the right words. "She's a little shy. On account of … the work, you know."

The smell is what he meant. The smell. I prickled with embarrassment.

"There's nothing to be ashamed of in the scent of hard work," Josiah said gently. I felt his fingers touch my chin and lift my head so that he could look at me. "Believe me, I know all about that. Separating the hemp fibres is a most arduous job, and the retting pits are notorious for their smells, but it has to be done. It has to be done."

His green eyes locked onto mine, silently reassuring me that I had nothing to be ashamed of.

"And when one realises that it is also the smell of profit, one soon comes to embrace it." He allowed himself a knowing chuckle.

"Indeed, Mr Roope." My father nodded vigorously, barely able to believe his luck.

"And there is nothing that a bar of God's soap cannot fix."

My father took the hint with a vengeance.

On the day Mr Roope was invited for afternoon tea, my mother plunged me into the tin bath in front of the kitchen fire and scrubbed me raw with soap and a horse-hair brush. This wasn't the tender touch of a nurturing mother; it was a violent scouring performed in order to get me off their hands.

"I thought you didn't believe in cleanliness," I said as my skin turned red.

"Shut up, now." Mother poured a jug of water over my head, making me cough and splutter.

"Was it really so much to ask? For all these years?"

"Fine gentlemen don't want no stench of the yard," she muttered to herself. "Should've scrubbed you before ever letting you out."

Never has a child been made to feel so worthless.

Mr Roope, on the other hand, was to be treated like royalty. As my parents prepared the room for our guest, possessions I didn't even know we had emerged. Fine cutlery, a blue and white china tea set, a crystal milk jug, and lace doilies for every setting. Apparently, it was all from my mother's dowry.

Josiah Roope, of course, took it in his stride and didn't once comment on the china, pretending that he believed this was how we always ate.

The conversation was stilted. Since my parents were too frightened to say much lest they spoil my chances, Mr Roope ended up waxing lyrical about himself.

"It's a good business, is ropemaking. The world always needs securing. Do you know how much rope goes into the rigging of a ship?"

My parents stared at him wide-eyed, not even daring to guess.

"Thirty-one miles," Roope declared. "Thirty-one miles of rope in each of His Majesty's ships of the line. Without the ropemakers, we would have no Navy. And without the Navy, we would have no empire. I tell you, even though some may see me just as a modest Norwich businessman, my work is of national importance. And I'm proud of it."

My parents nodded gravely, their simple faces glowing with admiration.

"Not excessively proud, of course," Roope corrected himself. "For pride is a sin. One does not build a successful business through pride. One builds it through thrift, sobriety, hard work, and prayer."

"Indeed. Indeed," my father murmured.

"National importance," my mother cooed. "Fancy that."

"I confess, my sense of duty has involved sacrifice. My devotion to the rope means that I have been married to my work."

"I'm sure many married men would happily make that trade," my father quipped. Mother glared at him disapprovingly.

"But now that I am turning fifty…" Josiah paused, waiting.

"Goodness me, Mr Roope!" My mother took the bait. "You don't look a day over forty."

"The gift of sobriety," Josiah smiled. "Yet it is true. Fifty beckons, which is why I have decided to acquire a wife who can bear me a son."

This was the moment everything had been building to — the tea set, the doilies, the scrubbing brush.

"Who is to be the lucky lady?" my father asked, trying to sound nonchalant.

"That is where I thought…" Mr Roope's eyes fell on me. "Perhaps … Arabella is a most enchanting young woman."

Young. That was the problem. He was fifty, and I was eighteen. Was this really my only way out of the stink of the tannery?

Roope turned to my father. "If I were to overlook the considerable difference in our stations, perhaps your daughter could overlook the difference in our ages?"

"You have earned the right to have whatever you want, Mr Roope," my father said without even glancing in my direction. "Arabella will be most happy."

And that was it. My life arranged.

After tea, Mr Roope and I walked in the field behind the cottage. A slow, awkward walk, full of silences. I think a part of him felt for me, and he tried to cheer me up with his philosophy.

"In many ways, marriage is like ropemaking, Arabella. On their own, the individual strands of hemp are weak and fragile, but when they twist around each other, they strengthen each other. And the more they twist, the stronger they become. Who would have thought that friction alone could create something so strong?"

He looked at me, anxious to see whether his words of wisdom had hit home.

"Is it true you also make rope for the hangman, Mr Roope?"

He didn't quite know what to make of that. "Not, er, not anymore. That was in the early days."

"I see."

"Not much money in the short drop."

"And do you have a room for bathing?" I asked.

"Why, of course." He seemed greatly relieved to be on safer ground. "Hot and cold water are essential elements in my household."

"That's good to hear."

"Cleanliness is how we celebrate God."

I smiled. Things were starting to look hopeful. "And tell me, Mr Roope —"

"Josiah, please."

"If we were married, could you teach me to read and write?"

He looked at me and blinked. "You've had no schooling?"

"No, sir, I'm ashamed to say."

"No shame, girl. None at all. And it would be my pleasure, my privilege to teach you."

"Really? Even at my age?"

"Dearest Arabella, to learn is to be young, however old. Reading will unlock a world of riches that will change your life forever. I promise."

I reached out and took his hand.

Finally, here was a man who could rescue me from the ignorance of my parents.

SIX

My husband's house was a land of wonder. An imposing four-storey building overlooking a small park at the corner of Princes Street and Tombland, it had me under its spell from the moment I walked through the heavy oak doors.

For several weeks after the wedding, I would just wander from room to room, running my fingers over the gleaming surfaces, gazing at my reflection in Josiah's treasury of silver plate, admiring the ledgers in his study, immersing my face in the folds of heavy curtain that adorned the high windows.

And the smells… Rich cotton, beeswax polish, the different soaps the housemaids used to keep the rooms pristine; it was paradise. As promised, there was an abundance of hot and cold water, and no limit on the number of times a week I could bathe. Finally, I had extricated myself from the terrible smell of dead animals and taken a step towards enlightenment.

Josiah loved to watch me as I admired his house, and I really think it gave him pleasure to see me so happy. He had worked hard to build a prosperous business, and he took nothing for granted. Our marriage may have been strange, but it had all the elements of success; we were bound together not so much by love, but by the satisfaction of mutual needs, and that should have been enough.

Yet as the months passed and I became accustomed to material comforts, the true price I was paying started to become apparent. Evening meals were characterised by worthy food and tedious conversation about rope and hemp and the minutiae of the factory. It was either that or silence.

After dinner Josiah would retire to his study to work through the accounts, while I was left on my own to embroider yet another cushion. I do believe reconciling the ledgers had become an obsession for him.

As was the calendar, which hung above the bed like a Sword of Damocles. Josiah recorded my monthly cycles as he tried to predict when I would be most fertile. Because this is what the marriage was really about, providing an heir. It was Josiah's deepest longing to paint "& Son" on the sign above the gates of the rope shed, and I had to endure his sweaty exertions in bed to satisfy that longing. My desires were of secondary importance, and the fact that I was only just out of childhood myself made his obsession even more distasteful to me. Was this all that life had to offer? Children begetting children in an endless cycle?

On this, my husband was depressingly aligned with my parents. They came to dinner just once, and as they shuffled around on the tour of the house after dessert, they made their admiration of Josiah's achievements abundantly clear, until they came to the bathroom. My mother turned her nose up at the gleaming copper tub, and my father refused even to touch the taps.

"That's why there's no children," my father pronounced. "You bathe too much."

Sensing my restless spirit, Josiah engaged a tutor to teach me how to read and write, and this hour soon became the highlight of my day. Knowing that the reward for study would eventually be the whole of Western literature, I became an exemplary student. Whatever lettering exercises were set, I repeated tirelessly until they were perfect. When he asked me to read two pages, I would read six. Whenever I was out and about in Norwich, I would choose the longest route possible so that I could read all the street signs and study every notice in the shop windows.

Finally, when I felt worthy enough, I ventured into Chase's Bookshop to buy my very first novel.

I had intended to acquire something romantic with heroic knights and delicate ladies, but instead emerged with *Robinson Crusoe*, which the sales assistant assured me was the most extraordinary story of stoicism and survival on a deserted island.

Anxious to learn about this kindred spirit, I practically ran back to the house, threw myself into the great armchair by the fire, and began. The sun set, the kitchen maid came and went, but I was lost to the real world. *That evil influence which carried me first away from my father's house, which hurried me into the wild and indigested notion of raising my fortune —*

"What on earth are you doing?"

I looked up to see my husband standing over me.

"What has been prepared for supper?"

"Josiah, this is the most extraordinary tale! Have you heard of it?"

He plucked the book from my hands and examined it while I explained.

"Some say it is a true account, others that the whole thing is fiction. But it doesn't matter. The story is so —"

"No, Arabella! This is not right. This is not why I taught you to read."

"What?"

"This is profane rubbish." His brow furrowed.

"It's a very famous book."

"Not as famous as the Bible. That is the only book that matters in this house, Arabella. The only book. Do you understand?"

I looked at him, trying to work out whether he was playing a joke on me. "Are you being serious, Josiah?"

"All the wisdom there is to be had can be found in the Bible. It has a thousand pages for you to explore. Go where you want, Arabella, as long as it is in the Holy Land." He put my book in his pocket, then turned and walked towards the door. "Now go and find out what has been left in the kitchen for me."

And that was the last I ever saw of *Robinson Crusoe*.

SEVEN

That glimpse of independence must have scared Josiah, because not long after he secured me a job, presumably to keep me occupied until my womb obliged.

For several years, he had run the top floor of his townhouse as lodgings for respectable travellers and prospective clients. These had been particularly useful when working on Navy contracts, as the procurement officers had to travel considerable distances, and generous hospitality always helped to sweeten the deal. Now Josiah dismissed the housekeeper who had nurtured this business, and installed me in the position instead.

Immediately my days were filled with the business of bookings and linen, of menus and water closets. It made my dull life, in a dull city, with a dull husband who was a dull lover, bearable.

Until Chevalier John Taylor arrived.

It was a Wednesday afternoon when the mud-spattered coach from London pulled in along Queen Street. Before it had even rolled to a stop, the coach was surrounded by a gaggle of yelping urchins, curious to see what foreigners had dared to venture out into the wilds of East Anglia. I pulled the shutters aside and gazed down onto the street. The carriage door was flung back, and out stepped a human peacock.

The chevalier was wrapped in a red and black cape that covered his silk knee-length coat and breeches. On his head, a tricorne with a long green feather was perched atop a full-bottomed wig.

The urchins fell silent and gazed upon the spectacle in wonder. The chevalier drew a deep breath and looked proudly to his left, then to his right. He dipped into his purse and scattered a few pennies into the air above the boys, who yelped with joy and started scrambling in the dirt to retrieve them.

The chevalier chuckled to himself, then gave some instructions to the driver, who started to unload a set of matching trunks from the coach. They didn't just match each other, they also matched the chevalier's clothes, which is presumably why they were not allowed to travel with the common luggage on the roof.

While the driver wrestled with the trunks, the chevalier strode back and forth with a confident swagger, stretching his limbs.

A haycart pulled up behind the coach; unable to get past, the farmer called out a few choice words. But rather than help the driver to unload his trunks more quickly, the chevalier made a quip to the farmer, who started to laugh. The two of them watched the driver sweat out the last of the luggage and haul it to the side of the road, then the chevalier made a great show of guiding the haycart safely past.

He had only been in Norwich for a matter of minutes, yet already everyone was dancing to the chevalier's tune.

Three heavy knocks on the side door sent me hurrying down the staircase that serviced the guest rooms. I slid back the bolts and swung open the door to reveal the red-faced coach driver, who now appeared to have been seconded into the chevalier's service.

"He wants to know if you got his letter, reserving a room?"

On the opposite side of the road, the chevalier stood casually winding his pocket watch as he waited for his minion to sort the details.

"There's been a mistake," I said, shaking my head. "We've had no reservation letter about tonight."

"From London. He's from London, and don't he know it!"

I glanced across the road just as the chevalier looked up. He stopped winding, and his eyes fastened onto me, running up and down my body, taking in everything about me.

I looked back at the driver. "Perhaps you should try the lodging house in Castle Meadow."

"He says it's this one. He insists." The driver was getting exasperated. "And I really haven't got time for this. Got to get the horses changed…"

As I saw the chevalier striding towards us, I edged back and tried to close the door, but the driver blocked it with his foot.

"Please, miss," he whispered urgently. "I just want to get rid of him."

"Don't be a lobcock!" The chevalier clamped a hand on the driver's shoulder and spun him round. "You're blocking the footpath, man!" He pointed to the pile of his own trunks. "The pedestrians of Norwich deserve better. Now, fetch the luggage over here." He pushed the driver away then turned to me, took off his hat and bowed extravagantly. "You, madam, must be the famed beauty of Norwich whose praises they sing."

"I'm sorry. I … I think you must be mistaken, sir."

"No, no." He flashed me a playful smile. "I refuse to believe there can be another woman in this city as alluring as you."

"I … I…"

"This precise address was given to me in my London club." He took a notebook from his coat and flicked through the pages.

"London has heard of us?" I stammered.

"Oh, yes. Heard of, and celebrated, Miss…"

"Roope. Mrs Arabella Roope."

"That's right. I have your name here." He read from a page in his notebook: "*Refined lodgings near the city centre, run by a woman who is the epitome of style and beauty. Highly recommended.*"

"You heard that in London?"

"Indeed I did. Which is why I instructed my people to make all the necessary arrangements. It appears they have failed, for which I beg your indulgence." He reached out and took my hand. His gloves were deerskin calf. "Arabella, I have travelled over hill and through dale to be with you. I have passed through hamlets such as Pox-in-the-Marsh and Fart-on-the-Water to reach this great city. Will you now take pity on a weary traveller in need of shelter?"

I should have pushed him away, or at the very least scolded him for his boldness, but the chevalier's easy smile was hard to resist. It was as if he could shrug off any obstacle that was impudent enough to block his path.

"As it happens, we do have a vacant room," I stammered.

"Madam, you have made me the happiest man in Christendom." Then he turned and shouted at the urchins, "You! Help the driver with my luggage!"

"It'll cost you!" came the reply.

"I have already paid! Those farthings weren't charity — they were an advance!"

It was quite a palaver getting all his trunks up the staircase to the top landing. The driver and urchins huffed and cursed and banged their shins, but not once did the chevalier offer to help. He took great care never to touch the luggage, as that was clearly beneath him.

As the final trunk was heaved into place on the top landing, the urchins waited for a few more coins, but the chevalier just pushed them down the stairs with his foot, then started striding around the space.

"What a charming establishment." He inspected the paintings on the wall with the knowing gaze of a connoisseur. "Provincial interiors make such a refreshing change from London."

Realising he too had now become invisible, the driver cursed under his breath and slunk down the stairs.

"Is that a Chippendale?" The chevalier sat in one of the armchairs by the dresser, trying it out for comfort before rising again. "He does turn a fine piece of wood, does Thomas."

He continued his restless pacing, opening the doors to all the rooms without asking permission or even knocking. It was pure chance that the residents had left for the day.

"Ah, now this is the room for me," he said, entering the largest suite that overlooked the river.

"I'm afraid this one is already taken, sir."

He opened the windows and breathed in deeply. "I'll take it for a week."

"As I said, this room isn't available."

"Then write sorrow on my bosom, for you have crushed all hope that was within me." A great sadness came upon him that seemed to drain the energy from the room.

"I'm sorry. There's nothing I can do," I stammered.

"Such a tragedy." His gaze roamed appreciatively across the room. "The light here is so … so conducive to concentration, which is a vital component of my work."

"Are you a painter?"

"No, no. I am that to which all painters are enslaved. I am an artist of the human body: a surgeon." He stepped close to me and held up his hands, marvelling at them. "See how steady they are. Not a tremble or twitch. The slightest shake is the difference between life and death."

His hands were pale, smooth, utterly unused to any form of manual labour. The nails were immaculately trimmed, and the fingers long and slender. They were definitely hands you could trust.

"Now compare them to yours."

"Oh, no," I said, hiding my hands behind my back. "Mine have seen too much of the world already."

"Nonsense!" He leant close, took my hand, and held it up to the light as if it was a medical specimen. "You seem to be trembling, Arabella," he whispered as he gently touched my fingers. "I must remember not to put my life in your hands."

I pulled myself free.

"Are you really turning me down?" The chevalier looked crestfallen. "Denying me the inspiring lightness of this room? Condemning me to second best? Throwing me into the jaws of darkness?"

"Well, perhaps I could move this guest to the back…"

"A fine decision! Done in the name of medical science."

"He's a procurement man for the Navy Board. The light is of no importance to him."

"Wasted on such a pudding-headed fellow."

"Hush now. He's a good customer."

"You are a charming creature, Mistress Roope. Utterly charming." The chevalier swung into action, directing me where to hang his clothes, and how to position his personal items. One whole drawer of the dressing table was to be dedicated to his perfumes and scents, another to his soaps and powders. "There is one thing I must ask you not to touch under any circumstances, Arabella." He picked up the smallest of the trunks and placed it carefully on the bed. "This is forbidden to you."

"What is it?" I said, gazing at the box in wonder. "Holy relics?"

"Far more valuable." He undid the clasps and opened the lid, revealing a shining array of strange and specialised tools, each one finely machined to perfection. "No-one must ever come between a surgeon and his instruments," he whispered. "Aren't they beautiful?"

There was a set of scalpels, some pointed probes and hooks, small clamps, and other instruments that were too bizarre to describe.

"Apart from that," he said, snapping the clasps shut again, "you can put everything away while I take in the sights of fair Norwich."

Then he picked up his hat and was gone, leaving me with the aura of his fine colognes, and all the unpacking still to do.

Each trunk was like an exotic treasure chest; to open the lid was to enter a world of refinement and wealth.

There were delicate silk stockings in three distinct colours, shirts of Egyptian cotton, a different waistcoat for every day of the week, beautifully tailored breeches and day coats, three different wigs of varying formality, and more silver-buckled shoes than I had seen in my life. One small trunk was devoted entirely to the chevalier's gloves, most of them leather, some of them cotton, no doubt to protect those precious hands.

But most enticing of all were the toiletry trunks, with face powders, lotions and lip-colourings; manicure tools, tweezers, combs, and a set of ivory-backed hairbrushes. This was grooming as an art form, displaying a surgeon's intense respect for the human body, and it made my husband and everything in his house seem heavy and dull and ugly.

I noticed the chevalier had left his notebook on the side table; curious to see what else had been written about me, I picked it up and flicked through the pages. There were lists of names, some crossed out, some with amounts of money marked against them; there were phrases written in foreign languages, and some anatomical sketches of the human eye; but nowhere could I find any reference to me or the guesthouse. Perhaps I was mistaken; perhaps he had a second notebook that he kept about his person.

No matter. The aura of the man was so intense, it banished all doubt.

Longing to absorb the chevalier's sophistication, I slid his formal black wig onto my head and dressed the curls around my bare shoulders. Then I gazed in the mirror, imagining myself as some fine lady in a London ballroom, turning away suitors with a haughty eye.

I unclasped his box of cosmetics, delicately brushed some powder onto my cheeks, applied gloss to my brows, and dabbed the crimson lip-colour onto my mouth. Now I even smelled like him, and my skin started to tingle with warmth.

EIGHT

Josiah Roope liked to slurp his soup. He always joked that it was a sign of appreciation; I thought it was disgusting.

I studied him now, watching his fat fingers clasp the spoon too tightly, noticing the tuft of bristles on his top lip that he'd missed when shaving, and the liver spots emerging on his cheeks. Everything about my husband now seemed ill-favoured. Had he always been this way? Was I only just seeing the truth? Even the way he crossed the room irritated me, waddling with heavy feet, so different to the chevalier's confident stride.

Josiah was ten years older than the chevalier, but it might as well have been thirty years.

"Where is he now?" *Slurp*. "All the other lodgers are in for the night." Josiah glanced at the grandfather clock.

"I believe he had business in the city."

"At this hour?"

"He is a surgeon. Illness has no respect for the clock."

"Huh. More than likely the Watch will pick him up, roaming the streets in a drunken stupor."

"Josiah, maybe we should invite the chevalier to dinner. With us."

His spoon froze mid-air. "Why?"

"He seems interesting."

"I don't trust those types."

"But you've never met him."

"You can always judge a man by his luggage. Those fancy trunks…"

Suddenly I glimpsed my parents in him. Beneath all his nice possessions, Josiah had that same leaden attitude and closed mind.

"But think of the people he might know," I ventured. "An eminent surgeon will have treated all sorts of men in high places."

"I already have my contacts at the Admiralty."

"But what about the East India Company? Imagine having a rope contract with them."

"Does he know anyone there?"

"Why don't we find out?"

Josiah finished his bowl of soup in silence. I could see his mind running the numbers, for he always blinked a little faster when thinking about money. "Well, I suppose…" He offered me an indulgent smile. "If you think it's a promising idea, Arabella, what harm can it do?"

The calendar spared me from Josiah's grunting exertions, but just to be sure, I spent a long time at my nightly toilet, so that when I snuck into bed he was already snoring.

I slid a pillow between us, anxious that he shouldn't accidentally touch me and become aroused, but I didn't close my eyes; I lay there listening for the chevalier's return. For that entire evening, one ear had been on the side door, waiting for his distinctive footsteps and ebullient voice.

What was he doing out so late at night? Who was he seeing? Did he have a secret lover here in Norwich?

Finally, just as the grandfather clock in the hall struck one, there was a rattling at the door, followed by a banging and cursing. My ever-cautious husband had locked the guest entrance before retiring to bed, possibly to spite the dashing surgeon.

I threw on a nightgown, grabbed the keys and hurried down the back stairs.

"Quiet down! I'm coming! You'll wake the whole house." I hauled open the door and was greeted by an expansive smile.

"Once again, you have saved me, Arabella!"

Drink had made him charming rather than boorish; perhaps that was how it worked in London.

As he entered the hallway, he clasped my hands. "Do you know the Allemande?"

"What?"

"The most fashionable dance in Europe. It's all about hands."

"Shame on you! Get to sleep now." My feeble attempt at scolding him was met with a laugh.

"I hold your hand as you turn under my arm." He spun me round. "Now you hold me as I turn under you." He attempted a twirl but lost his balance and stumbled into me. I could smell the sweet wine on his breath.

"Enough with you!" I pulled away. "We have guests trying to sleep."

"Who cares about pen-pushers and bureaucrats?"

"My husband, actually."

"Ah. The worthy Mr Roope."

"Who has extended you the honour of a dinner invitation."

"Me?" He stopped flirting and considered this new development. His eyes seemed to be calculating something.

"Do you accept?"

The chevalier smiled again. "It would be my pleasure, Arabella. My absolute pleasure."

"Well, then. Tomorrow evening."

"Then I'd best get some rest. Sleep off the wine. Must be on my best behaviour for the worthy Mr Roope."

I watched as he crept up the stairs making a great show of stealth. As he turned the corner, he glanced back at me darkly. "We will continue our dance tomorrow," he whispered.

I knew it was going to be a difficult meal the moment the soup was served. I had tried to persuade Josiah to choose a different menu, but he was a creature of habit. The chevalier, of course, rose to the occasion with effortless style, skimming his spoon across the surface, always away from himself, and allowing a moment's pause for the drips to fall. Then with a graceful hand movement, he put the edge of the spoon to his lips. Perfect, and silent.

The chevalier endured my husband's slurping with great stoicism, but when Josiah finally tipped the bowl to scoop up the dregs, he offered me a sympathetic smile, as if to say, 'You are a saint to endure this boorish behaviour.' At least, that's what I thought his expression was saying.

Our guest seemed to sense that conversation was the best way to lighten the mood. "So, Mr Roope, this is quite a business you have established."

"It is. Biggest ropemaker in East Anglia."

"Impressive. A lifetime's work, no doubt?"

"Well, that's an interesting story. As a boy, I had been apprenticed to a sailmaker, but I saw an opportunity in rope. So I nurtured my idea and went to the guild to borrow five guineas — this was thirty years ago, mind, when a guinea could buy —"

Suddenly the chevalier burst out laughing. "So now we have an answer to the eternal question: how long is a piece of rope? Thirty years!" He laughed enthusiastically at his own joke.

Josiah let him calm down, then continued. "First I had to serve out my apprenticeship; it was one of the conditions —"

"I don't believe in long apprenticeships," the chevalier interrupted. "You either have the talent, or you don't. It can't be forced."

"Nevertheless," Josiah plodded on, "they say it takes a man seven years to master something."

"'They' being the dull-witted, I assume?"

"On the contrary —"

"Kings are born great. Aristocrats are born to rule. They don't need apprenticeships."

"Being an aristocrat is not a skill; it is an accident of birth."

"On the contrary, Mr Roope. Defending the land, maintaining the greatness of the kingdom. These are heavy burdens the aristocrat bears."

My husband looked at him searchingly. "That is a curious title you bear. 'Chevalier' is unusual in British aristocracy, is it not?"

"We are an exclusive breed."

"Less than a baronet, but more than a squire, perhaps?"

"No, no, my good Roope. You've got the wrong end of it altogether."

"Do enlighten me." Josiah had sensed a weakness and was determined to press it.

"I am the youngest son of Lord Taylor of London. I'm sure you've heard of us — a great and ancient family. The peerage obviously passed to my older brother, which is why I have adopted the French title, 'Chevalier,' to illuminate the superiority of my blood."

Roope nodded to himself. "But really, you are just plain Mr Taylor."

The chevalier stopped eating. "I am not plain anything. I think you'll find, sir, that 'plain' is for the provinces. Not the metropolitan nobility."

"Empire is built on the industry of the provinces." Josiah had found his stride. "The untitled men of business who know how to build things with their hands are what has made this country great."

"Hands are not enough. Sweat is nothing without leadership, which comes from the superior class."

"Indeed, Mr Taylor."

The chevalier put down his cutlery with a heavy clink; he was not going to take the slight. "Would a plain 'mister' perform the most intricate surgery known to man? Would a 'mister' have the courage to take a scalpel to the human eye?"

"You're an eye surgeon?" For the first time Josiah let down his guard.

"I do not saw bones or deal with the lesser organs. Not for me is the distasteful dabbling in human entrails. The human eye is the greatest of all God's creations. To distinguish colour and form, to focus from the farthest horizon to the smallest wrinkle on your own hand, to understand beauty and symmetry … these are the wonders and mysteries of the eye. And it is my calling to perform the most delicate surgery on this most intricate of creations."

The chevalier pushed his chair back and started to pace the dining room. "If my scalpel goes but the thickness of a hair beyond where it should, the results could prove fatal. There is no calling back, no passing that way twice. Once the error is made, repentance is in vain. And like all true artists, I have confronted adversity and turned it to my advantage, just as a dull stone sharpens the knife. With no chance of inheriting family money, I have had to rely on my own natural talents. I trained under the surgeon William Cheselden at the renowned St Thomas' Hospital in London."

"I have heard of it," Josiah said, nodding.

"An adequate school. Yet I quickly outgrew my tutors and have pioneered my own brilliant techniques for operating on cataracts, curing retinal blindness and treating other assorted maladies of the eye."

"That is most impressive, Chevalier," Josiah said humbly. "I meant no offence."

"And to set the record straight," the chevalier said with a hint of disdain, "I have published no less than forty-five treatises on the eye and its defects, many of which have been translated into foreign languages. The only reason I have come to Norwich is to negotiate with some financiers. Once I have raised the capital to build a mobile operating theatre, I believe that my innovations will make me the toast of Europe. The eye surgeon to kings and Popes. But if you wish to be pedantic and call me 'mister,' then that is your business." Calmly, he sat down, picked up his knife and fork and resumed his meal.

I think that was when I fell in love with him. This was a man who soared high above all others.

Josiah raised his wine glass. "A toast, Chevalier. To your remarkable talents. I was too quick to judge you, for which I apologise."

The chevalier picked up his glass, and with an easy smile returned the favour. "To your generous hospitality, Mr Roope."

"Perhaps we can help, sir?" I ventured. "My husband knows many of the financiers in Norwich."

"I have to be very selective," the chevalier frowned. "There are more men keen to invest than I can consider."

"But we could assist. We could organise a luncheon with businessmen here in Norwich, and help you decide who would make a reliable investor."

The chevalier considered it. "Perhaps if I extended my stay, it might be possible."

"Stay another week. At our expense," I offered.

"Of course," Josiah said cautiously, "I would need to have proof of these new techniques of yours."

"You have doubts, sir?" Again that cold glance from the chevalier.

"It's much like ropemaking. No matter how powerful and strong a rope looks, it is only when it is tested that its true quality is revealed."

"Ah," the chevalier smiled. "Now I understand your meaning. You have a friend whose eyesight is failing, perhaps?"

Josiah nodded pensively. "Yes. I do."

"I thought as much, and I know how distressing that is, Mr Roope."

"You didn't tell me this, Josiah. Who is it?" I asked.

"Poor Mather is ashamed of his condition. He has tried to keep it a secret."

"Assure him he has nothing to fear," the chevalier said. "It would be my pleasure to offer a consultation without any cost."

"He is not looking for charity."

"And I am not offering it. I am merely putting my years of experience at your disposal. There is no surgeon in Norwich capable of examining your friend's eyes with expertise such as mine, and I would consider it an honour to help."

Josiah reached out and clasped the chevalier's hand. "You are a good man, sir. A good man."

NINE

Mr Mather was a silent, sober, rather dull man. He and my husband had been in business together for over twenty years, patiently growing the rope factory and cultivating new clients. Josiah frequently talked about what a blessing it was to have a trusted partner with whom he could shoulder the burden of bad times and celebrate the good fortune of success. Josiah and Mather saved each other from the loneliness of leadership, and this had become the foundation of a reliable friendship.

Now we were all seated in Mr Mather's dark-panelled study, watching the chevalier pray. Josiah's hands were also clasped, his head bowed. Mrs Mather looked pale and pious, while her husband looked worried.

Finally the chevalier crossed himself and rose from his knees. "Shall we begin?" Here was a vastly different man to the one who had flirted with me on the stairs a few nights earlier; now his absolute focus was on the patient.

"I'm hoping it is just the natural process of getting older," Mather said.

"Nature can be a difficult mistress," the chevalier frowned. "When did you first notice something amiss?"

"Michaelmas, two years ago. I was struggling to read the smallest numbers in the ledger, so I purchased a magnifying glass."

"Both eyes were the same?"

"Yes. But the magnifying glass seemed to solve the problem."

"Tell him about the fall at Easter," Mrs Mather whispered to her husband.

"That was an accident," Mather replied.

"Tell him."

"Everything that may be relevant must be disclosed, Mr Mather," the chevalier said firmly.

"When things are not put back in their proper place, I stumble over them. It is only natural."

"Every day it happens," his wife added.

"It is carelessness, nothing more. I am often distracted."

"Denying your condition will only make it worse, Mr Mather. Never delay when it comes to the eyes. Time is of the essence."

Mr Mather looked disconsolate. "The truth is, my sight has been getting worse, sir. Every month that passes, the world becomes darker. I fear it is slipping away from me."

"Then we must fight back." The chevalier opened his case of instruments and prepared for the examination. Onto his forehead he strapped a delicate, curved mirror to focus the light; on the bridge of his nose he clipped a magnification lens. He then picked up a small steel clamp. "Hold still." But as he loomed forward, Mr Mather recoiled. "There is nothing to fear," the chevalier smiled. "It is just an examination. You will just feel a little discomfort."

Mrs Mather gripped her husband's hand, then the chevalier applied the clamp to Mather's right eye, peeling back the lid and opening the screw wide so that it was impossible to blink. He leaned forward, focussing the light on Mather's eyeball, and peered through the lens with intense concentration. "Write this down, Arabella."

I did as I was told.

"Outer edge, three over eight." There was a long silence of intense concentration. "Inner edge, five over eight." He moved his head slightly, peering into the iris from the opposite angle.

"Occlusion, four. Radial damage … seven. Retina obscured to six."

He leant back, deep in thought.

"Well?" Mr Mather asked.

The chevalier said nothing but proceeded to transfer the clamp to the other eye, where he conducted a similar examination, dictating another set of obscure numbers.

When he was finished, the chevalier held out his hand, beckoning me for the notes. He studied them, then consulted a bound volume of mathematical tables, nodding occasionally.

Finally he took off his instruments, put them away carefully, and turned to Mr Mather. "You have cataracts in both eyes that need couching. The operation can be done, but because of the peculiarities of your lenses, it will be complex and expensive."

"Couching? I've never heard of couching. Doesn't sound too bad." Mr Mather was trying to be brave.

"I will use a sharp scalpel to pierce either edge of the cornea in your right eye. Then, drawing upon my considerable experience, I will slide a long needle into your eyeball, with which I will break up part of the vitreous jelly to create a small cavity within the eye chamber. I will then take a second needle, insert it through the cornea, hook it into the faulty lens and push it downwards, into the cavity and out of the field of vision. I will then repeat the procedure for your left eye. The operation will be less painful if you get drunk prior to surgery."

A terrible silence descended.

"Drunk?" Mather stuttered. "But I don't really drink."

"Then you'd better start."

"What about laudanum?"

"It won't stop the pain; it will merely relax your muscles. You'll still feel everything, but you will be unable to struggle.

And in any case, the quantities required would probably kill you."

It was at this point that Mrs Mather fainted.

A dose of smelling salts helped Mrs Mather recover her senses; regaining her composure was not so easy.

"His eyes! His eyes!" she wailed. "God help the poor man! God help him!" She succumbed to hysterical sobbing.

She was ushered into the care of a housemaid, then my husband and Mr Mather withdrew to the study to discuss the matter in private.

"I am torn, Josiah, utterly torn." Mather huddled beside the fire, staring at the glowing embers, savouring every bright lick of flame as if it might be the last he would see.

"Whatever your decision, I will support it."

"But there is no easy choice."

"There is also no dodging the truth," Josiah said gently. "Once a rope starts to fray…"

"It will fail. Indeed."

"So it is with your eyes."

"But the operation he describes … the agony of it."

"I will be by your side," Josiah promised. "Believe me, if I could take some of your pain, I would. But…"

"He says it will all be done in an afternoon. Then the fear will be gone." Mather picked up the fire tongs and prodded the coals, sending up a shower of sparks. "Whereas creeping blindness … my dear wife's face fading into obscurity … the world receding before me until all is consumed by darkness. That pain would torment me for the rest of my life."

"It is a cruel choice."

Mr Mather frowned. "Not to mention the cost…"

"Do not even consider it," Josiah urged. "The business will pay for it."

"No —"

"It is an expense we will share. I insist."

"I am a lucky man to count you as a friend, Josiah."

The two men hugged awkwardly, a rare display of emotion, but heartfelt.

"God has sent this challenge to test us. Like a rope."

"We will not break. We will hold fast."

The chevalier decided to operate that Friday morning. I was tasked with ensuring his complete peace of mind in readiness for the surgery — whatever food or material comfort he required was to be provided without question; the other lodging rooms were left vacant to ensure nothing disturbed his sleep, and all kitchen deliveries were diverted to the far side of the house.

In the hours immediately before operating, the chevalier underwent a remarkable transformation; it was like watching a priest prepare for a holy sacrament. He meditated, then he prayed; he spent hours polishing his surgical instruments until the steel gleamed. Then he dressed himself in black breeches and a black jacket with close-fitting sleeves but expansive shoulders to allow for easy movement. His hair was slicked back tightly, and he wore shoes with flat soles to maintain a perfectly balanced posture.

"How do I look?" He turned to me.

"Like a man about to do God's work."

"Do you see this?" He picked up a strange collar that had been stiffened with rods, then he screwed a metal block into one end. "This will fit around Mr Mather's neck, like so." He fitted the contraption around me. "It will be your job to keep it in position during the operation."

"Me?"

"Can I rely on you, Arabella?"

"But I have no medical training."

"Nor do you require it. You are there to support me. And I need this collar to be held firmly in position throughout the operation."

"What does it do?"

He adjusted the metal block so that it was by my left cheek, then he leaned close and rested the outer edge of his hand on the long edge of the block. "This is how one maintains a steady hand, you see? The weight of the hand is taken by the collar, leaving the fingers relaxed and still." His fingers touched my face. They were cool and dry, without the slightest tremor. "How does it feel?"

"Perfect."

He stroked my cheek gently.

"How do you stay so calm?" I whispered.

"I am calm because I am not afraid."

"Mr Mather is terrified."

"No doubt. This will be a difficult morning for him, but I am strong. Only the fearless can take a razor-sharp scalpel and cut into a living eye, not with the intention of hurting, but of healing."

"Where do you find such courage?"

"When ordinary men make mistakes, they simply correct them, but the eye surgeon must be right first time, and every time. I must cut with precision and confidence, and I must never doubt myself. The surgeon who has doubts is finished. This is not a calling for the fainthearted."

Mr Mather was strapped into a high-backed dining chair by Josiah, who carefully tightened the buckles, binding human legs to chair legs, arms of flesh to arms of wood.

"Hold still," Josiah said as he wrapped a leather belt around Mr Mather's forehead and tightened it to the chair back. "Ready now?"

Mr Mather looked up at Josiah with a glassy stare; he had drunk a bottle of whiskey for breakfast, but there was no merriment in his drunkenness, only dread.

The chevalier examined all the leather bindings, making sure they were tight. "The slightest movement could ruin my work," he said. When he was finished, he nodded to Mrs Mather. "You can kiss him now."

With tears streaming down her cheeks, Mrs Mather leant forward and kissed her husband tenderly. "Be brave, my darling." Then she flung her arms around him, refusing to let go. The housekeeper prised her away and took her to the kitchen.

"Let me stay," Josiah said quietly.

"I will not tolerate any squeamishness, Mr Roope. No wincing or protestation."

"I understand."

"This is not a procedure for the timid."

"No, sir."

The chevalier turned to me. "The collar, please."

I fitted the device around Mr Mather's neck exactly as I had been instructed.

"And so to work." The chevalier picked up a small clamp and moved forward. Immediately Mr Mather recoiled in fear. He tried to move his head away, but the bindings held him fast. "Try not to struggle, Mr Mather."

"No, please! Must be another way!" he moaned, barely coherent in his drunken state.

"Give him the stick," the chevalier instructed.

Josiah wedged a piece of wood into Mather's mouth and secured it with a cord.

"When it hurts, bite harder," the chevalier advised. He slid the jaws of the steel clamp under Mather's top eyelid, hooked them into the flesh at the bottom of the eye, then turned the screw so that it was impossible for Mather to blink. "Good man."

The chevalier picked up a small scalpel and rested his hand on the metal block so that the blade floated just above the eye.

Mr Mather's screams echoed through the house. I saw his teeth bite deep into the stick. Josiah looked away, unable to watch, but I was mesmerised by the chevalier's utter focus; he had blocked out the entire world to concentrate on the patient's eyes.

Gently he slid the sharp blade across the eyeball, making a first incision. As the white of the eye pulled apart and fluid oozed out, I felt a wave of nausea.

"Look at me, Arabella."

I focussed on the chevalier's face, marvelling at his composure as he cut deeper into Mather's delicate eye.

"Is it nearly done?" I whispered.

"I have barely started." He put down the scalpel and picked up a probe with a small metal hook on the end. As he moved the hook towards the incision, Mr Mather started to scream again.

The chevalier paused and gave an impatient sigh. "How else can I scoop out the jelly?"

At which point Mr Mather passed out.

"Finally," the chevalier said. "The man's screams were most distracting."

Unencumbered by any human suffering, the chevalier concentrated as he again rested his hand on the metal block and slid the instrument into the incision; the hook disappeared into Mr Mather's eyeball.

There was some blood as he dug around in the vitreous jelly, and I must confess, as it spilled onto the floor I had to look away.

"The block! Keep it in position," the chevalier said impatiently. Quickly I regained my concentration and did as I was told.

Inwardly I scolded myself for being weak. I was just a passive observer; the chevalier was the man actually performing the surgery. And yet how could one not feel for Mr Mather? Think of the discomfort when a speck of dust enters your eye momentarily; now imagine the horrors of scalpels and hooks.

Yet somehow the chevalier had found a way to rise above all that as he manipulated the eyeball with a blunt stick, then impaled the fine lens on the hook and dragged it down.

Finally he removed the instruments and studied his work. "Perfect," he declared. Then, humming to himself contentedly, he took a fine needle and thread, and proceeded to sew up the wound on the surface of the eyeball as if it was nothing more than a piece of silk rather than delicate living tissue.

"Most satisfactory."

I looked at the eye — it was monstrously bloodshot, the lid was bruised and bloody, the whole thing swollen out of shape.

"Now for the other one," the chevalier said calmly.

And it began all over again.

It was a relief to see the bandages finally emerge from the chevalier's instrument box. As he wrapped them round Mather's head, the horrors of the maimed eyes disappeared from view. Bloody pools on the floor were the only testament to what had happened.

"The smelling salts, please, Arabella."

"Shouldn't we undo his straps first?"

"Trust me on this."

I wafted the pungent phial of salts under Mr Mather's nose, and gradually he started to stir. At first he was groggy and confused, but as he tried to open his eyes the horrors of what he had just endured flooded back. He started to struggle violently, trying to break free from his shackles.

"Now, now, Mr Mather," the chevalier said with calm authority. "It's all over. The procedure is done."

"I can't open —"

"Your eyes have been securely bandaged so that they can heal."

"Let me go!"

"You must be calm before I release the straps."

"Get away from me!"

Finally, Josiah found his voice. "It's me, I'm here, old friend," he whispered into Mather's ear. "Everything is done. It is finished."

It was the only voice in the room that Mr Mather seemed to trust, and he stopped writhing.

"If I release the bindings, will you remain calm?"

"Yes."

The chevalier nodded to Josiah, who loosened all the leather straps and held his friend's hand.

"Listen to me very carefully," the chevalier began. "Healing is a critical period, and you must follow my instructions precisely. The bandages will be kept in place for five days. During that time there must be no sudden or violent movements of the head. Try not to cough or sneeze or laugh."

"Laugh?" Josiah looked at the chevalier in disbelief. "About what?"

"When you sleep, make sure that your head is propped upright with pillows. Do not sleep face down; we need to keep pressure off the surface of the eye. Eat only soft food for the next three days — soup, gruel and porridge, as chewing might send vibrations through the skull. I will check up on you every morning and evening. There is nothing to be frightened of, Mr Mather; the worst is behind you. Do you understand?"

"What about crying?" Mather whispered. "Can I weep?"

"Come, don't be so melodramatic," the chevalier smiled. "You are on the mend now."

"I can't… I can't remember everything you said…"

"Don't worry," Josiah reassured. "I will stay by your side while the bandages are on."

"God bless you." Mather clasped Josiah's arm.

"I will send over fresh clothes for you, dear." I kissed Josiah on his forehead. "Everything will be arranged."

"And talking of domestic arrangements," the chevalier said, stretching his arms, "I'm pretty peckish myself."

"You can eat? After that?" Josiah was so pale he seemed on the verge of throwing up.

"Surgery is immensely taxing. One must keep one's strength up."

"Very well," said Josiah, nodding. "Arabella, take the chevalier home and make sure he is looked after."

"Of course."

The chevalier turned to me and smiled. "Shall we?"

TEN

The moment we walked into the house, the chevalier flopped onto a chaise longue with a dramatic sigh. "Put a drink in my hand, Arabella. Your finest brandy."

I hurried to the cabinet, poured a large glass, and placed it in his hand. He took a swig and rolled it around his mouth.

"This is when it hits. When I let go of the concentration, I am smothered with exhaustion." He closed his eyes. "Help me, please."

I knelt, untied his laces, slid off his shoes and gently massaged his stockinged feet.

"Mmm. Yet it is my shoulders that feel the cramp."

I put a cushion under his feet, then moved behind his head, rubbing his back.

"You're good at this," he purred.

"I can feel the tension. Like knots."

"Don't forget the neck."

My fingers obliged. "Who would have thought such delicate surgery could be so gruelling?"

"Each muscle and sinew must be focussed on the single point of the scalpel. The oculist is a man of immense physical as well as mental stamina. Hence the ravenous appetite."

I took the hint. While the chevalier sipped brandy by the fire, I prepared a rich leg of roasted mutton, served with batter pudding and artichoke; dessert was to be blancmange garnished with almonds and raisins.

As we ate together, I saw his strength gradually return; the serious-minded surgeon was replaced by the urbane aristocrat. He told me about all the latest etiquette and customs that were now fashionable at court, how to greet nobles with sincerity, and how to greet them while simultaneously snubbing them. He persuaded me to lay out the many different pieces of cutlery in the house, then proceeded to show me the perfect technique for eating with each one. He showed me how female courtiers use their fans to flirt, to warn, and to cool themselves while coquettishly raising the temperature of admirers.

"But most intriguing of all," he said with a dark smile, "are the politics of décolletage."

"I don't understand. Politics of…?"

"The cleavage."

"Oh."

The chevalier shook his head. "Your husband would not approve."

"My husband is not here."

"It is not for prim, provincial minds."

"You really think we are so naïve?" I leaned forward, drawing his eyes down to my neckline.

"Too many buttons, Arabella," he whispered.

"Do London women not care for decency?"

"They care more for power. Their ability to mesmerise an entire room with a few inches of flesh is a wonder to behold." His fingers reached out and undid the top button of my blouse.

"But there are limits, surely?"

"Not when it comes to the neckline." He undid another button and stared admiringly at my breasts. "I swear, had you been born into a different class, the whole of London would now be at your feet."

Perhaps I should have brushed his hand away, but I had been born into the smell of piss and rotting animal brains, and here was this brilliant aristocrat admiring me.

"Do you know of balneotherapy, Arabella? It is quite a revolution."

"For the eyes?"

"For everything but. It is a method of treating diseases by bathing the body in hot water. It has been pioneered in the great spas of Europe: Baden-Baden, Vienna, Marienbad."

"How can bathing be a cure?"

"Perhaps I can demonstrate, if you will permit?"

And so, on the pretext of learning about cures, I prepared the chevalier a bath. He laid out his personal collection of fragrant oils for me to experiment with. The smells were so rich, I can almost taste them now … lemon and honeycomb … amberwood and mandarin … vanilla and ginger. As the room filled with steam, the cocktail of aromatic vapours spread through the house.

I glanced up. The chevalier was standing in the doorway, dressed only in a muslin bathing robe, gazing at me as I stirred the water. As he approached, his eyes remained locked on me. Then as he climbed into the bath, he gently took me in his arms and lifted me into the waters with him.

I am not proud of what I did. But I am only human. You must understand, I was not just making love to a man; he embodied a life of glamour and indulgence, of excitement and power. He was London at its finest; I was having sex with one of the great cities of the world.

It was the first time in my life I had known such wanton pleasure, the first time I had been so completely satisfied.

I drifted into an easy sleep, but when I awoke, the chevalier was sitting in the corner chair, his head in his hands.

"Is something the matter?"

Silence.

"Don't worry about my husband." I hurried over. "He'll never find out."

The chevalier looked up at me — his cheeks were wet with tears. "You make me so happy, Arabella."

"And you, me." I kissed his tears away.

"Which only makes it worse."

"I don't understand."

"We are powerless. Utterly powerless."

I couldn't bear to see him so defeated. "Then let me help."

He started pacing the room in a state of agitation. "England is such a small, mean-spirited country. Its people know the cost of everything, but the value of nothing. We are surrounded by philistines and ignorance! Pious prigs are strangling us, Arabella. They think that stoicism is a virtue, that if one is losing one's sight, it must be accepted as God's will. Hang the Gods, I say! If God wanted us to be blind, why did he give us eyes in the first place? My God has given me the genius to fight disease, to restore sight to the blind just as Christ did on the road to Jericho."

"Mr Mather didn't accept his blindness," I ventured.

"Exactly! And how would he have fared had not chance put me here? No-one else could have helped him as I have done. There are no oculists for a hundred miles! The English are obsessed with their bowels; nothing else matters. Look how I struggle to raise money."

"Are your meetings not going well?"

He shook his head mournfully. "'What is the expected return on my capital?' they ask. 'There needs to be collateral for the investment.' Small-minded imbeciles."

"You must persevere."

"Inspired by you, Arabella, I refuse to give up. Because I know that if I had the money to build a fully equipped mobile operating theatre, I would become the leading oculist in Europe."

I put my arms around him and kissed the top of his head. "One patient at a time. You have cured Mr Mather; you have done God's work in this city."

He looked up at me with such gratitude. "You are so wise. And beautiful."

"And I am yours."

I kissed him, and we made love again.

The pleasure … it was so delicious. He taught me things … positions… It was as far from the calendar above the bed as it was possible to get. Josiah wanted a son, but the chevalier wanted to feel alive.

Day blurred into night. The doors remained locked; all domestic routines were abandoned in the hedonistic rush. This man was the embodiment of everything I had longed for without knowing it.

Why should I wither away in provincial Norwich, wasting my youth and beauty, when I could be living to the full and dedicating my time to supporting a medical genius? Had God not put this man in my path to save me? His eye surgery defies Fate; he changes the destiny of his patients, so why could he not change my destiny?

The following morning I unwrapped myself from the chevalier's arms and crept down to the kitchens to prepare us a syllabub. Cream mixed with wine, brandy, and lemon juice, with nutmeg sprinkled on top — a perfect breakfast for lovers.

But when I carried it upstairs to the chevalier's room, he was fully dressed and packing all his possessions.

"What are you doing?"

"It is better this way."

"No! You cannot leave."

He loaded his anatomy books neatly into one of the trunks. "Once Mather's bandages are removed, my work here is finished."

"But I am not work!"

"That's not what I meant, Arabella."

"And we still have two more days."

He stopped momentarily. "You know I must find patrons to support my surgical art. That is the whole purpose —"

"There are wealthy men here in Norwich." Defiantly I started to take his possessions out of the trunks again.

"Please, don't make this more difficult."

"I won't let you leave!"

"Stop this!"

"You can't just come into my life and turn it upside down!"

"But I have no choice."

"We always have a choice."

He reached out to touch me, but I pulled away.

"Arabella, this hurts me as much as it hurts you. But pain is the way of the world."

I watched in silence as he finished packing his possessions. Every bottle of perfume and oil, every pair of fine gloves and polished shoes that were stowed away felt like another year added to my prison sentence. All I could see ahead was a vast expanse of provincial ignorance, endless days reading nothing but the Bible, endless nights being subjected to the grunting exertions of Josiah Roope; and all this followed by old age and death.

Like Mephistopheles, I had tasted the eternal joy of Heaven, and to lose it would be ten thousand Hells.

"What if I could get the money for you?"

The chevalier hesitated, then snapped the trunk buckles shut. "I fear I have exhausted Norwich."

"But I know where my husband's money is kept."

"Mr Roope is too cautious. My plan needs bold investors."

"Which is why I wouldn't ask him."

He studied me. "What exactly are you suggesting, Arabella?"

"I know where the key to his strongbox is hidden. We can use his gold to escape to Europe. Together. Where we can marry."

"You mean steal his money?"

"Your talent will take the Continent by storm. We will never have to return to this wretched country to face any consequences."

The chevalier looked at me with a strange expression. I have wondered about that moment many times since; there was satisfaction, there was the glint of a predator, and there was even a touch of humility. But he quickly masked it all with a charming smile. "Do not joke about such things."

"You don't take me seriously?"

"You are talking about a criminal act!"

"And what is seducing another man's wife? Are we not merely being honest?"

"Passion is not a crime."

"I don't love my husband. I have never loved him. Truth be told, he will be well rid of me — then he can find a more compliant woman to bear him children."

"But to take his money…" The chevalier frowned.

"It is simply compensation for the years I have already wasted."

"I do believe you are in earnest, Arabella Taylor."

"Deadly."

But just as he seemed to be on the verge of agreeing, he shook his head. "It's impossible. *Primum non nocere.* It is my professional oath. *First, do no harm.* I heal people, I don't wound them."

"Then heal me."

"Doing the right thing is never easy, Arabella. But it must be done all the same. I fear we must sacrifice our love for one another. That is our destiny."

"I have made sacrifices my entire life! Now I want what is right for me." I leant forward and kissed him. "Is this not right for you?" I kissed him again, stroking his cheek. "Is this not our destiny?"

Suddenly he pulled me towards him and kissed me as if he wanted to consume me. He held my face in his hands and gazed at me. "You have a very persuasive tongue."

"So do you."

At that moment, I would have defied anyone to say how something that felt so good could be wrong in God's eyes. The chevalier's love for me swept all else aside.

Wrapped in his arms as the coach sped towards the port of Great Yarmouth, I believed that he was a genius who could restore sight to the blind, and that we were escaping to a new life.

I had no time for pain; I thought only of pleasure, and love, and the future. We had a strongbox full of money, we had ambition, and we had each other. Europe awaited.

I was to learn too late that the wheels of Justice may turn slowly, but they will grind exceedingly small.

PART THREE: DOCTOR HARVEY

ELEVEN

"Justice?" My voice echoes in the stark prison cell. "You have the audacity to talk about justice?"

Arabella studies me calmly. "You have not heard my full confession."

"Nor do I wish to! You betray your first husband, a man who plucked you from the filth of poverty. And now you have destroyed your second husband, a gentleman and a surgeon? This confession is a sordid affair."

"Is that how you diagnose your patients, Doctor Harvey? A superficial examination followed by a rash judgement?"

"There is nothing rash about my judgement. You have confessed to more crimes than most men know in their entire lives. If you think this will help your case, you are deluded."

"You have not been listening carefully enough."

"I am out of patience with you." I stand up to leave. "You are an adulterer, a thief and a liar." I hammer on the cell door to summon the guard.

"You think you are so established in this world, Doctor Harvey. But in your heart, and in your skin, you know what it means to be worthless. Deep down, you and I are not so different."

I turn to look at her — so utterly unwavering in her self-belief. "Make your peace with God," I suggest.

"I have nothing to repent because I do not set the rules. I merely play the game."

There is a rattle of keys, the heavy oak door swings open and I am free.

As the constable escorts me from the prison, he sees how agitated I am and wisely remains silent. Maybe the Birds of Prey are right. Why parade the humiliation and suffering of innocent men through a lurid court trial? Everyone's dignity will be spared if Arabella is shipped straight to an asylum. She is clearly following a different morality to the rest of us, and if that isn't madness, what is?

When I get back to my surgery, there is an empty carriage waiting outside. I assume a new patient has arrived unannounced, but as I enter the hall, Joseph hurries to meet me.

"Doctor Harvey, you have been summoned by the marquess of Lansdowne."

"Is he ill?"

"He didn't say. But he's sent a carriage."

"Let me talk to the chevalier first."

"You're too late, Doctor Harvey. He has gone on ahead."

"What do you mean?"

"The marquess sent for him shortly after you left."

I feel a flash of anger at the way these aristocrats are interfering with my investigation. Yet what choice do I have but to do as they instruct? They are dangerous men to resist. "What do they want with the chevalier?"

Joseph shrugs. "I'm not sure, Doctor Harvey. But they told me to make him look as presentable as possible."

The carriage journeys for five miles out of the city, then pulls through some iron gates in an anonymous-looking wall and enters the vast private estate of the marquess of Lansdowne.

Its rolling meadows, punctuated with a perfectly placed lake, are empty except for some well-behaved sheep and a couple of ant-like gardeners toiling over a tree stump. These optics are all about exuding power without seeming to try too hard. Mature trees form a natural driveway to the imposing mansion, as if placed there by God; in fact, each one has been hauled across the county by brute force and raised with elaborate scaffolds.

The Humbling of the Visitor continues inside, as a footman leads me down long corridors, turning left and right when I least expect it. At one point I swear we have gone in a circle.

Finally I am ushered into what the footman announces as the East Library, where there are no books, just a single long table at which are sat the chevalier and a grey-haired artist making pencil sketches. Rather than approach, I wait by the door, eavesdropping on their conversation.

"Perhaps a blindfold might look more dramatic?" the chevalier suggests. "A classical illusion to the Blind Seer. Or Lady Justice, maybe?" The man seems in remarkably good spirits considering the ordeal he has so recently endured.

"It could look most striking, Chevalier," the artist agrees.

"Or would the darkened glasses look more enigmatic?" The chevalier puts on his shaded spectacles to demonstrate. "Heroic rather than humble, should be the guiding principle."

"Astride a horse, perhaps, sir?"

"I have never cared much for horses." The chevalier pulls a sour face. "But what about in an operating theatre? Observing an operation using just my hearing, advising young students."

"That would indeed be an arresting image."

"You could put me on the dais, in the centre of the frame, with all the students looking up at me for guidance."

"Yes, yes." The artist makes another sketch with fast, bold flourishes. "This is good. Very good."

Without warning, the floorboard under my foot creaks.

"Who's there?" the chevalier demands.

I have no choice but to approach. "Good afternoon, Chevalier."

"Ah, Doctor Harvey, this is Thomas Bardwell, a renowned portrait painter, up from London."

"Don't let me interrupt." I try to sound casual.

"I was just finishing," Bardwell says as he puts his sketchpads into a large leather holdall.

"Show Doctor Harvey your ideas."

Bardwell obliges, and I look at his flattering pencil studies of the chevalier's face from various angles.

"Do some thinking, Bardwell, and come back with a few more compositions," the chevalier instructs.

I watch in silence as the artist leaves. "A portrait? This is unexpected," I observe.

"It's a gift from the marquess of Lansdowne. A most charming surprise. My portrait will soon be hanging in the Assembly Rooms here in Bath."

"Such a pity it is a portrait you will never actually see."

"I am not the point," the chevalier smiles. "It is for the future generations who will gaze admiringly at my legacy. 'There was a great surgeon,' they will observe as they drink tea from dainty china cups."

And suddenly I am not so sure about this man. Where is his sense of outrage? Why hasn't he asked me about what Arabella has confessed? What kind of an arrangement has he struck with Lansdowne while I have been at the gaol?

I put the drawings back on the table. "So the marquess summoned you today?"

"He sent his own carriage. Wonderfully appointed. Apparently Bardwell was here in Bath, and the marquess wasted no time. Evidently, he made some enquiries and discovered just how significant a man I am."

"Evidently."

"The marquess is very keen to keep me in Bath for as long as possible, and all at his expense. Most generous."

Is this the voice of a man who has been tragically abused, I wonder? Or is it the euphoria of someone who has outwitted justice, and cannot believe his luck?

Perhaps I have been too quick to judge Arabella.

One of the servants announces that supper has been prepared, and promptly wheels the chevalier away. A few moments later, another set of doors opens and the marquess of Lansdowne enters, flanked by Viscount Melville and the earl of Stratford. Do they always hunt in packs?

"So, have you brought the committal papers?" Lansdowne asks.

"No, my lord."

"Why? What's the delay?"

"I have only just begun my examination of Lady Taylor."

"But that's just a formality. We all know the conclusion you're going to reach, Harvey."

Stratford gives an impatient sigh. "If it was up to me, she'd be burnt to death. Like the witch she is. An example to all women who raise a hand against us."

The others nod their agreement. I study their faces and realise why the chevalier's emasculation is terrifying to these men. They all have wives and mistresses and wilful daughters who need to be controlled; God forbid those women should get wind of any precedent set by Arabella.

But how can I defy the marquess without incurring his wrath?

"My lords, an interesting possibility has arisen," I begin. "I have reason to believe that this scandal has the potential to reach far beyond the city of Bath."

"Which is precisely why it needs to be smothered," Melville grumbles.

"The chevalier was a prominent surgeon in London until just a few years ago. He treated all the great families, and it may well be that some of those in positions of power could be compromised by all this. Once we know the full extent of the scandal, there may be an opportunity for you to … settle old scores, or deal with people who may have wronged your lordships in the past. Scandal can always be exploited by the canny."

Now they are tempted. I can see it in their eyes. There's nothing an aristocrat loves more that settling a grudge.

"If you give me a little more time with Lady Arabella, who knows what I can unearth?"

The three men exchange wary glances.

"We'll discuss it in private," Lansdowne pronounces, then beckons for a servant to show me out.

TWELVE

I arrive back at the gaol the following morning to find confusion amongst the guards, because Arabella has asked for a small mirror.

"What if she uses the glass to harm herself?" The constable shakes his head gravely. "I wouldn't have agreed. Never. But the sergeant overruled me."

"I'll wager she offered him a sweetener," the junior guard smirks.

"Enough of that. We don't know it for sure."

"Perhaps she just wants to maintain her grooming," I suggest.

"Wouldn't know. Never had such a fine lady in gaol before."

"Is she a difficult prisoner?" I ask.

"Quite the opposite, sir. Very obedient."

"And the food? How does she find that?"

"Eats it without complaint."

"Not an easy task," the junior mutters.

"Does she sleep well?"

"There she's a strange one." The constable hesitates. "I've never actually seen her with her eyes closed. She lies on the bench as if she's sleeping, but her eyes are open. Even when you check through the spyhole in the middle of the night, her eyes stay open."

"Like the Devil," the junior adds.

They take me to her cell, but before I enter, I study her through the spyhole. For someone who doesn't sleep, she looks remarkably well; her face is clear and calm. The mirror has been propped on a high ledge to cast a reflection onto the far wall, and she is running her fingers across the puddle of light, feeling its warmth on the whitewashed stone.

The constable unlocks the door and lets me in; Arabella doesn't even glance round. "I knew you would change your mind."

"Just because I listen, it doesn't mean I believe you. Or trust you."

"Trust. Now, there's a strange word. To accept without evidence. Only a fool would do that. Sit down, Doctor Harvey."

The stool is exactly where I left it yesterday. I resent the way she takes control, but I am now on a quest to discover the truth. So I sit.

"We were on the run," she begins, "with Josiah's gold and silver hidden in our trunks. We knew that we had to get far away from Norwich as quickly as possible, to avoid the wrath of my husband. So once we had crossed the English Channel, we headed east in a series of waggons and river barges, our luggage piled high around us.

"At each town and frontier, the chevalier checked the maps carefully; we were speeding through the Netherlands, intending to cross the German States, then head deep into Prussia. Europe is such a chaos of changing borders that the chevalier knew it was the perfect place to detach ourselves from the consequences of what we had done.

"We passed so many strange and mysterious places: gothic walled cities that loomed out of the mists, castles on top of wooded hills, bridges over steep and jagged ravines. The danger was all part of the thrill, and it drew us closer together. That, and the sex. You must remember, until then I had only ever known one man, and the things the chevalier taught me

… how was I to know what was normal, and what was aberrant?"

"Enough of this!" I snap.

"Must you interrupt, Doctor Harvey?"

"You are taking me for a fool!"

"And you are behaving like a prig."

"All you are doing is romanticising a sordid crime. You stole from your husband then abandoned him. Do not turn your shameful behaviour into a salacious adventure story. You were criminals on the run."

"And yet, Doctor Harvey, you return for more."

"Because it is my job."

"Really? Or maybe it is the vicarious thrill that attracts you." Her dark eyes study me closely. "Or perhaps you are frightened that I might be right. That God is on the side of a violent and abusive woman."

"Not the God I believe in."

"Do you know how many times the word 'vengeance' appears in the Bible, Doctor Harvey? Fifty-two times. It's not all love and forgiveness in the Good Book. I think my favourite is Psalms Fifty-Eight. 'The righteous shall rejoice when he seeth the vengeance: he shall wash his feet in the blood of the wicked.'"

"You would really cloak your crimes in the Bible?"

"Justice is justice, Doctor Harvey. Now keep listening, and please, no more interruptions."

PART FOUR: ARABELLA

THIRTEEN

We finally crossed into the Free State of Thuringia and stopped at Eisenach on the River Hörsel, a town dominated by a huge castle that loomed from the wooded hillside.

I cannot describe the relief to be out of the perpetual motion of carriages; to stretch out, to sleep on a bed that was not bumping and jolting, to drink from a cup without half the contents spilling down my chin. But it was no accident that we were here. The chevalier had picked this town because it was home to the Mosengel Workshop that has built some of the finest church organs in Europe; now he wanted them to build a vehicle tailored to his oculist arts, a mobile laboratory and operating theatre — the Eye Waggon.

"Have you ever seen inside a church organ?" Mosengel the Younger was the grandson of the founder; he was tall, thin and nervy, with an unruly mop of black hair. "It is one of the most complex machines ever made by the human hand."

You could sense the man's dedication; he must have shown people round his workshop a hundred times, yet his enthusiasm never dulled. Patiently he showed us how huge banks of pipes connected to keyboards via hundreds of intricate rods and joints; proudly he presented his craftsmen — carpenters, metalworkers, engineers, engravers and finishers.

"Constructing an organ is like performing surgery, Chevalier. Music is to us what sight is to you."

"Which is precisely why we are here, Herr Mosengel."

As Mosengel guided us through the workshops, we saw wood being intricately carved, ivory shaped, gold leaf delicately inlaid.

"Each instrument is like a child to us," he said. "It may leave the workshop, but it never leaves our care."

"And I believe the Eye Waggon will be every bit as complex."

"We do not fear that word, Chevalier. We embrace it."

"Just as well. At its heart I need an operating theatre, with all my instruments perfectly positioned."

"We will build the space around your body's exact measurements. It will fit you like a glove." Mosengel grabbed a sewing tape. "Arms up, please." He darted around the chevalier's body, taking a complete set of measurements.

"The waggon also needs a small bed chamber," the chevalier continued. "As well as storage lockers, and provision for a well-hidden strongbox."

"We have some excellent locksmiths here in Eisenach."

"I want every surface to be highly polished, reflecting the optical excellence of my art. It is these details that are so important."

"Indeed, Chevalier. And not just the visuals, but the sound." Mosengel was really getting into his stride. "Every latch and handle will close with a reassuring click — smooth and perfect. For it is the things we touch most that create the deepest impression. Like the actions on a keyboard, every moving part must be precise."

"Yes, yes. I like this," the chevalier nodded. "But above all else, the Eye Waggon needs to exude wonder. It will be a place where miracles happen. Patients must feel as if they are entering a magician's laboratory, a mysterious emporium where nature is conquered. After all, that is what they are paying so handsomely for. Splendour, power, mystery, Herr Mosengel. These are to be your guiding lights."

Mosengel wound the sewing tape up carefully. "You do understand, Chevalier, that level of excellence is only possible if each component is created without compromise?"

"I despise the word. There can be no compromise in eye surgery."

"And your budget reflects that?"

"We didn't travel halfway across Europe on a shoestring, Herr Mosengel."

"In which case, I suggest we use only the very best materials."

He opened a door onto one of the smaller drying rooms, which was stacked with exotic timber, its smell as rich as coffee. Mosengel selected a plank, pulled it from the rack and dusted it lovingly with a cloth. "Mahogany from Cuba. It has been drying all winter."

The chevalier ran his hand over the smooth surface. "Beautiful. Such a colour."

"And that is before it is treated." Mosengel put the plank back in its place like a parent putting his infant to bed. "For decorative metals, I suggest copper rather than brass."

"Naturally."

"Silver rather than pewter."

"Agreed. But steel for the mechanicals, surely?"

"For strength, yes. And we have been experimenting with hydraulic systems for powering organ bellows; it occurs to me that this could be modified into a suspension system for the Eye Waggon."

"I think you have read Arabella's mind," the chevalier said, smiling at me. "Isn't that right, my love?"

"Herr Mosengel, if you could smooth the ride, I would worship you forever," I replied. "We have travelled for so many weeks in such discomfort."

Mosengel studied us closely. "Where exactly have you come from?"

"The Netherlands. Before that, some time in France. And Belgium," the chevalier said vaguely.

"Then you have already travelled past many great organ workshops to get here. Which is strange, perhaps?"

"But your reputation," the chevalier said solemnly. "No-one has a reputation like yours."

"You flatter me."

Did Mosengel suspect we were trying to evade the authorities in England?

"Such a sophisticated project will require a large down payment," he said pointedly.

"I would expect no less," the chevalier smiled.

"Then let me fetch my cost surveyor." Mosengel hurried from the room, leaving us momentarily alone.

"Why are you so worried, Arabella?" The chevalier stroked my cheek.

"The cost will be enormous."

"Do you not want me to have the best? Is my art not worthy?"

"Why do decorative fittings have to be in silver?"

He leant close and kissed me gently. "Do not fret about the expense. It is Roope's money, and he is not here to object."

"When it is gone, what then?"

"The finest surgeons need the finest equipment, so that they can charge the highest fees."

Mosengel returned with an older man in tow, who carried a large, pristine ledger. "We will itemise your costs in here."

The chevalier took the book and leafed through the hundreds of blank pages, all neatly ruled and full of promise. "Have your craftsmen start work today," he commanded.

While the craftsmen toiled, we shopped.

The chevalier set up accounts with the most renowned tailors and wigmakers in the province, and we assembled a wardrobe of the finest clothes ever to adorn the human body. Waistcoats, frock coats, breeches, stockings and shoes; close-bodied gowns, Brunswick gowns, silk chemises … we were reinventing ourselves in fabric. The cost was eye-watering, but the chevalier insisted, "To reflect the exceptional nature of one's aristocratic breeding, one must be exceptionally well dressed."

To add a flourish to his new image, the chevalier treated himself to a long, black walking cane embossed with gold trim and topped with a silver knob. The moment it was placed in his hand, his entire bearing changed. Now the chevalier walked down the street with swagger, pointing imperiously with the cane, waving pedestrians aside, impudently prodding those who were too slow to move.

"You see, Arabella," he explained in the privacy of our rooms, "this is not about vanity, it is about power. This is how an aristocrat wields his birth-right."

He handed me the walking cane so that I could feel its weight and authority.

"But at times it makes you appear … rude," I ventured.

The chevalier laughed. "You are so charming."

"Prodding people who stand in your way? Is that what a gentleman does?"

"I am merely reinforcing the social hierarchy. The man with the cane is the superior man."

I handed the wretched thing back to him.

"You do not approve?"

"Let's not talk about it."

"Arabella? What did I do wrong? The cane is nothing to do with you."

"Isn't it?"

"Stop speaking in riddles, woman."

"If that cane is a daily reminder to the world of your superiority, then what does that make me? Nothing."

"Nonsense!"

"It's the truth, and you know it." I tried to force back tears of shame.

"You are with me, Arabella. And that transforms you." He reached out and pulled me close, kissing the back of my neck.

"Why are you interested in someone low-born?"

"Because I love you."

"Until you find someone of better rank." I pulled away. "Then you will cast me off."

"Never. I swear."

"Fine clothes cannot hide who I really am. People will sense the truth."

"I promise —"

"Behind my back they will laugh at me. A pigeon strutting like a peacock in borrowed feathers."

"Arabella, you are defined by me." He looked at me solemnly. "You are the moon, basking in the reflected sunlight that radiates from me. And like the moon, you are beautiful and hypnotic."

"And when people learn the truth, it will humiliate us both."

He took a silk handkerchief and dried the tears from my cheeks. "We will continue the lessons we started in Norwich. I will teach you how to conquer the world with grace and etiquette. My earnest project shall be the creation of Lady Arabella Taylor."

"You cannot just make up something like that."

"I already have." He drew up a chair and sat me down. "Listen carefully to the new truth. I have decided that you can trace your ancestry back to a mistress of Charles II; he had so many, they lost count. Your line was ennobled, as is fitting for the royal seed, but that Dutch prig William III took legal action to strip your family of its title. The dispute rumbled on for years, until a settlement was reached that left you with money and status, but a discreet title: the Keeper of the Beehives."

I stared at him. "No-one will believe that."

"Why not? They have the Groom of the Stool, the Clerk of the Green Cloth, the Master of the Buckhounds — why not a Keeper of the Beehives?"

I considered my new title; it did have a certain poetry to it.

"And like the bees —" he rubbed himself against me, his hand sliding between my legs — "you also have sweet honey."

I laughed and playfully pushed him away.

"So now that you have your story," the chevalier continued, "you must live the part in everything you do. Remember: etiquette is to people what warmth is to wax. It shapes them to your will."

So our lessons continued. But it went far beyond dancing and cutlery, for now he was teaching me the art of superiority. We spent many days perfecting the 'look of disdain'.

"It must come from deep inside," the chevalier explained, "from a conviction that you are always right because of who you are. Your breeding gives you an innate wisdom that the meek will never possess. You are right because you are an aristocrat. And if you should need to change your mind, it can be done in such a way as to bolster your exceptionalism. Never say, 'I was wrong' or 'I stand corrected.' Instead, make a quip in Latin (any words you can think of — no-one will call you out on it), then remark, 'It is always so stimulating to meet a man who is an expert in their field; I will consider your arguments further.' The next time you meet, simply claim that you have always held those beliefs. If anyone dares to remind you that you used to believe the opposite, you remark, 'Do you doubt me, sir?' and deploy the haughty look of disdain."

"Will people not think me a liar?"

"Humility is not for aristocrats, Arabella. It makes the inferior classes feel nervous. They need the whip-hand of strong leadership. I have found the English lower classes love to tug their forelocks and doff their caps. The rich man in his castle, the poor man at his gate. That is how everyone likes it. Especially the poor."

Over the following weeks, I proved to be an exemplary student, and the chevalier was a first-class teacher.

My mistake was never to question *why* he had perfected the art of duplicity.

FOURTEEN

When they wheeled the finished Eye Waggon into the presentation hall, it was still shrouded in cotton sheets. And it was heavy; it took four carpenters just to haul it from the workshop.

Stepping onto a small wooden dais, Mosengel cleared his throat and read from a piece of paper, "It gives me immense pleasure to present you with the completed artefact — a mobile operating theatre for the eyes. May she bring healing and enlightenment wherever she travels."

There was polite applause from the craftsmen, then Mosengel pulled a red sash cord, and the sheets fell away to reveal the most strangely beautiful carriage I have ever seen. It was immense: seven yards long and nearly three wide, supported on double axles front and back. Steel straps around the mahogany carcass made it look a little like a strongbox on wheels, and its panels were covered with huge, carved eyes, each one beautifully painted. Engraved on the strap under the top railings, and highlighted in gold leaf, was the Latin motto, *Qui Visum, Vitam Dat*, meaning 'He who gives sight, gives life.'

A smile of pure joy broke across the chevalier's face. "I love it!"

"Allow me to demonstrate," Mosengel said, inviting us to follow him around the waggon. "The driver's perch has been fitted with a canopy that can be extended to protect against rain, so that travelling is safe in all conditions." He pulled a lever that extended the canopy in a smooth motion. "Under the driver's box is a small sleeping compartment." He swung open a panel to reveal a narrow bunk with a mattress. "Not for everyday use, but essential when you cannot reach a town. For you, however, sleeping on the journey is all part of the pleasure."

He opened the front door with a precise click, to reveal a luxurious travelling and sleeping compartment. The bed folded into a large plush sofa, lockers were cunningly positioned in every available space, there was even a small wash basin with a pump handle to draw water.

"Very sensual, Herr Mosengel." I ran my hands over the plush cushions and silk bedding. "I'm impressed."

"But there is an even more private space," he said with a glint in his eye. He slid aside a flap and wound a crank handle, and the bed swung up to reveal a hatch in the floor. "Please, take a look."

The chevalier opened the hatch to reveal a mass of pipework and steel struts.

"The suspension system," Mosengel beamed.

"Impressive."

"But look closer. What is hidden between the pipes?"

We peered into the gloom; hidden among the mechanics was a cast iron safe, built into the chassis.

"Perfect," the chevalier muttered.

"Only accessed from the living quarters," Mosengel whispered. "And only if you know it is there, and only if you have both keys."

"Could the whole safe be stolen?" the chevalier asked.

"You would have to cut the waggon into pieces to release the strongbox."

"And what if someone wanted to steal the waggon itself?"

"The steering mechanism is locked by a master key, which only you have." Mosengel handed him a large, complex key, with teeth jutting in multiple directions. "But no-one would dare. The carved eyes on the outside — they are not just for decoration; they give the impression that you are being watched at all times."

"Clever."

"It's a trick the Church has used for centuries. Why do you think there are so many cherubs staring down at you from cathedral rafters?" Mosengel stepped back outside. "But the best is yet to come."

He led us to the waggon's main door; as he opened it, a small set of steps slid out of the chassis, inviting us to enter.

"Behold the operating theatre."

We climbed into an extraordinary room with a glass-panelled roof that flooded the space with natural light.

In the centre was a padded chair mounted on a platform, with a series of levers and crank handles jutting out of the framework. "The chair is fully articulated, adjustable in three axes to ensure perfect positioning of the patient. Every joint is lockable, and there are straps on the pivoting arms and headrests."

"No longer any need for an assistant to hold the patient down." The chevalier nodded. "That's good."

"Stand there, if you please," Herr Mosengel instructed.

The chevalier took a position next to the chair as if he was about to perform an operation, then Mosengel released a catch and a metal arm suspended from the ceiling slid across the room.

"The delivery system."

The chevalier looked at the metal tree in wonder: numerous mechanical sprigs held magnifying glasses, forceps, scalpels, mirrors, and various surgical instruments.

"All the essentials at your fingertips." Mosengel smiled. "And if you turn around…"

The chevalier did as he was told; Mosengel revealed a set of cabinets with more instruments, bandages, dressings, and numerous medical reference books, all artfully arranged.

"We have also installed some opticon devices." He pointed to a series of small sliding shutters dotted around the room. I pulled one aside and looked out — a lens gave me a comprehensive view of the space outside the waggon.

"I do love a peephole," the chevalier quipped.

"Built into the pupils of the carved eyes, they are the perfect way of seeing if the next patient has arrived."

"Genius!" The chevalier reached out and hugged Mosengel warmly. "You have excelled yourself, sir!"

The German seemed a little embarrassed at the display of affection and extricated himself. "There is more." He made his way to the back of the space. "What good is all this if people don't know you have arrived?" He pulled another set of brass levers and the back wall dropped down to become a presentation stage. "For pitching your services in market squares," he explained. "And as you present, people will be able to see the wonderful surgery behind you."

The chevalier strutted out onto the platform, raising his arms in the air like a politician in session. "Here I shall defeat blindness once and for all!" he declared. "Here you shall see genius outwit nature! Man shall no longer live in fear of the dark!" He laughed, then leapt from the platform and worked his way down the line of craftsmen, shaking the hand of each man in turn, until finally he was face to face with Mosengel. "You have performed a miracle, sir."

"It's nothing compared to the miracle of eye surgery," Mosengel said modestly.

"And with this vehicle you have enabled genius to flourish."

"We also took the liberty of hiring you a driver, who we have trained in the mechanics of the Eye Waggon. He will be with you at all times for adjustments and maintenance."

"I have never known such service, Herr Mosengel. You put the English to shame."

"There is just the matter of the final balance to pay." Rather awkwardly, he handed a sealed envelope to the chevalier, who smiled and brushed it aside.

"Arabella will settle the account, won't you, my love?"

The entire staff of Mosengel's workshop lined up to watch as the waggon pulled smoothly out onto the cobbled streets of Eisenach, drawn by six powerful horses, then sped through the imposing St Nicholas' Gate and out into the wooded countryside.

This was the high point. We were new and brilliant, and the chevalier was now the 'Peripatetic Oculist to European Nobility'. Wherever we travelled, we would turn darkness to light.

We stopped at a few small towns to practise our presentation and enable the chevalier to test the workings of the operating theatre on some minor cases.

In Göttingen, he treated a lady of distinction who had a defect of the upper eyelids, so that in order to see she had to throw her head back. The chevalier was quite familiar with this condition, and delicately cut part of her eyelids away then sewed the lips of the wound together, leaving the woman astonished and delighted.

In Northeim, he was approached by a prominent member of the Hanseatic League whose life had been blighted by a squint; ever since childhood he had endured the mockery of strangers. Undaunted, the chevalier made him a pair of spectacles with the good eye blacked out, forcing him to use his poor eye. Then over the course of a week, he used needles to prick the merchant's eyeball and all the surrounding tissue, to stimulate the nerves. Finally, he made a series of delicate incisions to cut the muscles that were pulling the eye to one side. When the spectacles were finally removed, the merchant gazed at himself in the mirror and was so grateful he burst into tears and pressed a purse of gold into the chevalier's hands.

So we worked our way northward, gradually tackling increasingly complex cases and filling our strongbox with gold and silver. The Eye Waggon would park a mile outside the chosen town, so that the driver could be sent ahead on foot to distribute handbills and posters heralding the arrival of 'the most gifted eye surgeon in all Europe'. We would let anticipation ferment overnight, then the following morning the Eye Waggon would roll into town with solemn fanfare and set up in the main square. Children were always the first to arrive, wide-eyed at the magnificently strange carriage, and mesmerised by the way the stage unfolded from the vehicle. They would run to tell their parents about the wonder, so that by the afternoon a large crowd invariably gathered around the waggon.

At this point the driver would emerge, ringing a handbell like a town crier, and deliver in resounding tones a speech written by the chevalier.

"Between the hours of eleven and one, on the sixteenth day of August 1703, did Nature and the midwife give our matchless Chevalier-Surgeon to the world. No sooner did the infant begin to distinguish objects, than he expressed the greatest aversion to all spots and blemishes, either on garments or on the countenances of those to whom he came near. In particular, he could not bear the slightest flaw or defect on pairs of spectacles, which he often broke in his attempt to clean them. This pursuit of visual perfection has been the toil and study of the chevalier's life these forty years past.

"The nature of Good, my worthy citizens, is to communicate itself. Good is not selfish or solitary. Good is no good except as it is diffused. Good, like a dunghill, is good for nothing until it is spread about with great liberality. And it is a dedication to the good of his fellow man that burns at the heart of our surgeon's Grand Tour. He has taken a vow before God to share his genius and bring Enlightenment to every town and city of Europe. You here today, you noble citizens and honest tradesmen, are honoured to receive the great and renowned Chevalier-Surgeon, Dr John Taylor."

The driver sounded the bell again, and the crowd gasped as the chevalier stepped out of the waggon and stood proudly in the centre of the stage.

For a few moments, he said nothing. He just let the crowd gaze upon his fine clothes and haughty demeanour. Then he raised his beloved cane in a grand flourish and began. "I am like a blazing comet! Travelling through the vast expanses of Nature, visiting every country in its course, amazing the learned with brilliance, and scaring the ignorant with idle terrors. Like a comet, I am wondered at by all." He swept his cane over the crowd in a great arc. "From the lofty height of the firmament, I look down upon you, but it is with eyes of pity and compassion for your many ailments and infirmities."

There was a murmur of gratitude in the crowd that their frailties had been acknowledged.

"Fear not! My healing dews shall descend upon you. My medicine, like Manna in the Wilderness, shall fall in showers around you, and restore your peace. For I am the Man of Knowledge. I am your champion in the cause of health. I will trample down the Dragon of Disease. I will fight him; I will pull out his sting and send him packing!"

At this point, the crowd would invariably burst into applause, but the chevalier had not finished.

"Yet have we all not come to fear the fraudulent apothecaries who rob the purses of the public? Have we all not suffered in hospitals that wear charity on their faces but have knavery in their hearts?"

Here there would be grim nods of recognition among the crowd.

"Only a fool would put his trust in my words alone. For words are cheap; they are a false coin that flatters and deceives. Proof is what you demand! Proof! And that is what I humbly present to you now…"

This was my cue to step out of the waggon onto the stage, holding up the Book of Testimonials for all to see. It was a weighty manuscript, impressively bound in antique leather, and embossed on the cover with the Hippocratic symbol.

The chevalier had first shown me the book when we were in Eisenach, waiting for the Eye Waggon to be completed. I think it was his most treasured possession, even more so than his surgical instruments, for it was kept in the most securely fastened of his trunks. He always handled it with the reverence due to a holy relic.

"Twenty years ago," he explained in the privacy of our lodgings, "not long after completing my training, I did my first tour of Europe. I was astonished at their primitive knowledge of eye surgery. I had barely performed half a dozen operations when word of my skill spread like wildfire. I was summoned by the great and the good across the continent to reverse the cruel ravages of blindness that had debilitated doges and bishops. They paid me well, but the real treasures were the testimonials they gave." As he leafed through the book, I saw that each page was written in a different hand and embossed with a unique seal, but all of them were united in singing the praises of the chevalier's skill. He was a 'médecin sans égal', a 'chirug von Gott geschickt', an 'operatore di miracoli'.

"This is why I have returned to Europe," he said solemnly, "to fulfil my calling."

Without doubt, it was an impressive volume, and it was invariably the object that new patients were keen to examine, which is why the chevalier had a special glass case built to house it. Ordinary people were not allowed to actually touch its pages; only I was given that privilege.

When the stage presentation was complete, the chevalier would withdraw inside the waggon, remaining mysteriously elusive. The driver then set up a small table on which he placed the appointments diary, and a lengthy queue would form. I would sit on a raised platform behind the driver, back leaning against the waggon, from where I would listen to the prospective patients as they described their ailments. What no-one could see was that the chevalier was secretly positioned inside the waggon, where he could look out through one of the opticons and assess each patient for himself. He would then whisper to me 'treat' or 'reject' and I would deliver the verdict, then the driver would duly fill up the appointments diary.

It may seem overly theatrical, but the chevalier knew it was vital to maintain an air of mystery. He did not want to sully his hands with petty diagnoses; he was all about elusive genius. He did not prescribe mere spectacles; he performed grand surgeries on complex cases. And there was sound economic rationale to the selection process: it was important to filter out the poor, as they would never be able to afford expensive treatments, and one way or another, we had to pay for the Eye

Waggon. "In any case," the chevalier would often declare, "they are only poor because they are stupid, so why should I waste my talent on them?"

In truth, they were just cannon-fodder; the chevalier wanted them in the crowd to create an air of excitement, but he was really after the town's merchant classes and aristocrats. We always kept a keen eye out for the servants they would send to make enquiries.

Once the diary was full of affluent patients, the driver would disperse the crowd and close the waggon doors. We would remain inside for the night, an enigmatic presence in the heart of the town.

The following day, each client would be invited inside for a private consultation with the chevalier. Finally they would get close to him and could marvel at the technology in the operating theatre, which the chevalier never tired of showing off.

He would conduct a solemn examination of each patient, liberally sprinkling his diagnoses with Latin terminology. Then treatment would be agreed, and a fee paid.

The chevalier performed all the operations inside the Eye Waggon, where the facility Mosengel had created proved to be exemplary. The makeshift procedures that I had witnessed in Norwich were a thing of the past; inside this new operating theatre everything had been arranged to make the surgery less traumatic for the patient, whilst allowing greater precision for the chevalier.

It was remarkable to watch him work; he was fast and relaxed as he sliced into living eyes, and would often hum folk tunes to distract himself from the agonised cries of his patients. It added a strange air of flippancy to the surgery, but as the chevalier frequently pointed out, it was his relaxed attitude that made him such a good surgeon. "To be tense is to fail," he would declare.

Confidence: it was all about confidence.

Post-surgery, the patients' eyes would be tightly bound with bandages, and they would be entrusted to their family for the aftercare; only the very richest would be accompanied home by the chevalier. All the necessary treatments and poultices were included in the cost of surgery, as the chevalier was adamant that he didn't want his patients falling into the hands of unscrupulous apothecaries. He would supply laxatives and large doses of mercury, as well as ointments made from slaughtered pigeons, pulverized sugar, and baked salt, which were to be rubbed into the eyes after the dressings were removed.

The most important stipulation concerned timing: patients were forbidden from removing their eye bandages for ten days. This was deemed vital to the success of the operation.

From Monday through to Saturday the chevalier would work, morning until dusk, performing as many operations as he could. On the seventh day, he would rest, as the Lord commands. Then on the eighth day we would vanish. The driver was invariably awake before dawn, packing up the Eye Waggon and harnessing the horses, and we would leave before anyone was stirring. As a rule, we never just moved to a neighbouring town; the chevalier insisted that we always headed to a different province where he could repeat the entire process.

At first, I did question the urgency of this timetable. "Should not a surgeon always follow the treatment through to its conclusion?" I asked.

The chevalier gave an indulgent smile. "Healing needs time," he assured me. "Mother Nature is a slow worker. If we wait, we might be waiting for months, and who would bear the cost of that?"

That was the point: money. The chevalier had created a well-oiled and highly lucrative machine. He had such confidence, such bravura. He seemed untouchable, and he knew it. Why else would town after town fall under his spell?

It was only as we approached Konigsberg that things started to change.

FIFTEEN

The Vistula Spit stretches out into the grey Baltic like a discarded rope floating on the water. A great wooded curve poised delicately between two seas, it is one of the wonders of northern Europe. As we were to pass close, the chevalier decided to spend an afternoon exploring this strange natural phenomenon.

While the driver organised a picnic in the shade of some trees, the chevalier and I took off our shoes and paddled in the breaking waves. The sun was shining, and there was warmth in the air; it was a welcome moment of peace and solitude.

Quickly bored of the water, the chevalier decided to make pictures in the sand instead. He gathered armfuls of stones, and together we arranged them to create a huge eye on the beach, gazing up at the heavens, unblinking. We worked from either side, and when we met at the iris, he held me in his arms and together we watched the sun sink towards the Baltic horizon.

It was a perfect moment: the strongbox was full of gold, and we were free and in love. Suddenly I realised why the chevalier had brought me here: to propose. To make me his wife. I was alive with excitement at the thought and started laughing and joking without a care.

Yet he seemed nervous, hesitant. Perhaps he was waiting for the sun to glow deep red, perfecting the romance of the setting.

"Are you happy?" He kissed my hair.

"Happier than I ever thought possible."

"I could not have achieved this without you, Arabella. You know that?"

"And without you, I would be languishing in the misery of a dull, provincial life."

He fell silent again. I imagined that he was steeling himself for the moment.

The sun set. Dusk washed across the spit.

Finally he whispered, "I have a gift for you." He pressed a velvet box into my hands.

"A gift? Whatever for?"

"So that you never forget me."

I laughed and affected surprise, but as I looked at the box it was immediately clear that it was too large for a ring. Hurriedly I untied the bow and removed the lid, revealing a diamond brooch shaped like an eye.

Not trusting myself to speak, I stared at the jewel in silence, but the chevalier knew something was wrong.

"It was very expensive." He took the brooch from the box, but as he pinned it to my blouse, a tear dropped from my cheek onto his hand.

"Tears of joy?" he smiled.

"It's the wrong gift!"

He looked at me, bewildered.

"You made a promise."

"Did I? About what?"

Infuriated by his nonchalance, I turned my back on him and strode down to the water.

"Arabella! What on earth's got into you?" He chased after me. "What are you talking about?"

"Marriage!" I hissed.

"What?"

"You promised we would be married."

"But you already have a husband."

"In a different world!"

"Ah."

That would have been the perfect moment for him to go down on his knees, beg forgiveness and propose. He could have redeemed himself and changed the course of our lives. But he didn't.

"Marriage is a petty, bourgeois institution for the meek and fearful!" he scoffed. "You are above such small-minded conceits, Arabella. We both are. We are free-thinkers, mavericks pushing back the frontiers of human knowledge. Everything about us is bold and new and daring! Petty social conventions are for little people, not for the likes of us."

I stared at him in disbelief.

"Can you not feel the thrill of the unorthodox? Does it not quicken your blood that we are outside the rules that constrain others?" He went to clasp my hands, but I pulled away. "Arabella, you are so funny. Everything you have done has been bold and decisive. You have broken free at every step. Extricating yourself from your monstrous parents, bending Roope to your will before tossing him aside; that is the woman I love. Not some young girl blushing behind her wedding veil." Chuckling to himself, he walked back up the beach to finish off the last of the picnic.

For the rest of the evening, he waxed lyrical, trying to lighten the mood, but his words were blown away on the indifferent Baltic wind. The chill clung to us like damp as the driver packed the small camp away, and it followed us back into the Eye Waggon. Or rather, it followed me.

The chevalier let the incident slip effortlessly from his mind, and as the waggon sped into the gloaming, he lit a pipe and started to hum a little tune to himself. It wasn't selfishness; it was beyond that. I felt hurt and rejected and humiliated, and he was humming contentedly.

Although I learn slowly, I learn thoroughly, and this lesson was not lost on me. It was the first time I had glimpsed the truth about the chevalier: the world was only there to serve him.

Even the most beautiful city looks miserable in the drizzle; so it was with Konigsberg. The damp had seeped through massive stone walls and penetrated the souls of the Prussians within.

We set up the Eye Waggon in the central square as usual, but the town burghers here seemed wary and suspicious. When the chevalier stepped onto the stage to deliver his fine speech, he was shocked to discover only a sparse crowd, huddled in small clumps to ward off the Baltic chill. Rather than taking flight, his soaring rhetoric soaked up the rain and sank to the shiny cobbles.

Only one person paid close attention: a round-faced man with startled eyes. Judging from his clothes he was some kind of city official, for he seemed inordinately proud of the chain of office around his neck. A subordinate stood next to him, holding an umbrella over his master's head.

When the presentation was over, the meagre crowd dispersed in a sulky silence, but the official stepped forward and rapped on the stage with his cane.

"How long are you intending to stay?" he demanded.

"That depends," the chevalier deflected.

"This is not an answer."

"And who is asking?"

"Stadtschreiber Duddengrat." How this town clerk loved his official title. I found him repulsive, but the chevalier immediately sensed that this little man could be trouble and needed to be managed.

"Herr Duddengrat, I have found there is nothing like a brandy to fend off the chill," he said with a small bow. "Would you do me the honour of stepping inside?"

Duly flattered, Duddengrat dismissed his subordinate and we entered the Eye Waggon, where the chevalier set about charming the official with fine Armagnac and a small purse of silver coin.

"Do the good citizens of Konigsberg have perfect eyesight?" the chevalier inquired.

"Not at all. The long winter nights take their toll, you understand?"

"Then why are people so suspicious? I am a man of science. Of medicine. I bring hope."

Duddengrat sighed. The chevalier signalled to me, and I topped up the official's brandy glass.

"Whatever you say to me in this waggon, Stadtschreiber, remains confidential."

"There have been rumours, Chevalier. Conflicting rumours, you understand?" Duddengrat was clearly uncomfortable, but he had taken our silver and was duty bound to give something in return.

"Rumours about me?" The chevalier affected surprise.

"Some say that you work miracles. Others … others are not so kind."

"Go on."

"Some have suggested that you are like … how do you say? A butcher."

The chevalier went a little pale. "Because I spill some blood?"

"Because you leave people blinded. In pain. With infections. Maybe worse."

The chevalier remained silent. Hurriedly I poured him another drink, which he slugged down. "I am mortified," he said finally.

"This is nothing personal, Chevalier," Duddengrat added quickly. "I do not make a judgement, you understand? I merely report what I have heard. But this is why people are suspicious. Why they stay away."

"They are wrong," I said. "Quite wrong."

"No doubt."

"And I know exactly where these scurrilous rumours have originated." The chevalier had found his stride again. "Professional jealousy."

"Is that so?"

"My arrival in a town invariably exposes the mediocrity of the local surgeons. Finally people realise how poorly they have been served, and that their doctors are quacks. Believe me, Stadtschreiber, there is nothing like a ham-fisted surgeon to stick the jealous knife into a colleague's reputation."

"No doubt, no doubt."

"But I appreciate your candour, Herr Duddengrat, and I can assure you that by the time I leave, all Konigsberg will be singing my praises." As he spoke, the chevalier discreetly pressed some more silver into the town clerk's hand. "You understand?"

"I believe I do."

Duddengrat was barely out of the waggon when the chevalier's façade crumbled.

"Spineless catchfart! Who does he think he is? Blackmailing me, extorting money! I am a highly trained surgeon! Not some jumped-up bureaucrat whose career is built on kissing the arse of the local prince."

"Perhaps we should pack up and move on," I suggested.

"And let him win?"

"There are plenty of other towns."

"I will not give him the satisfaction!"

"Why swim against the tide?"

"Only the wicked flee. I am entirely innocent. A victim of these baseless slanders."

"Please, let us go where we are welcomed."

"Arabella, I will not be defeated by superstition and ignorance. My vocation, my calling, is to shine the light of knowledge into the darkness of ignorance. Konigsberg must learn some respect."

The following morning, the chevalier changed his appearance. He picked a sombre black silk gown from his wardrobe and wore a short legal periwig. Then, plucking a weighty volume at random from the bookshelf, he went for a walk. His route had been carefully planned: along the riverbank, then round the island in the Pregel River on which Konigsberg's striking cathedral sits. This was a route favoured by the city's elites and intellectuals, but while the chevalier ensured that he was seen, he made a point of talking to no-one. Instead, he clasped the book tightly and walked slowly, round and round the island, back and forth across the seven bridges, head bowed as if deep in thought. It was a splendid affectation of gravitas.

On his return to the Eye Waggon, he announced his intention to open a second front in his attempt to take the city: a charm offensive.

"You are the perfect weapon, Arabella," he said as he went through my wardrobe, looking for a dress.

"Me?"

"This is the moment to deploy all the etiquette I have taught you."

"But you are the surgeon. I cannot talk about medicine."

"Nor would I want you to. Your job is to endear yourself to the chattering classes of Konigsberg. Flirt, seduce, charm — I don't care how you do it, but once there, you must sing my praises. Make sure everyone knows about my fine medical pedigree and the long list of miraculous cures I have left in my wake." He selected a pale blue dress and held it up to me. "Perfect."

"I'd really rather not." I put the dress back.

"What did you say?"

"I am tired of these games."

The silence thickened around us.

Suddenly he grabbed my arm and pulled me roughly towards him.

"You're hurting me!"

"Do not defy me."

"Let go!" I tried to wriggle free, but he tightened his grip.

"If my reputation fails, this whole enterprise fails. And if that happens, you will be cast back into the tedium and obscurity whence I plucked you." He shook me like a rag doll, demanding obedience. "Do you understand?"

I scratched his hand, forcing him to let go. "Don't ever touch me like that."

"In future, dearest Arabella, you would do well to remember: never defy me. Is that clear?"

I was too shocked to answer; all I could do was stare at him.

"*Is that clear?*" he bellowed.

"Yes," I whispered. "Perfectly."

SIXTEEN

I had to wear long gloves to cover the bruises on my arms, but the deception didn't end there. Even though only a handful of people had seen the presentation in the market square, it was important that I wasn't recognised, to which end a large, powdered wig and two beauty marks were deployed.

At that time, Konigsberg was famous for its gaming salons, attracting precisely the type of wealthy clientele we were pursuing, so it was decided I would start there. With the driver posing as my servant, I presented myself as a wealthy English widow on a grand tour of Europe.

An imposing townhouse on Lanagasse contained a dozen rooms of diverse sizes, each with a different table in play. The staircase was busy with servants ferrying drinks and refreshments to the patrons; in the darker corners, courtesans were already seducing some of the evening's winners. But I had a very clear purpose: to find prospective clients and warm them to the idea of the 'famous English surgeon', whilst being as vague as possible about any specific connection I might have to him.

As soon as I stepped into the salon, the benefit of the social training the chevalier had given me became apparent. I knew how to conduct myself and how to greet others. I understood the complex etiquette of the gaming tables, when to smile and when to be haughty, how to lose gracefully, and when I did win, how to take it as no more than my due. The chevalier may have been a selfish man, but he certainly knew his way around the rulebook of manners.

At the piquet table, I spotted a pair of older men. They looked like brothers and were clearly struggling to see in the candlelight. They wore thick spectacles and had to hold the cards close to their eyes, yet none of this prevented them from placing extravagant bets. They were most definitely in need of eye surgery, so I secured a seat at the table and started to eavesdrop on their conversation. But as I studied the brothers, I gradually became aware that someone else was studying *me*. I glanced up and caught the eye of a tall man, around thirty years old, with a thoughtful face. He held some gaming chips in his hand, but seemed more interested in watching than playing … in watching me in particular.

Every time I glanced up, I caught his eye, until finally he ventured a charming smile. I looked away; flirtation was supposed to be for my mission, not my own pleasure.

There was a ripple of applause at the table — I had been so busy looking at the stranger I lost track of the game, and now one of the brothers was scooping up his winnings. Flushed with triumph, the two of them decided to retire for some celebratory drinks. I followed them, intent on striking up conversation, but just as I reached the door someone collided with me, sending my gaming chips scattering across the floor.

"Forgive me, madam!"

Irritated, I bent down to pick them up, and found myself crouching next to the same man who had been watching me.

"A thousand apologies. I am not normally so clumsy." Quickly he gathered the chips and pressed them into my hand. "What can I do to make amends?"

"That won't be necessary." I saw the two brothers disappear into one of the dice rooms and tried to follow, but the young man stepped in front of me.

"A drink, perhaps? This salon is famous for its cognacs."

I studied his face — he had kind eyes and wore a subtle bergamot cologne. "There is no harm done, sir."

"Maybe not to you, but my conscience is wounded. Please, allow me to atone, madam."

His words may have been earnest, but he delivered them with an irreverent smile.

"If you insist," I said, relenting.

"It would be an honour."

"Lady Arabella." I extended my hand; he took it and gave a small bow.

"Dr Max Ostermann."

This was interesting — a medical man. I would need to tread carefully.

He guided me through the crowded room, found a small table and pulled up two seats. Then he instructed a servant to bring us some drinks.

"You are new to the city, Lady Arabella?"

"Indeed."

"There are so many fine things to see in Konigsberg, yet you come to a gaming salon?"

"To be honest, cards are not one of my indulgences, but a salon is the perfect place to meet interesting people. Such as yourself," I smiled.

"Your husband is in one of the other rooms, perhaps?"

I gave him my cover story, peppering it with my noble lineage, then adding emotional heft by describing my struggle to recover from the grief at burying my husband. Dr Ostermann listened intently and seemed genuinely moved.

"But tell me," I said, keen to move the conversation onto firmer ground, "what is a doctor doing in a gaming salon?"

"Like you, I must say it is not really a passion. The chips won't leave my hands for the entire evening. I am only here because prospective patients are here."

"Drumming up business?"

"Perhaps." He gave a mischievous smile.

"Very shrewd. I don't doubt there will be some heart problems, given how many people are losing."

Dr Ostermann laughed. The drinks arrived, and we toasted each other.

"I am fascinated by your English traditions." He leant forward in his chair. "All the titles and social ranks, but forgive me, I have never heard of this Keeper of the Beehives you talk about."

"Really?"

"Really."

"Well, it's hardly surprising. Even King George doesn't know who he employs. There are so many courtiers."

"Indeed, indeed. But you wear the title beautifully." He raised his glass.

"Thank you." I sipped the spirit, grateful for a few moments to gather my thoughts.

"Were you aware that another Englishman has arrived in our city?"

"Really? I had no idea."

"Quite a coincidence."

"Travelling is all the rage among the English."

"Not to the Baltics, so much. It's too cold." Ostermann's brow furrowed. "The English prefer to escape from their damp little island to the warmth of Italy."

"Have you travelled widely, Dr Ostermann?"

"Some. In Russia. And Sweden. But this intrepid Englishman, he is a surgeon who calls himself the chevalier. You have heard of him, perhaps?"

I frowned as if wracking my memories. Ostermann's gaze never left my face.

"Now you mention it," I began, "there is a man, an oculist, widely celebrated for his skills. Perhaps it is the same man?"

"He has the most extraordinary carriage from which he operates. It is parked right here, in the town square."

"Really? I hadn't noticed."

"It must have cost a small fortune."

"Then he is surely a man of considerable skill to afford such a waggon?"

"Not necessarily." Ostermann swirled the cognac around his glass.

"What do you mean?"

"Word of his arrival has preceded him."

"He is that famous?"

"The word is not flattering. To be quite honest, they say he is a fraud, an imposter who is utterly incompetent."

I concentrated hard on not moving a muscle.

"This is quite shocking, no?"

"It is scandalous," I agreed, "if true. But should you really be repeating such wild rumours?"

"We take medicine very seriously in Prussia."

"But to defame a man's reputation … you have spoken to some of his patients, I assume?"

"Not yet."

"Then it is just a rumour. And frankly, Dr Ostermann, I despise rumours."

"Prussia may be a big kingdom, but word travels fast. This chevalier claims to have testimonials proving his worth. Yet I am led to believe that the documents are all false."

"The documents are false?"

"Forgeries," he said, nodding gravely. "Though very good ones."

"How dreadful." I had a desperate urge to get away from this inquisitive doctor, but I had to be careful not to arouse suspicion. "Tell me, Dr Ostermann, do you know how to play Black Maria?"

"Is this an English game?"

"Very popular in the London salons. I noticed they are playing it on the upper floor. Would you like me to teach you?"

"Of course. I love learning new things."

I managed to distract him with cards for another hour, then I made my excuses and left.

He bowed low at the salon door and kissed my hand. "It has been a pleasure, Lady Arabella. I hope it won't be the last time."

"Thank you for taking care of me."

"It's the least I could do."

As I hurried across the street, accompanied by the driver, I did the one thing the chevalier had always warned me never to do: I looked back. Dr Ostermann was watching me from an upstairs balcony, his serious eyes studying my every step.

The chevalier was stunned. His face went pale; he slumped into a chair, closed his eyes, and breathed deeply. Gradually shock and disbelief morphed into fury. "How dare he defame me?"

"I'm sure Ostermann is the source of all these rumours."

"Ostermann? What kind of a name is that?"

"He seems to be well regarded. A lot of people in the salon knew him."

"He is clearly nothing but a gambler! A card-shark! Why else would he be keeping such low company?"

"I fear he has been using the tables to warn people about us."

"*Poison* people against me!"

"They clearly listen."

The chevalier stared at me. "You sound rather taken with him yourself."

"No. Not at all."

"The man is quite obviously jealous of my accomplishments. Of my skill and reputation. This is the calumny of a failure! I should have expected it."

"But how do we counter? We are strangers. This is his hometown."

"I shall confront the lickspittle and teach him a lesson he will never forget."

"Perhaps we should just leave. There are plenty of other —"

"Would you have me run away from malicious lies? That is the coward's way, Arabella. And I am no coward."

At nine o'clock the following morning, the chevalier barged into Dr Ostermann's surgery. This was the last place I wanted to be, but the chevalier insisted on bringing me face to face with his accuser. With flagrant disregard for protocol, he pushed past the protesting secretary and walked straight into the consulting room, where Ostermann was peering into a patient's ear.

"A word, sir!" the chevalier demanded.

The doctor didn't even look up. "This is the English fraud I was talking about, Herr Wolfsteiner," he said to his patient.

"And you, sir, are a liar and a cheat," the chevalier replied with disdain.

Wolfsteiner peered over his glasses at the chevalier. "He has the face of a bully. I shall leave you to teach him a lesson, Dr Ostermann." He picked up his hat and left without giving us another glance.

"So you do know him, Lady Arabella," Ostermann said politely.

"You have slandered a good man, Dr Ostermann. I'm hoping that this business can be set straight."

"Can you not see that your ridiculous charade is over?" He looked at me with contempt. "'Keeper of the Beehives'? Do you think we are all idiots? I doubt you are even an aristocrat."

The chevalier stepped in front of me protectively. "We have heard about your barbarous Prussian ways, and we have tried to make allowances. For my own part, I can shrug off the harmful lies that you have so wilfully perpetuated, but I will not have Lady Arabella's good name dragged into gutter. I have to warn you, Ostermann, unless I receive an immediate and public apology, along with a full retraction of your baseless slanders, I will seek redress through the courts."

Dr Ostermann considered the offer in silence, then calmly shook his head. "There will be no apology because I have said nothing that is not true. It is my belief, 'Chevalier', that you are a fraud and a butcher, a man who has lied his way to fame and left nothing but a litany of maimed patients in his wake."

"Apologise!" The chevalier was trembling with rage.

"Furthermore, I have reason to believe that the testimonials you are so keen to show off at every opportunity, are fake. Forged signatures on a tissue of lies, with fraudulent seals."

"Liar!"

"You are, sir, as we say in Prussia, a greased piglet. But you will not slip away this time."

"Forget the courts!" the chevalier thundered. "I demand satisfaction!"

"Is that how doctors settle a dispute? With a duel?"

Sensing Ostermann's reluctance, the chevalier pressed harder. "To the death. That is the English way, and I demand no less."

"Very well. If you insist."

"I do. Pistols it is."

Ostermann frowned. "As the accused, I believe it is my right to choose the weapons."

The chevalier gave a contemptuous shrug. "What do the mighty Prussians prefer? Walking sticks?"

Calmly Dr Ostermann crossed the room and opened a large set of cupboard doors to reveal a gleaming armoury of swords, all neatly mounted and polished. "These."

The chevalier blinked as he looked at the weapons.

"Rapier, foil, épée or sabre?" the doctor asked.

The chevalier was momentarily speechless; panic was etched across his face.

Dr Ostermann remained chillingly calm. "Well? What is it to be?"

I wasn't sure whether the chevalier actually knew the difference between the swords. "Let it be rapiers," he said finally.

"Very well. Ask my secretary to find some free time in my diary."

With that Ostermann closed the cupboard doors, sat down at his desk, and calmly carried on with his work. It occurred to me that he really did not look like the sort of man to spread malicious gossip lightly.

"Where are you going?" I chased after the chevalier as he marched towards the cathedral. "Are you really intending to see this through?"

No reply.

"Please! Wait!"

He didn't.

"There must be another way of settling this."

"I have endured intolerable insults! There is only one way that honour can be satisfied."

"But have you ever fought a duel?"

Finally he looked at me. "I am an aristocrat! It's in our blood."

"When? When did you last fight?"

"It doesn't matter."

"Ostermann has an arsenal in his surgery!"

The chevalier didn't stop walking until we got to one of the bridges over the Pregel. His hands gripped the stone balustrade as he stared down into the grey waters. "God, I hate the Prussians," he said quietly.

It was hard not to feel sorry for him. As he stared at the cold, indifferent river, the chevalier looked suddenly vulnerable. It is a sad spectacle to see a man stripped of his bravura, and all his energy and ebullience crumble to dust. He was out of his depth, but didn't dare admit it.

I looped my arm through his. "If you can wield a scalpel, surely you can wield a rapier."

He considered it, then took my hand. "Yes … you're right, Arabella. A blade is a blade."

"Perhaps all one needs is a little practice."

Selmeyer was reputed to be the best swordsmith in Konigsberg, so that was where we started. His workshop was on the outskirts of the city, where all the smoke and hammering from the foundry was absorbed into the dense pine forest, but Selmeyer also had an upmarket showroom on Untere Laak.

"I wish to buy a sword." The chevalier strode into the showroom with all his old confidence returned, and cast an expert eye across the racks of weapons. "A rapier. Your finest."

Sensing the possibility of a lucrative sale, Selmeyer himself emerged from the office to take over the presentation. He ushered the chevalier towards a cabinet containing a host of glinting swords, finely engraved and beautifully polished. The chevalier plucked out the richest looking one and ran his fingers along the blade.

"An excellent choice," Selmeyer nodded.

Suddenly the chevalier spun round and started slashing the air dramatically, as if he were in a fight to the death. "Not bad," he pronounced.

"Er, perhaps a sabre would suit you better?" Selmeyer suggested.

"No. It has to be a rapier." He slashed the air again, delighting in his power.

"Forgive me, but the rapier is for thrusting, not slashing."

"I do know how to use a sword." The chevalier cast his most haughty look. "But listening to the sound it makes through the air is the quickest way to assess the quality of a blade."

"Interesting," Selmeyer muttered. "I did not know this."

The chevalier slashed the air a few more times, then lunged forward dramatically, thrusting the tip of the sword towards Selmeyer, who cleared his throat.

"Might I suggest this one, Chevalier?" He plucked a longer blade from the cabinet.

The chevalier took it from him and felt its weight.

"You have a tight grip," Selmeyer noted.

"It is the English way."

"Ah."

"Why? How do the Prussians do it?"

Selmeyer demonstrated. "Hold it like a bird — tight enough to control, without hurting it."

The chevalier tried it.

"And finger through the pas-d'âne." He adjusted the chevalier's grip.

"Interesting." The chevalier made a few moves with the sword. "Yes, this also feels good. I think I'll try it. When in Prussia, and all that." He strutted across the shop, dramatically thrusting as he went.

Selmeyer looked worried. "What is the purpose of the sword? Ceremonial, perhaps?"

"I am defending my honour," the chevalier said gravely.

"Oh. Against whom?"

"The liar Ostermann."

"Not Dr Ostermann?" Selmeyer asked anxiously.

"Soon to be the late Dr Ostermann."

There was silence as Selmeyer took in the magnitude of the problem. He studied the chevalier as he thrust his way around the showroom.

"Chevalier, you might find it helpful to use a different stance."

"I have found that in duelling, it pays to be light on one's feet."

"Light, yes. But not unstable. Perhaps if you kept a wider base..." He put his hands on the chevalier's body to make some adjustments. "And roll your shoulder back to take the weight of the sword onto your whole body…"

By now the chevalier was starting to look like a bad dancer. He waddled forward awkwardly; then, aware of how ridiculous he looked, he started slashing the air again with a great sense of drama.

"Interesting technique," Selmeyer observed.

"Hah! Like you, my opponent will not be expecting the slash. Which is why I find it so effective."

Selmeyer looked unconvinced. "They say that he who masters the thrust will always beat he who masters the cut."

"But it is precisely because you follow the rules that I am able to outmanoeuvre you."

"Perhaps."

"Use surprise to destabilise your opponent." The chevalier pointed to the rack of swords. "Pick one up. I'll prove it."

"No, no. I believe you."

"Go ahead, attack me." The chevalier braced.

"I'd rather not."

"Come on, man!"

Reluctantly Selmeyer selected a rapier and settled into a perfect stance.

"*En garde!*" the chevalier declared.

With lightning speed, Selmeyer stepped forward; moments later the chevalier's sword was on the ground, and Selmeyer's tip was pressed to his throat.

After a moment of shock, the chevalier laughed. "Cunning. I might have known you'd keep the best sword for yourself. But I have discovered your secret." The chevalier took the rapier from Selmeyer's hand and admired it. "I'll buy this one."

"Very good, Chevalier."

"Does it come with any extras?"

"Extras?"

"Belt? Scabbard? Sharpening stone?"

"You may be assured that the rapier will be in perfect condition when it leaves us."

"Have it ready for me tomorrow." The chevalier turned to go, but Selmeyer gave an awkward cough.

"For duelling swords, no credit is extended, Chevalier. I will require full payment today."

"Do you not trust me?"

"It is not a question of trust, Chevalier, but one of mathematics. Two men walk into a duel, but only one walks away."

SEVENTEEN

You can watch a great painter at work; you can wear his clothes, adopt his posture in front of an easel, imitate the way he moves his brush across the canvas, but that doesn't mean you will be able to paint a masterpiece. So it was with the chevalier and duelling.

We found a clearing in the wooded hills outside the city, and I watched as he tried to master sword fighting in an afternoon. He went through all manner of exercises: cutting, stabbing, slicing, even driving the rapier into a tree trunk; but every thrust threw him off balance, and every attack left him vulnerable.

It was obvious to me: this was a man who had seen but never done. Ostermann would destroy him in a few lethal strokes. And where would that leave me? Stranded, in disgrace, a thousand miles from anything I could call home.

The chevalier broke from the drills to recover his breath and drink some wine. "Why do you look at me like that, Arabella?"

"Like what?"

"As if you doubt me."

"I don't want to see you hurt. That is all."

"My reputation has already been maimed by that liar Ostermann." He swiped the rapier across some poppy heads, sending them flying into the gloom. "If he had the faintest idea about the complexities of eye surgery, he would not be so quick to make accusations of negligence."

"I know."

"Actually, I don't think you do. Even though you have seen me work on countless occasions." He sat down on a fallen tree trunk and swigged some more wine. "Sometimes ... sometimes it feels as if I am fighting an invisible enemy. No matter how perfect my technique, certain patients are cursed. It's as if they are doomed to blindness. No matter what I do, the procedure..." He hesitated, struggling to say the word. "Fails," he finally whispered.

It was the first time I had ever heard him admit to failure. Words were cheap to the chevalier. He would say anything to anyone to get what he wanted, yet he struggled with this simple, haunting word.

"There is only so much a man can do to fight Destiny," he admitted. "Perhaps Nature is jealous of my genius. Perhaps it is God's way of demanding humility; I cannot know. But what I do know is that dwelling on cases that have not worked would paralyse me. It would render me incapable of ever picking up a scalpel again. That is what Ostermann wants: to paralyse me. And I cannot allow that to happen."

He finished the wine and stood up, rapier balanced in his hand, pretending that he was ready to take on the world, but sensing in his heart that he was going to die. It was impossible not to be moved by his vulnerability.

"There is another way," I said.

"I'm afraid not." He swung at the air with his sword. "Honour is everything."

I walked over to him and put my hand on his arm, lowering the sword. "*Primum non nocere*. First, do no harm."

"It's too late for that. And in any case, Ostermann is not a patient, he's a vindictive liar."

"An oath is an oath. And the Hippocratic Oath is most sacred of all. 'I swear to abstain from all intentional wrongdoing'."

"Ostermann is a cancer that must be removed from my life."

"I have no interest in him, only in you. And you are a man of medicine. You heal, you do not harm."

"Arabella, you do not understand: if I honour my professional oath, I will dishonour my good name."

"But if you knowingly turn a blade on another man to kill him, what is there left to live for?"

I could see his mind working: he had glimpsed a way out of this predicament.

"You must protect your craft, and your hands, for the sake of your future patients," I pressed.

"And let him strut about the streets of Konigsberg, repeating his malicious lies?"

"Let Ostermann have his day. We will never set foot in Prussia again. We can forget about him and move on. But if he harms you in this pointless duel, think of the hundreds of patients that you will never be able to treat. Can you really let them suffer? Would you abandon them just to satisfy your honour?"

The chevalier stepped further into the clearing and swirled the sword, beheading mushrooms with a vengeance; yet all the while I could see he was calculating.

Finally he sheathed the rapier and turned to me. "Out of love and respect for you, Arabella, I will do as you wish. As an English gentleman, I value my honour like a precious jewel; but if you insist, I will reluctantly drop my claim."

I hugged him. "It is my wish. It is."

"Then we must leave this city."

"Thank you." I kissed him tenderly.

"We were never in Konigsberg. And this never happened," he said. "It is to be forgotten. Do you understand?"

"Of course."

"Very well." He started to whistle as he gathered up his things.

"There is just one thing I need to know," I said.

"Where we're going next?"

"Tell me, are any of the testimonials forged?"

The chevalier froze. "What did you say?"

"I just…"

His eyes glistened with moisture. "What have I done to be such a disappointment to you, Arabella?"

"I didn't mean —"

"I have treated you with nothing but kindness and respect. I have lavished money and affection on you without hesitation because I love you. But if you have lost faith in me…"

"No! I haven't. I swear."

He looked down, and I saw a tear drop onto his shoe. I went to comfort him, but he pulled away.

"If even you doubt me, then the future is truly dark."

"Please, forget I ever asked."

"I confess, there have been deceptions. I have told lies, but I have told them solely to protect *you*, Arabella. No-one would have accepted you had they known the truth about the squalor and poverty and ignorance into which you were born. 'Lady Arabella', 'the Keeper of the Beehives' — yes, those are lies, but they are lies that come from love."

"And I am grateful."

"It's not about gratitude. It's about justice. You are so much more than the cards you were dealt at birth. I sensed that the moment we first met, and I so desperately wanted to help that it clouded my better judgement. But you're right: lies do not sit well on a surgeon's shoulders. I accept that now. If you want the deceit to finish, just say the word and I will take you home. I will accompany you back to England, where you can live as you were destined to live, without any more deceit. But I must continue my chosen path because my destiny is to restore sight to the blind, and to push at the frontiers of medical knowledge. If I must do it alone, it will break my heart, but so be it."

As the chevalier looked at me, I could see a profound sadness in his eyes.

"Please, forgive me for even asking."

"Very well." He opened his arms, and I went to him.

"But we must leave Konigsberg immediately," I urged. "This city is no good for us. It has been tearing us apart from the moment we arrived."

As we sped south, cocooned in the Eye Waggon, we made love. It had taken courage for the chevalier to admit his vulnerability, and that strengthened the bond between us. So we lost ourselves in desire, and all the tensions that had grown between us dissolved. We only had each other, and we had to believe in each other; that was the way to stay strong.

How could I have known that his arousal was contingent on cravings that were degenerate? That the intimacy between us was rooted in perversion? There was no-one else in my life to teach me, only him. And he exploited that.

Escaping from Prussia was the right decision, for as soon as we crossed the Polish frontier, our luck started to change. A letter was waiting for us from Herr Mosengel, the craftsman who had constructed the Eye Waggon. The chevalier opened it cautiously, but as he read the letter, he started to relax.

"This is excellent." He gave me the envelope. "There is a church organist whom Mosengel has known for years; they grew up in the same town. Apparently, he's a prolific composer, but is now losing his eyesight. They want to know if we can detour to Leipzig to see the man."

"I doubt he'll be able to afford you," I said, scanning the letter. "It says here he has nine children. On an organist's salary. How does that work?"

"Maybe he can sell one of them to raise the money," the chevalier quipped. "In any case, it's worth making the trip, and an excellent way to silence my critics. When I cure a blind church organist, it will be as if I have divine powers. I will be a gift from God, the protector of His music."

"If you healed the Pope, maybe. But a poor church organist?"

"I have a good feeling about this, Arabella. Who knows, this Bach chap might even compose a piece of music for me, out of gratitude. *Anthem to the Chevalier!*"

It was spring 1750 when the Eye Waggon rolled into the impressively fortified city of Leipzig, but the chevalier was fast asleep and quite uninterested in architecture. The driver found a spot on the great market square in the shadow of the town hall, and while he went to get water and fodder for the horses, I decided to explore.

Immediately I could tell that this was an enlightened city, dominated by a great university, for the squares were full of students laughing and disputing, and it seemed as if every other street contained a bookshop. Time flew by as I browsed shelves that groaned under thousands of volumes written in many different languages.

I wandered along crowded alleys and around sheltered courtyards, until eventually I found myself standing in front of the striking gothic façade of the Thomaskirche. But it wasn't the building that caught my attention; it was the music floating out of the open doors.

I was familiar with the dull hymns that droned out of English churches every Sunday, and I had endured plenty of oom-pah bands as we travelled across the German states, but this … this was like no music I had ever heard. On the surface it was simple and delicate, just a human voice and a violin; but they were wrapped around each other with such perfect intimacy, the music seemed to shape time itself.

The beauty of that sound clasped my hand and drew me up the stone steps into the body of the church. It was a curious space; the walls were shades of white and grey, while the columns that lined the nave were painted with climbing palm leaves which stretched out along the cross-ribs of the ceiling. Yet the sublime grace of that music burst from the confines of the modest church. It was a sound so full of longing, alluring in its simplicity yet overpowering in its emotion.

In those moments, all the pain and regret in my life seemed to resolve into forgiveness. Sin and guilt were lifted from my shoulders, and replaced with a profound love.

In the sanctuary, I saw a young man singing and an older man standing next to him, playing the violin. The two of them gently swayed together, as if in a trance. By the violinist's side, propped against his music stand, was a white walking cane.

This was him. This was Johann Sebastian Bach.

EIGHTEEN

There was a moment of perfect silence as the final notes faded, then violinist and singer relaxed. I watched as they exchanged a few words; Bach seemed to be offering some advice about phrasing. Even from where I was standing, I could see the respect and affection the student had for the composer. With great attentiveness he put Bach's violin back in its case, gathered up the music and gently placed the white stick in his hand. They parted with warm words and a smile.

As Bach made his way down the nave, it was apparent that though his vision was failing, it had not yet gone entirely, and the stick was perhaps more to make him feel secure than to guide his way. He struck me as a modest man with a thoughtful face, and none of the swagger that one might expect from a composer. Yet despite this, I found myself holding my breath as he passed; it was as if I dreaded being noticed.

But Thomaskirche was Bach's church; he had worked there for nearly three decades and he knew everyone who frequented it. As he drew level, he stopped and peered towards me.

"That looks like a new silhouette."

It was halfway between a question and a statement, and I didn't know how to respond.

"If it's the Martin Luther window you're looking for, that is on the opposite wall."

"Thank you."

He gave a little bow and started to walk away.

"Are you the organist here?" I hurried after him.

"I wish it was that simple." He gave a strange little laugh. "Cantor would be more accurate."

"I'm afraid I don't know the term."

"If only I could say the same."

"Are you one of the priests?"

"That would be too easy. I'm the one who runs three choirs, teaches at the school, supervises the city's religious and civic music, and deals with an army of bureaucrats, all for a hundred crowns a year. In my spare time I get to compose."

"What about sleep?"

"Yes … I vaguely remember that. Had a good night's sleep ten years ago, I recall."

"Is Leipzig really such a slavedriver?"

"The upside is that I get paid extra for funeral music. So when the Lord taketh through a hard winter, he giveth back to the humble cantor."

I couldn't help laughing. "I cannot believe anyone so cynical could have written such a beautiful piece of music."

Bach stopped and peered at me through his failing eyes. "Thank you. People don't often say that. In this city I'm just another service, like the ratcatcher."

"Well, that was quite a rat."

Bach stepped closer, trying to see my face more clearly. He extended his hand. "Sebastian Bach."

"Arabella Taylor."

"You are a long way from home. Your accent is not local."

"Tell me, Herr Bach —"

"Sebastian, please."

"Sebastian. Where does music like that come from?"

He shrugged. "I work hard at it. Anyone who works just as hard can write music that is just as good."

"I think you're too modest."

"Only because I have nothing to boast about."

"Then Leipzig needs to wake up."

"Amen to that. But no-one in this city listens properly. That aria you just heard, I composed it over twenty years ago for Good Friday, in this very church. It was part of a sacred oratorio, but the Deputy Burgermeister didn't like it, so it's only been performed twice."

"That must be soul-destroying."

"Only if you care. I'm beyond that now. I no longer write music for people."

"But who else is there?"

"God." Bach looked up at the gothic vaulting. "I write for God. As long as He listens, nothing else matters."

"And what does He think?"

"Perhaps I'll find out when I'm dead." He gave an irreverent chuckle.

"Please, don't say things like that."

"Forgive my crude humour."

"I don't understand how anyone could hear your music and not be moved."

"Watch and learn." His arm gestured to the main doors, where a fawning priest was greeting a merchant and his portly wife. "The good burghers will soon teach you that skill."

Bach dodged into the side aisle to avoid the priest, and I followed.

"You know, I have always wanted to sing, but never had a chance to learn," I said. "Your music has rekindled those longings."

"It's never too late. Give me a scale."

"Now?"

"Of course."

"Here?" I was embarrassed.

"The acoustics are perfect." He looked at me with such expectation that it was difficult to refuse. I cleared my throat and sang a tentative scale.

"Hmm." He considered it for a few moments. "Very raw. But a nice tone. There is something to work with."

"Thank you."

"You should take lessons when you get home. Which is where, exactly?"

I hesitated. "England."

Bach's face lit up. "I thought so!"

"But I have been travelling for many months."

"You are not with the famous eye surgeon, by any chance? From London?" he asked eagerly.

"I … I do know him."

"Hallelujah!" Bach laughed. "You've come!"

"We are only passing through —"

"I wrote to Mosengel but heard nothing. I assumed you'd moved on, but this is marvellous news! Did you receive the letter?"

"I really couldn't say."

"Naturally, I appreciate the chevalier will be much in demand in Leipzig. Every merchant has his pockets stuffed with gold. But if you could arrange an introduction, I will be forever in your debt." Bach clasped my hand. "My world is slipping into darkness, Arabella. Every day it grows dimmer. My beautiful wife and children are becoming shadows. It's almost impossible now to make out the staves. Composition is painfully slow, and there is still so much to write. But if your surgeon could restore my sight … I cannot tell you what that would mean."

I desperately wanted to protect this man; to turn him down would be cruel, but to let him see the chevalier … perhaps that would be crueller.

"Will you do this for me, Arabella?"

Johann Sebastian Bach sat down in the operating chair; the chevalier swung over the delivery system and positioned a powerful magnifying lens in front of his eyes to conduct the examination. Anna Magdalena sat next to her husband, holding his hand.

I watched as the chevalier studied each of the composer's eyes in turn; now and then he made little noises as if deep in thought, and occasionally he called out some numbers which I dutifully wrote down. With absolute trust, Bach had put himself in the chevalier's hands; I was the only one in that small room who harboured doubts. I could only pray that I was wrong.

"They're in a bad way, Herr Bach," the chevalier finally pronounced as he folded the magnifying lenses away. "And without surgical intervention, I'm afraid blindness is inevitable."

Bach sat forward and ran his fingers through his cropped hair. "I have long feared this day."

Anna put an arm around her husband and kissed his forehead. "He spends so much time working by candlelight. Could that have caused the damage?"

"But night is the only time I have to compose."

"How often have I told you? It's not right." She scolded him with such love. "This city would work you to death."

"Wrestling with the staves never harmed anyone. It's the fistfights that have done for me."

"That was years ago, Sebastian."

"Bare knuckles on the side of the head?" the chevalier lamented. "That would do it."

"But I had to defend myself," Bach protested.

"He was always getting into tavern brawls," Anna explained. "You know young men."

"Walk away from a fight in this city and you're finished," Bach insisted. "Fight back or be damned."

"You'd think an organist would have more respect for his hands," Anna sighed.

"Please. Blame is a fruitless exercise," the chevalier intervened. "What is done, is done. All that matters is where we go from here."

"So there is a cure?" Bach asked.

"Of course." The chevalier consulted his notebooks. "You have cataracts; your lenses have clouded over. Both eyes need to be couched, which means removing each lens from the line of vision. It is something I have expert knowledge of. The operation can be done in a morning."

"Then we have a plan!" Finally Bach could see a way out of the darkness.

"But … it will be costly," the chevalier warned.

"How costly?"

"One must remember that the procedure will completely restore sight to both eyes. You will be able to play and compose, and even get into brawls again if you wish." The chevalier chuckled.

"Don't give him ideas," Anna scolded.

"But how much will it cost?" Worry had returned to Bach's brow.

"A hundred crowns."

"That is a year's salary," Bach whispered.

"You must remember, to be blind is to be dead amongst the living," the chevalier pronounced. "To be shut out of the light, to be deprived of its sweetness is to be in the most lamented of all states. So it follows that the man who restores this invaluable sense can never be sufficiently rewarded."

Anna looked at the lenses and surgical instruments that lined the walls. "Somehow we will have to find the money, Sebastian."

"Where? At the end of a rainbow? Hanging from the magic money tree? I simply do not have it. Unlike music, it cannot be conjured from nothing."

"Perhaps the city could pay for it?" the chevalier suggested.

"Ah, that English humour," Bach replied. "So dry."

"You are a servant of Leipzig; you look after their music. Now is their chance to look after you."

"Last summer I was taken ill. Rather than pay for a doctor, the City Elders held auditions to find my replacement without even waiting to see if I would recover." Bach gave a grim laugh to try and hide the hurt he felt.

"Then now is their chance to make amends," Anna insisted.

"If I write to the Council asking for money, they will use the letter as irrefutable evidence that I have lost my mind and send me straight to the madhouse."

"Surely there must be someone who is responsible for your wellbeing? Some patron of the arts?" the chevalier pressed.

"Oh, I have plenty of masters. Twenty-four of them, to be precise. Assessors, Burgermeisters, Deputy Burgermeisters, rectors."

"Not one of them has a kind heart?"

"If they do, I have not seen it these past thirty years."

"That is difficult indeed," the chevalier frowned.

"Is there not an alternative procedure?" Bach asked. "Some treatment that will not ruin me?"

"Let me see…" The chevalier studied his notes in silence, then slowly shook his head. "I'm afraid not. And I have such a pressing schedule. The Elector of Frankfurt is waiting for me, so I shall be leaving Leipzig shortly."

"And so it ends." Bach stood up. "Men dig gold out of the ground, only to be enslaved by it." He shook the chevalier's hand. "But thank you for your time."

"Wait, there must be another way," Anna said, but Bach was already out of the door.

"There is not a second to waste," he called out. "Music has to be written before the darkness falls."

Reluctantly Anna hurried after her husband. As the waggon door clicked shut, I felt myself breathe again; deep in my soul I sensed that somehow everyone had just been spared.

Immediately the chevalier went to one of the opticons and watched Bach walk away across the square. "Do you think I overplayed my hand? I want to push him, but I also want him to return."

"You did the right thing," I reassured. "We should move on. Find another city."

"Quite the opposite. We must play this one out."

"You heard him: he has no money."

"*Someone* in this place has money. Look at it — underground sewers, streetlights, modern buildings; these Heinies are wealthy."

"But Bach clearly isn't."

"Which is perfect." The chevalier turned to me with a knowing smile. "I want him to go to the city's rich and powerful with a begging bowl. The more he spreads the word about me, the greater will be my reputation for saving the music of Leipzig. A latter-day Christ healing a Bach rather than a Bartimaeus."

"And what if no-one steps forward? Surely we are wasting our time here."

Suddenly there was a knock at the door. I opened it to find Anna Magdalena; this time she was on her own.

"That was quick." The chevalier ushered her inside. "You have thought of a benefactor?"

"Not yet." Anna shook her head. "But we are desperate not to miss this opportunity. So, what if Sebastian gives Lady Arabella singing lessons, absolutely free, while we try to raise the money?"

"Singing lessons?"

"At least that would make it worth your while staying in Leipzig a little longer. And my husband is a fine musician. The finest I have ever known. Even though the authorities think so little of him, I know they are wrong."

The situation was slipping away from me. "That is truly kind, but I cannot sing. Really, it would be pointless."

"Sebastian will be very patient. And there is nothing he doesn't know about the human voice."

"I appreciate that, but —"

"It is an excellent idea!" the chevalier interrupted. "Perfectly charming."

"But it is not you who will be singing." I tried to close this down.

"Ah, but think of the pleasure I will get from listening to you." The chevalier took Anna's hand and kissed it. "We have an agreement. I will write to Frankfurt and tell the Elector that I have been unavoidably delayed."

"Thank you! Thank you so much. This means the world to us." Anna turned to me. "Shall we say noon? Our house is next to the Thomaskirche."

"Very well."

"He is a wonderful teacher, Lady Arabella. You will never forget this time."

NINETEEN

Those weeks in Leipzig were the most stimulating of my life. All the fine clothes and material comforts that had previously given me such pleasure shrivelled to nothing; you cannot imagine what it was like to be coached by a man so possessed of musical genius.

That first morning, as Anna Magdalena opened the door to the schoolhouse building where the Bach family had their apartments, music flooded out — a cacophony of beauty from every room.

"Forgive me, have I come at a bad time?" I apologised.

"No, no. This is normal," Anna laughed.

"But it sounds as if the maestro is busy."

"There are harpsichords on every floor. Five in all! Can you believe it?" she said as she ushered me up the stairs. "Someone is always rehearsing or teaching. We've found that if the choirboys aren't singing, they're usually fighting."

She showed me into a music room at the front of the house, overlooking the Thomaskirche. It was modest in size, but full of different instruments; a violin hung from a hook on the wall, three flutes were perched on a window ledge, a trumpet lay on top of the harpsichord, and huge piles of musical manuscripts were dotted across the floorboards.

Suddenly the door flew open, and Sebastian entered. "Ready to start?"

He strode across the room and sat down at the keyboard. Despite the clutter, the composer knew precisely where everything was, and even though his eyes were failing, he never once tripped or stumbled.

"Is this where you compose, maestro?"

"No, no," he chuckled. "I don't need instruments to compose, just a desk and a goose quill. And it's Sebastian, not maestro."

"But do you really have time to teach me? With all your other commitments?"

"There is no need to feel nervous, Arabella."

"I must apologise in advance, for I have no singing experience."

Bach shook his head. "Everyone can sing. They just need the right teacher. And today, that is me."

So we began — with posture, breathing, tempo and pitch. The instant Bach opened the door to that world, his entire presence transformed. His concentration was absolute. He had passion and dedication and humility such as I had never witnessed; his whole being seemed to resonate with music.

As he moved around me, correcting my technique by gently touching my jaw, my nose, my diaphragm, Sebastian became a young man again, light and quick on his feet.

It made me feel like a clumsy giant lumbering through an intricate doll's house, and I blushed at the roughness of the sounds coming from my mouth. But Sebastian never mocked me or looked down on me with pity; my desire to learn was my vindication. That I even wanted to put my hand into the stream of music and taste a few drops was enough for Bach, and he saw me as a fellow traveller on the mysterious journey that had taken him across vast and beautiful oceans.

Once I had mastered the rudiments of ascending and descending intervals, he instructed me to sing through an entire set of vocal exercises, and as I sang, he would sit at the harpsichord and improvise harmonies around my voice. The music poured effortlessly from his fingers, and a smile would touch Sebastian's face as all the worries and pressures of his life vanished. When he was with music, nothing could harm him.

We both knew that I was possessed of little talent, but as his notes danced around my simple voice, there was the illusion that we were creating music together. For those few hours, I understood what real beauty was.

Stepping back into the ordinary world after the lessons was always difficult; the clatter and confusion of Leipzig's streets immediately started to erode the fleeting perfection of music. Hoping to prolong the sense of elation, I took to browsing in the city's bookshops, and eventually found my way to the university library. Its vast collection of books included many in the original English, and it was here that I hid every afternoon, reading anything and everything that caught my eye: poetry, novels, books of philosophy and religion. Much of it I struggled to understand, but that didn't matter; the important thing was to reach for a better world.

Unfortunately, each evening I had to return to the chevalier.

"Why do you always come in with that smirk on your face, Arabella?" He was in the middle of conducting an audit of his money, recording the results neatly in a ledger.

"Is it a crime to find culture enriching?"

"I'd like to see 'culture' fill your belly or keep you warm in winter."

"Must you do this?"

"I'll do what I want."

"Perhaps it's best I go for a walk." I turned to leave, but the chevalier blocked the door.

"You do know why Bach is teaching you? The real reason?"

"He needs time to raise the money."

"You're so naïve. I've seen how he leers at you."

"Don't be absurd."

"Maestro, this! Maestro that! The Great Man ogling your breasts. 'Oh, no. I'm just studying your breathing.'"

"Don't judge everyone by your own motives."

"The moment you leave, I'll wager he scurries to the closet and starts boxing the Jesuit."

"Stop it!"

"Ah, yes. The old 'right-handed fugue'." He roared with laughter at his own crude humour. The chevalier wanted to sully everything that had been given to me.

"Just let me be!" I pushed him aside, swung open the door and disappeared into the streets, trying to rekindle memories of the music lesson. There is nothing quite as ugly as a jealous man.

After a fortnight, the chevalier became anxious that Bach still hadn't raised the money, so he called him into the Eye Waggon and performed a minor operation to whet the composer's appetite. Using an exceptionally fine needle, he put a pinprick hole in each of the cataracts clouding Bach's eyes. It wasn't a cure, but the sudden increase in light gave Bach a tantalising glimpse of what could be achieved, and he redoubled his efforts to secure funding for the full procedure.

For my own part, I didn't care if he never raised the money; already his talent had enriched my life beyond measure, and I couldn't bear the thought of Sebastian subjecting himself to the pain and uncertainty of surgery.

But idleness did not sit well with the chevalier. In an effort to dull his impatience, he started drinking heavily in the notorious Auerbachs Keller. When he returned he would taunt me, mocking me as I tried to practise my singing, deliberately making obscene noises.

On the third Friday, I returned to the Eye Waggon to discover that the chevalier had been drinking for the entire afternoon.

"Lover-boy sent something for you." He tossed a small scroll across the room. "One of his spawn delivered it."

I loosened the ribbon and unfurled a handwritten sheet of music. Inscribed across the top were the words 'Für Arabella' and underneath was a beautiful aria, signed J.S. Bach. My eyes scanned the notes, hearing the plaintive melody unfold in my mind.

Suddenly it was snatched from me.

"Is this what passes for composition in Heinie-land?" the chevalier said, peering at the manuscript. He started singing the tune in deliberately clumsy tones. "That's not real music."

"Don't be so ignorant!"

"This is pedantic rubbish! Give me a real tune, an English tune!"

With drunken enthusiasm he started imitating a brass band, then bellowed at the top of his voice, "'*Rule, Britannia! Britannia, rule the waves! Britons never, never, never shall be slaves.*' Now that is a tune." He swigged some more brandy.

I had to get away from this philistine, but as I bent down to pick up the music, the chevalier raised his foot and pushed me over. "Oops. Sorry, my love."

I flew at him in a blind rage, fists flailing and thrashing; but the angrier I became, the more he laughed.

"Touchy, touchy," he mocked. "How the little songbird screeches now. More parrot than soprano."

"Leave me alone!"

He pushed me against the wall, then picked up the sheet music and right in front of my eyes he tore it in two.

"No!"

He kept tearing the paper into little pieces.

"Leave it!"

"Must try harder, Herr Bach!" Then he blew the paper like confetti, scattering it across the room. "Look, there's music in the air."

"You ignorant bastard!"

"Said the woman raised in the stink of pigs." The chevalier picked up his cane and strode out to continue drinking.

I spent the next few hours on my hands and knees, carefully gathering the shreds of paper and painstakingly trying to reconstruct the music. It was an almost impossible task, but I forced myself to concentrate so that I didn't have to deal with the rage I felt … rage against my own impotence in the face of such brute ignorance.

When it was finally done, I stared at the shreds pieced together on the table like a demented puzzle. All the beauty captured in the humble black dots was now scarred with a ragged spider web of vandalism.

But at least I had salvaged something. If I could stick the fragments onto a fresh piece of paper, preserving their order, then I would be able to get the music copied.

I searched through the cabinets, looking for paper and sealing wax, and finally found the chevalier's stationery cupboard in an obscure corner of the operating room. But as I took out some sheets of paper, I saw something glint at the back of the recess. I peered deeper and saw a small brass handle. My fingers reached inside, clicked the latch open, and a thin false wall came away in my hand. In the space behind it was a wooden box.

What was the chevalier hiding in here?

I removed the box and opened the lid to reveal dozens of small wooden handles, each with what looked like a coin attached to one end. They were wax seal stamps. Puzzled, I picked up each one in turn and studied the engraved symbols: the emblems of French dukes and Italian princes, of Spanish counts and German electors. These were the exact same seals that authenticated the precious documents in the Book of Testimonials.

Nausea overwhelmed me. I stumbled back into a chair. The Prussian doctor had been right; the testimonials were fake. The chevalier had forged them all.

Suddenly I heard a loud, uncouth singing echoing across the square outside. I peered through one of the opticons and saw the chevalier staggering along the colonnaded walkway beneath the town hall.

In a panic, I fumbled the seals back into the box and pushed it into the cupboard. There was no time to be neat. I clicked the secret compartment shut, and just managed to stuff all the papers in front of it when the waggon door was flung open.

"*Heart of oak are our ships, heart of oak are our men!*" the chevalier's drunken voice bellowed tunelessly. "*We always are ready, steady, boys, steady!*" He lunged forward to grab me, but I pushed him away.

"You stink of wine!"

"*We'll fight and we'll conquer again and again!*" He clambered through the small door into the sleeping quarters and collapsed on the bed. "Come here, woman! Let me conquer you again and again!"

I waited until he fell silent and his breathing became heavy before I crept through. There he lay, sleeping like a blacksmith's dog beside the anvil, fully clothed, legs splayed, spit dribbling from the corner of his mouth: The Benighted

Englishman. How he enjoyed mocking and destroying what he could never be.

The thought of getting into the same bed repulsed me. I didn't want to touch him or be near him, so I put some clothes in a bag and headed out to find a room at one of Leipzig's inns.

It was impossible to sleep.

The room was comfortable and well-appointed, and the night porter had gone to great lengths to make sure I had everything I needed; but what I really craved was peace of mind, and that he couldn't give.

As I lay awake, counting the quarterly chimes ringing from the town hall's clock tower and watching the shadows of the lamplighters' patrol move across the ceiling, a single thought circled in my mind: if Ostermann was right about the Book of Testimonials, was he also right about the chevalier's abilities as a surgeon? I knew that he had studied at the finest hospitals in London, that he had published learned books and pamphlets; but I also knew that the chevalier was very liberal with promises of miracle cures, yet rarely remained long enough to remove the bandages himself and witness the results. Every surgeon has some failures, but they should be the exception, not the rule, and any doubts I may have had were always banished by the Book of Testimonials. But if the testimonials were false … then what was left?

Dawn broke. I finally fell asleep and was only woken by a loud knocking at the door. It was one of the porters, delivering a beautifully wrapped package. I opened it to find a scroll of manuscript paper with a handwritten copy of the destroyed aria, along with a note from the chevalier containing two words: *I'm sorry*. All the fragments of torn paper had been gathered and placed in a mother-of-pearl snuff box.

Whatever my misgivings, at least I knew that it was now safe to return.

I arrived at the Eye Waggon to find it a hive of activity. Outside, the driver was washing the sides and polishing the brass fittings, while inside the chevalier was scrubbing down the operating chamber and checking his surgical equipment.

As soon as I entered, he drew me to him and held me close. "Do you forgive me?" he whispered.

"That was a cruel thing you did."

"I'm sorry."

"Cruel and thoughtless."

"I was drunk and out of my mind." He kissed me gently; I could smell the stale alcohol on his skin.

"Thank you for the gift," I replied.

"Had to haul a copyist out of bed to get it done in time." He laughed.

"At least the music is safe."

"Can I tell you something, Arabella?" He cradled my head in his hands.

"Of course." I felt myself soften in expectation of tenderness.

"If you ever leave without permission again, if you ever walk out on me, or spend the night in a strange bed, or behave as insolently as you did last night, I will throw you out of my life without a second thought. Is that clear?"

Shocked, I tried to pull away, but his grip was firm.

"You will be abandoned, a thousand miles from England, without money or connections or anyone to protect you. I daresay your only choices will be to turn beggar or whore. Have I made myself clear?"

I could feel the venom in his words.

"Do you understand?"

"Yes."

"But, dearest Arabella, if you show me love and affection and above all, remain loyal, then I will continue to offer you a life of luxury and indulgence. You are free to choose, but there will be no second chance." He kissed me again, then let go of my face.

I staggered backwards.

"Do we have an agreement?" he asked.

I think it was the first time I had felt genuine fear to be with him. If this was how he reacted to a single night's disobedience, God alone knew what he would do if I confronted him over the testimonials.

"I'm waiting for an answer, Arabella."

Perhaps he would kill me. Perhaps my body would be dumped in one of the pitch-black German forests. If anyone could get away with murder, it was the chevalier.

"I understand," I said quietly. "And I apologise for any offence caused. I ask only one thing: that we leave Leipzig."

"My work is not done."

"Bach will never raise the money for his operation. I've seen his house; money is a continual struggle."

"He is determined to see it through."

"How? He is too poor. No-one will extend him credit."

"You obviously haven't heard the good news," the chevalier smiled. "His wife, Anna Magdalena, came by this morning to make the payment."

It was the moment I had been dreading. "Where did they get it?"

"Some admirer or other. There's no accounting for taste." He shrugged. "Who cares? The important thing is, they raised the funds. The operation is booked for this afternoon."

He turned his attention back to the surgical instruments, but underneath his bonhomie he was pale and sweaty, and the reek of alcohol seemed to get stronger.

"No. You can't do it."

He turned and scrutinised me. "What did you say?"

"You can't operate like this. You're still drunk."

"I'll be fine."

"Look at your hands. They're trembling."

"Nothing that a brisk walk won't fix."

"At least leave it until you feel fresh."

"It's a routine operation. I could do it in my sleep."

"Please. For my sake —"

"Do you want another argument, Arabella? After everything we've just agreed?"

There was menace in his face, the veiled threat of the drinker spoiling for a fight. I should have done something, said something to make him change his mind, but I was frightened. To my shame, I remained silent.

"Good girl," he smiled. "Today I will do the operation. Tomorrow we will leave Leipzig, just as you ask."

All I could do was cling to the hope that the chevalier would live up to his own rhetoric.

TWENTY

The Bachs arrived at noon, full of nervous anticipation. Sebastian had shaved and wore a loose-fitting smock; Anna Magdalena was dressed smartly. As I greeted them outside the waggon, she clasped my hands. "Can I be with him? I really want to be there."

"I'm afraid there simply isn't room inside."

"I don't need a seat. I can stand."

"It's not a good idea. If you're not used to seeing surgery like this…"

The colour drained from her cheeks. "Is it so bad?"

"The chevalier has done this a hundred times. The best thing you can do is wait for your husband at home."

"But I can't settle to anything."

"Have you prepared a recovery room?"

"Not yet."

"Then that is something you can be busy with. Make sure it's quiet and not too bright. Somewhere he can rest and heal in peace."

"Very well." She embraced Sebastian and kissed him tenderly, promising him that all would be well; in truth she was trying to reassure herself.

Everything inside the surgical room was so perfectly designed, there had been no need for me to assist in any of the procedures for months, but in this case I insisted on staying. I wanted to watch every move the chevalier made.

Once Bach was firmly strapped into the operating chair, the chevalier inspected both eyes carefully with a magnifying glass. "You seem remarkably calm, Herr Bach."

"I have heard so much about you. This promises to be a new beginning for me."

"Indeed it will." The chevalier picked up a small clamp to hold back the eyelids. "Most people like to offer a prayer at this point."

"My whole life has been a prayer. Every piece of music I've written."

"Well, I'm sure God will show His gratitude by looking after you now." With that the chevalier applied the clamps so that it was impossible for Sebastian to blink. "Shall we begin?"

"I'm ready."

The gag was strapped into position. The chevalier picked up a scalpel and approached the right eyeball. Instinctively Bach tried to recoil, but he was tightly secured. Fearful cries came from behind the gag, but the chevalier didn't hesitate. "Hush now."

As the razor-sharp blade hovered over the glistening surface, I saw the chevalier's hand begin to tremble. He took a deep breath and wiped the sweat from his forehead, then made the first incision.

Blood and fluid oozed out as the white tissue peeled back. The chevalier made the second cut, but as he reached for the couching instrument, he stood bolt upright, sweating and pale.

"What is it?" I asked.

He looked dizzy and grabbed onto the wall to steady himself. Suddenly he pushed past me and burst out of the door. I hurried after, and found him leaning against one of the wheels, retching violently.

"Are you ill?"

He shook his head, burped, then vomited profusely over the cobbles. The moment it was out, he stood up, breathed deeply, and smiled. "Note to self: one less brandy next time."

Calmly he headed back to the steps, but I pulled him aside. "You're still drunk!"

"Just a little hungover. But I'll be fine now."

"You can't operate like this!"

"Well, I can't leave him with his eye sliced open." He pushed me out of the way. "If you're going to nag, you can stay outside."

I couldn't bear to witness it. I know that makes me a coward, but it's the truth. To stand and watch as the chevalier bludgeoned his way through the surgery was too dreadful a prospect. Instead, I went to Thomaskirche, knelt in front of the altar and prayed.

With all my heart, I begged God for mercy and forgiveness for my sins: for hating my parents, for betraying my husband, for the lies and deception, and for all the damaged people we had left in our wake. Above all, I asked that just for this one day, He could gift the chevalier with a moment of genius. We both knew he wasn't worthy of God's grace, but Bach surely was.

As the choir started to sing vespers, I finally rose from my knees and made my way out of the church.

I arrived back at the Eye Waggon to find Bach in a state of shock. Both of his eyes had been bandaged, obscuring the top half of his face, but I could see that his lips were pale and trembling; his breathing was erratic, and he seemed on the verge of panic.

"Sebastian?" I reached out to touch his hand, and he flinched. I could only imagine the fear and pain he had endured for the past hours. "Let us take you home now."

His body started to convulse as if he were about to cry.

"No!" the chevalier commanded. "No tears. It will damage the stitches."

Bach clenched his fists, struggling to control his emotions. His arms reached out, flailing in front of him. "Where is Anna?"

"I'll take you to her."

"I want my wife."

Carefully we guided his feet down the steps. The chevalier and the driver supported him, one under each arm, and walked him back across the market square to his house.

Silent tears ran down Anna Magdalena's face when she saw her husband. The man who that morning had left so full of energy and confidence, had been hollowed out; all that stood before her was a frightened husk. Quickly she wiped her eyes and wrapped her arms around him. "It's all right. I'm here. You're safe now. It's over."

Bach held onto her tightly, refusing to let go; she was the only thing that offered any comfort.

Once he was in his room, the chevalier took Anna aside to give her a set of medications. "Normally there is a charge for these, but out of respect for the maestro…" He pressed the potion bottles into her hands.

"Thank you, Chevalier."

"Rest is now the best medicine. Above all, do not remove the bandages for ten days."

"I understand."

The chevalier made his excuses and hurried away.

I went back into Sebastian's room one last time and stood at the foot of his bed, wondering what I could do to help this man. The whole house had fallen silent. No-one was rehearsing today; no harmonies were being aired for the first time. It was as if Music herself was holding her breath.

On the window ledge, Bach had left a composition he was working on. I moved the goose quill aside and looked at the title page: *Die Kunst der Fuge*. Perhaps he thought he would be able to complete it as he healed by dictating music to a student.

I turned back and looked at Sebastian, still trembling in shock. Would music ever flow from his heart again? Or had the chevalier silenced him?

Gently I touched his forehead and whispered, "Thank you."

"For what?" he mumbled.

"For helping me understand."

A trail of bloody water ran from the Eye Waggon to a cobbled drainage channel as the chevalier swilled down the operating chamber; the driver was busy harnessing the horses. They wanted a quick getaway.

"Is he cured?" I caught the chevalier's eye, but he looked away. "What happened during the operation?"

He bundled me into the waggon. "Make sure everything is properly stowed."

"Answer me!"

"I did everything I could."

"Your hands were shaking."

"Oh, so you're a surgeon now?"

"I saw it with my own eyes."

He busied himself packing surgical instruments into their cases. "What good does talking do now?"

"So it's true."

"I did the best I could."

"You should never have operated."

"You should never have upset me!"

"What?"

"I needed peace and calm to concentrate, and you destroyed that with your hysteria."

"You were drunk!"

"Because you drove me to it!"

"You were negligent, and you don't have the courage even to admit that?"

"Enough! Be quiet, woman."

"You can't run away from this."

"He just needs time to heal."

"Then let's wait here. Help him recover."

"First you wanted to go! Now you want to stay! Make up your mind!"

He opened one of the storage cabinets and reached for a bottle of brandy. "For Christ's sake." I slammed the door shut, almost trapping his hand.

"The fingers. Mind the fingers," he chided.

"Haven't you had enough to drink?"

"Do you want to take off his bandages with your own fair hands, Arabella? Is that it? Be the martyr? You who couldn't even bear to watch the operation."

"What will happen to him?"

The chevalier shrugged. "He'll be fine."

"Fine? That's not exactly a glowing testimonial, is it? Not something *you'd* write."

For a moment, the chevalier teetered on the edge of anger, unsure of exactly what I meant, or how much I knew. Then he laughed. "You can be quite the word-grubber."

We left in the dead of night, rolling silently out of Leipzig, careful to avoid the Watch patrols. As we headed west there was a dreadful, heavy atmosphere in the waggon; neither of us wanted to talk, but neither of us felt calm enough to sleep.

Yet as soon as Leipzig's walls slipped out of sight, the chevalier started humming contentedly to himself, and his old bonhomie returned. He took a deck of cards from his pocket and started shuffling them; it was a habit he had picked up when we were waiting for the waggon to be completed in Eisenach, and now he was trying to master as many different tricks as he could.

"Look, have you seen this one?" His hands pulsed back and forth. "It's called the Hindu shuffle." He took such childish pleasure in the cards. "Very good for cheating, I'm told. Hence the name."

I turned away and stared out of the window.

Before long he got bored with the cards and folded out the bed to sleep, leaving me alone with my thoughts.

I closed my eyes, but only to pray that God would look after a man who had spent his life celebrating the Divine. It was in vain.

I found out later that Sebastian had deteriorated very quickly. Within hours of the surgery, he was racked by a searing pain in his eyes that spread rapidly across his face and down his neck. As the infection worsened, a terrible fever took hold. Sweat poured off him and his entire body was gripped with agonising convulsions.

They say his cries of pain could be heard across Leipzig.

The doctors were called, but they could do nothing to bring the fever under control; Sebastian was unable to swallow even a spoonful of almond milk without throwing up. In desperation, Anna Magdalena summoned a barber-surgeon who attempted some bloodletting.

By noon the following day, his body was so weak he could no longer cry out; he just lay in his bed, whimpering like a wounded animal.

They say it was a blessing when he finally suffered apoplexy, rendering him unable to move.

We meandered west in the Eye Waggon, across the German states of Saxony, Hesse-Kassel and Westphalia, stopping only in obscure towns where the chevalier didn't even bother to drum up business. Uncharacteristically, he did everything he could to avoid attracting attention; perhaps deep in his soul he was doing penance.

Yet by the time we reached Cologne at the end of July, he felt sufficiently at one with the world again to take rooms in a grand hotel on the banks of the Rhine, so that he could wallow in a hot bath and indulge in an extravagant dinner.

The following morning, while the chevalier slept off seven courses, I rose early and went directly to Cologne Cathedral, still unfinished as it has been since the builders first broke ground in 1248. Two huge wooden cranes were perched on top of the tower stumps; they had been waiting in vain for the next shift of stonemasons for three centuries. My intention was to light a candle and pray for Sebastian's recovery, but as soon as I entered the church, I knew that something was wrong. A sombre fugue filled the cold air that swirled in the nave, and a black silk cloth had been draped around the organ loft.

Heavy with dread, I walked towards the altar, where a priest was kneeling in silent prayer. When he finished, he lit a candle and hurried away into the vestry.

I was alone in the cathedral with just the music, and I knew it was Bach's music, reaching out to me.

The piece finished. Footsteps creaked slowly on the wooden steps leading from the organ loft. I looked up and saw a young man with tears in his eyes.

"That was beautiful," I whispered.

"He taught me. Bach. I was his student in Leipzig."

"And he'd be proud."

"Not anymore. I received word yesterday. He is dead. The greatest organist who ever lived…" He stammered and fell silent.

Grief punched me. My legs felt weak, my mind dizzy. I slumped onto one of the pews.

"You knew him?" the young man asked.

"Briefly."

"The world will never see another man like him." He took a handkerchief from his coat, wiped his eyes, then walked down the nave to the main doors.

For a few moments I could do nothing. It was as if I too had been paralysed. I stared at the huge gold cross standing proudly in the centre of the altar. Why had God thrown this man away? What justice was that? How could a man like the chevalier be sleeping peacefully in his bed while Bach was lowered into a cold grave?

Rage overwhelmed me.

I heard myself scream, and the next moment I was standing before the altar, dragging down the cross, sweeping aside the candlesticks, hurling the chalice and paten to the stone floor. All I wanted was to hurt the same God who had stood by and done nothing while Bach was butchered to death.

They found me collapsed on the floor. To this day, I do not know how long I had been slumped there.

PART FIVE: DOCTOR HARVEY

TWENTY-ONE

The pain is still raw for her. Despite the gloom in the cell, I can see tears in Arabella's eyes.

"You did not wield the knife," I whisper. "You cannot blame yourself."

"But I do. And I always will."

There is nothing I can say to offer comfort. I am utterly out of my depth.

Without another word, I hammer on the door to summon the guards, then hurry away from the darkness of that prison.

I wander aimlessly through the streets of Bath, trying to clear the shadows from my soul. This city looks so civilised compared to the cruel world that Arabella's confession has drawn me into.

Eventually I find myself on Brock Street and decide to rest for a moment in King's Circus. Dodging the carriages ferrying people back from the Pump Rooms, I reach the stone paving in the centre and sit down on a bench. There is a faint sound of lapping water from the huge reservoir just beneath the stones under my feet.

Much as I try to distract myself by observing the comings and goings of the wealthy residents, my mind keeps circling back to Arabella, languishing in her lonely prison.

Would I have done anything different?

I try to convince myself that I would have spoken up, stopped the Chevalier from operating, saved Bach's life … but true courage is rare.

Once home, Joseph briefs me on the day's news as I take off my coat and boots. Fortunately, there are no patients demanding attention, and I ask him to rearrange my appointments so that the next two days are free. He offers to make me some hot chocolate, but I decline.

As I climb the stairs to my bedchamber, I notice the door to the guest room where the chevalier is staying has been left ajar. Silently I enter and stare at him, lying on white linen sheets, enjoying the sleep of the innocent. On the bedside table are more sketches from the portrait artist; the chevalier can't see them, yet still he wants to be close to these deceitful vanities intended to immortalise him.

Suddenly I feel a nausea of revulsion at the utter shamelessness of this man who has awoken dread ghosts in my own soul. For years I have locked them away, deep inside me, because I have never needed to dwell on them. Bath has been good to me, my practice thrives, and on the surface I am treated with respect. But if I am truly honest, when I look into the eyes of men like Lansdowne and Melville and Stratford, I see the same casual contempt that defines the chevalier.

I clamber up the steps into the loft and search among the cobweb-clutter until I find a wooden trunk. It has sat here, undisturbed, for so long. Thirty years ago I vowed to leave the past behind, but now it has caught up with me.

I wipe off a layer of dust and snap back the iron latches to reveal the only things my grandfather bequeathed me: the most valuable things in the world, and the most disgraceful.

An iron collar.

Chain shackles.

A slave badge.

His Deeds of Manumission.

This indenture witnesseth that I, George Sewell, of the City of Calcutta, have manumitted and made free Siddharth Christian Harvey, son of Kabir. So that in future he shall be free and of free condition, with all his goods and chattels, and shall be discharged of all obligation of bondage or servitude whatsoever.

I have my freedom, while countless thousands still do not because of the misplaced superiority of men like the chevalier: Company Men who straddle the globe in the name of Empire; men who will never be brought to justice.

My heart is heavy with guilt that I have been playing their game, laughing and dining with them, treating their ailments with such care.

In truth, I have been their fool.

PART SIX: ARABELLA

TWENTY-TWO

I remember waking up in the sanatorium in Bad Aachen. Who found me, how I got there, what the doctors diagnosed … these details remain a blank. But what I do recall is the chevalier's genuine concern, and his insistence that I receive the finest medical treatment.

He spent many hours by my bedside, holding my hand, stroking my hair, reassuring me that the doctors were doing everything in their power. In truth, all anyone could do was allow Nature to heal me in her own time.

And it was slow.

Weeks turned into months; through my window I watched the trees turn golden-red, then spidery-black, until the first snow flurries dusted the lawns white.

As my strength gradually recovered, the chevalier would wheel me in a chair to the hot spas, where nurses helped me bathe in marble-lined pools. My fellow patients were the nonpareil from across Europe: neurotic spinsters and sickly barons from Saxony lay next to bloated French aristocrats and emaciated dowagers. Not once did the chevalier complain about the cost of all this, though it must have been excessive. Perhaps guilt had unlocked his purse, and he was hoping that good works would redeem his sins. The only stipulation he made was that neither of us would ever talk of Leipzig again. "That city has destroyed you once," he said. "I will not allow it to haunt you."

It was when I was in this weakened state, that the chevalier humbly got onto one knee and asked me to be his wife. I was in no fit state to make such a decision; he had bombarded me with affection until my emotions were numb and my defences lay in ruins, but in truth, I was too much in his debt to have any real choice. If I turned him down, who would pay the doctors that were nursing me back to health? Where would I go? Who would keep me safe? I could not return to the poverty that had stalked my childhood, and at that moment I could not imagine a future that was not inextricably bound up with the chevalier. He may have broken me, but he had made me in the first place. Were it not for him, I would still be suffocating under the oppressive boredom and grinding perseverance of Josiah Roope.

We were married in Cologne Cathedral in March. The location was important to the chevalier: he was symbolically exorcising the demons that had taken possession of my soul. Now he was reclaiming it and making me his.

It was a fiercely cold day in the cathedral; without the hot breath of a congregation, the great stone pillars were like shafts of death in that gloomy space, drawing every shred of warmth into their hard hearts. The driver witnessed the ceremony, and the chevalier had rustled up a dozen or so society guests. A small choir sang some traditional hymns, but the organist was nowhere to be seen. The wedding breakfast was hosted in one of Cologne's finest restaurants, and there seemed to be much wine and good humour.

Finally, I had everything I thought I had longed for: respectability, status, wealth. But like the fabled Dead Sea fruit, it had turned to ash in my mouth.

A few days after the wedding we were on the move again, heading south, following the Rhine through Coblenz and Mannheim.

It was clear the chevalier wanted everything to be just as it was before my illness, but I needed life to revolve around something less venal. Reminding my husband that we were supposed to be on our honeymoon, I persuaded him to spend a few days sightseeing.

"Can there be anything duller than medieval ruins?" he grumbled.

"But think of the romance," I implored. "What woman doesn't love romance?"

Finally he relented, and a few days later we found ourselves on a boating lake near Heidelberg. It was a strange affair, a recreation that had been constructed entirely for the amusement of wealthy families. A Reichsgraf and his wife would perch in a boat that was rowed by men dressed as Venetian gondoliers; but they were just the brute force and had no control over their destinies, for the steering was in the hands of the passengers via a long tiller. Children, stifled in their Sunday best, were loaded into a second boat with a tutor or nanny, and that was towed by their parents' craft. The convoy would then float around artificial islands and under picturesque bridges, much to the bemusement of the swans.

"No! Certainly not," the chevalier said when I suggested we take a boat.

"Please."

"We're not infants."

"But it looks such fun."

"And I don't want to get this coat wet. It's sable."

I rested my head on his shoulder. "What could be more romantic than a boat? And this is our honeymoon."

"That excuse is starting to wear rather thin, Arabella." But the chevalier relented nonetheless.

Once we were on the water, I took control of the tiller. While my husband closed his eyes and started to doze off, I steered us towards the boating parties with boisterous children. Their delight at being on the lake was contagious. Somehow, just being afloat had freed them from the suffocating constraint of rules and decorum, and they happily ignored their fretful tutors.

We circled one particular boat of rebels who had thrown off the rope that tied them to their parents, and were now steering away as fast as they could. I waved at the mutineers, and they waved back excitedly. "Look at their little faces. They're quite charming."

"They're certainly noisy."

I steered towards a small rustic bridge. "When I was in the hospital, with the future so uncertain, I couldn't help wondering what will be left when I am gone."

"That is all behind us now, Arabella."

"Don't you ever think about your legacy?"

"I have published extensively. I am mentioned in the memoirs of kings and princes. My name will live on in medical history."

"But a treatise cannot love you. Or throw its arms around you. Or laugh at your jokes."

"That is why I have you, Arabella."

A scream went up behind us — the mutineers had discovered the joys of splashing each other, much to their tutor's horror.

"Huzzah!" I cried out.

"Don't encourage them," the chevalier said testily.

"Where is your sense of humour?"

"The answer is no."

"You don't want to be splashed?"

"I do not want children. So we are not having any."

"It hadn't really occurred to me." I looked away.

"There will be no cuckoos in my nest."

"And what about my feelings?"

"The thought of what childbirth will do to your body disgusts me, Arabella. You are perfect now, but babies will pull your hips out of shape, suck your breasts dry and turn you into a tearful wreck. I have just got you back, at great expense, and I have no intention of losing you again."

I fell silent in the face of his contempt. He removed my hand from the tiller and steered us towards a bank of willow trees. "Perhaps we can find a secluded spot where you can express your gratitude in a more visceral fashion," he said with a sly grin.

After that I lost interest in the honeymoon.

The chevalier's thoughts quickly turned back to work: his plan was to head into France, where he had heard there were rich pickings amongst the excessive wealth and decadence of the nobility, but as we crossed the border at Strasbourg, we were unexpectedly detained.

"Documents, please." Like border guards everywhere, the man was hostile and suspicious.

"Of course." The chevalier handed over a leather pouch.

As the guard opened it to pull out the papers, he saw two silver coins glinting in the bottom of the purse. He glared at the chevalier. "Papers only."

"Forgive me," the chevalier laughed. "An accident. They must have fallen in by mistake."

The guard studied the identity documents and travel permits. "Step out of the carriage, please."

"Is there a problem?" The chevalier was a picture of innocence.

"Please, sir. Step out of the carriage."

With a laboured sigh, the chevalier did as he was told. "My papers are all in order. We have been travelling for many months."

"You are the chevalier Dr John Taylor?"

"Ah, so you can read. That is indeed what it says on the documents."

"Answer the question. Is that you?"

"Yes."

The guard took the papers into a small building to consult with his superiors.

As the chevalier glanced at me, I saw a flash of unease in his eyes. "Let me do the talking."

"What do you think this is about?"

"Someone is always trying to make trouble. Probably that mad Ostermann chap from Konigsberg."

More likely it was someone from Leipzig. Bach's widow, perhaps.

Through the windows of the border post I could see the guard in earnest discussion with the officer in charge. When he emerged he was flanked by two armed soldiers. "You are to come with me."

"This is an insult! I am an English aristocrat —"

"Please, Chevalier. Don't make this difficult." The soldiers braced themselves for things to turn ugly.

"What about my wife?"

"Just you."

The chevalier turned to me and mustered a smile. "Set up in the main square. We may need to grease a few foreign palms."

As I watched my husband being taken away, escorted by armed guards, I felt a flicker of hope. Maybe God was listening after all.

By the time I arrived at the fort, the chevalier was visibly anxious. They had put him in a holding cell, and although he wasn't in manacles, he had not been extended any comforts.

"What do you think this is about?" I asked.

"How the hell would I know?" he snapped. "All these lobcocks do is kiss the rectum of the next bureaucrat up the ladder!"

"Here, I brought you this." I handed him some bread and cheese, along with a small bottle of wine. He ate in a moody silence, considering his options.

"How much do you think it will cost? To buy your way out of here?"

"What is the world coming to when an Englishman cannot roam freely throughout Europe without having to bow and scrape to petty officials?"

I sat with him quietly, watching the rain patter through a barred window high up in the wall. After what seemed like hours, we heard footsteps approaching. One of the guards escorted a man in a British military uniform towards us.

"Chevalier Taylor? I am Major Cleverly. Attaché to the English Ambassador in Paris."

"Whatever you are thinking, you are wrong. I am an innocent traveller."

"I apologise for the heavy-handed treatment. Perhaps the instructions were lost in translation." The major told the guard to unlock the cell. "An alert was sent to all the border crossings. You have been summoned to London by King George."

"Really?" The chevalier could sense that things were turning his way again. "The king is sick?"

"Mercifully, no. But someone in his service, a man for whom the king has great affection, is suffering. He needs your expert medical skills."

"I see." The chevalier closed his eyes, affecting an air of enigma, but I knew that secretly he was in ecstasy at this unexpected development. 'By royal command' was precisely the validation he had craved his entire life.

"Chevalier? Did you hear me?"

The chevalier stood up and cast a haughty look at Major Cleverly. "Here is what will happen. You will have me released from custody immediately and taken to the finest hotel in Strasbourg, an expense that will be met by the British government. Tomorrow we can talk over lunch."

"But the matter is urgent. Perhaps we could start the journey tonight?"

"Did you not hear me, Major Cleverly? I have given my instructions."

The reassertion of the chevalier's authority continued without mercy the following day. He insisted that we turn up an hour late for luncheon simply to keep Cleverly waiting, then ordered the most expensive items on the menu, along with a vintage wine. When the major finally managed to turn the conversation to London, the chevalier demanded a grovelling apology.

"I apologise unreservedly, sir. A formal complaint has been made to the French authorities."

"I should think so," the chevalier said, savouring his wine.

"Can I advise the ambassador that you will accept the king's invitation?"

The chevalier frowned. "I need to give it some thought."

"You would be well-advised to accept, sir."

"And you would be well-advised to learn some etiquette, considering the hurt and humiliation we suffered in a squalid French gaol."

"For which I once again apologise."

"Who exactly will I be treating?"

"I am not at liberty to say, Chevalier."

"You don't have a choice, Major. I have patients across Europe waiting for me. I will not abandon them on an anonymous whim."

"It is the composer, Handel," the major admitted reluctantly. "He is going blind."

"I have heard of him. Vaguely."

"He is the most famous composer in all Europe. And a particular favourite of King George. Hence the urgency."

"How bad is his sight?"

"Last year he was involved in a coach accident in the Netherlands. He was seriously injured. It seems the blindness started then."

"Interesting."

"So I can confirm you will come, Chevalier?"

"Let me discuss it with my wife."

"Of course." Cleverly looked at me expectantly.

"In private," the chevalier insisted. "If you would be so good as to wait outside?" He pointed to the window; rain was hammering down on the cobbles.

"Seriously?"

"I do not joke about work, Cleverly."

Reluctantly the major excused himself and left the restaurant. He tried to huddle under the flimsy window awnings, but the rain was too heavy.

With no-one observing him, the chevalier's whole demeanour changed. "Hah! The saints take care of the chevalier! The angels stoop to meet him! What a turn of events. The royal court is begging for my services."

"Surely you're not going to accept?"

"Of course I am. I always was." He glanced out to where the major was getting soaked. "I'm just toying with him."

"Shouldn't you leave composers alone?"

"Handel is the toast of London. He's favoured in all the highest circles. This will be the making of us, Arabella. Cure Handel, and all London will be at our feet."

"That's what you said before."

"Come now. We agreed never to mention Leipzig."

"Failure with Handel will be very public."

"For God's sake, woman! Have some faith in me."

"There will be nowhere to run this time. We are not talking about a provincial organist."

"There will be no need to run. I have learnt my lesson. Seeing how you suffered, Arabella, it changed me." He took my hand. "I never want to see you unhappy like that again."

"Then perhaps we should not take the risk."

"I am a reformed man. There will be no drinking before surgery, and no moving on until I have seen the healing process through to completion." Gently he kissed my fingers. "This is a new beginning for us. I swear on my mother's life. I have let myself down too many times in the past. Everything will be different in London."

Yet the chevalier sensed his rhetoric was losing its potency.

"Bach was going blind anyway," he urged. "Nature had decided his fate. But Handel — this is an eye injury. It is something completely different. I can give this composer his life back."

I wanted to believe him. More than that, I wanted to see England again. Perhaps in my own country, I would be less vulnerable to the chevalier's capricious nature.

TWENTY-THREE

We arrived in London like shining stars. The finest social circles were hot with anticipation and rife with gossip; everyone knew we were freshly returned from the most powerful courts in Europe, summoned by royal appointment to treat the much-loved composer, George Frideric Handel. We took a house in St James, in the very heart of fashionable London. While the driver tended the Eye Waggon in the mews coach-house at the rear (the race across Europe had taken its toll on the mechanics), the chevalier and I revelled in a whirl of soirées and lavish dinners. Every morning a steady stream of calling cards would arrive at the house, and extravagant bouquets of flowers were sent by aristocrats hoping to lure us to their private gatherings. London's best theatres sent us open invitations to enjoy their latest productions.

To feel so loved by complete strangers … one would need to have a very cold heart to remain unseduced.

As for Handel himself, he was the one man we couldn't get to meet. He was busy rehearsing two oratorios that were opening within days of each other, but his assistant had managed to schedule an appointment for the end of the month.

Handel may have been elusive, but his music was not; it surrounded us wherever we went. Unlike Bach, this composer knew what it meant to be celebrated; no London event was complete without someone performing Handel's music.

And it was beautiful music.

I remembered how fondly Bach had spoken of Handel, how he had travelled across Saxony to try and meet his fellow composer; now I understood why. To hear a soprano's voice cast such a delicate spell across a crowded room, was like being in a fairy-tale.

Let me weep over my cruel fate, and let me sigh for liberty.

This was beauty quite different to that created by Bach. It was not layered with complexity, but cried out from the heart with a single line of such purity and emotion. It was the longing of the human soul distilled into harmony.

Unfortunately, music wasn't the only entertainment our hosts expected; invariably, as guest of honour, the chevalier was called on to give an after-dinner oration. It was a task he relished.

"God said, 'Let there be light!' And there was light."

The table fell silent; all eyes turned to the chevalier, who held a dramatic pose for a few moments.

"What He should have added was, let there also be an eye surgeon, so that all of Creation can enjoy the wonders of daylight. But He didn't. And who am I to question the Lord's will?

"Alas, it was not long before the devious Serpent slithered under the garden gate, wound itself around the weeping willow, and corrupted His world. Blindness and suffering were the Serpent's gift to mankind. Blindness that creeps slowly upon some, gradually darkening their days; blindness that thrusts itself upon others without warning, plunging poor benighted souls into a pit of despair.

"But the world turns. And as day follows night, so a brave knight has arisen to challenge the darkness; the same knight-chevalier who stands before you now. Ladies and gentlemen, I have come into the Garden to hunt down the serpent of blindness and strike off his head!"

There was invariably some applause at this point, which the chevalier acknowledged with a modest bow.

"But I am not just a common knight. I am not an old curmudgeon in clanking armour that Chaucer would have mocked. I am a surgeon-knight, whose scalpel is his sword, whose learning is his shield, whose mighty Eye Waggon is his trusty steed! And under which flag do I fight? Whose colours do I champion? There is no single country that can limit my ambition, for the whole of mankind is my project. *Qui dat videre dat viver.* 'He who gives sight, gives life.' These are the noble words on my chivalric banner. For I am the opthalmiater, pontifical, imperial, and royal!"

More applause.

"Chivalry should not be a fusty idea in a dusty tome. I have taken a vow to uphold the five virtues of the knight: courage, mercy, generosity, faith, and hope.

"To take a blade to a fellow man's eye, not to wound but to heal ... if that is not courage, then I do not know what is. To fight a duel with a jealous rival, to have him on his knees at the point of your sword, begging to be spared despite his calumnies which have besmirched you, and still to spare him ... is that not mercy? And let us not forget the poor organist from Saxony who could barely afford bread, let alone surgery. And yet neither could he afford to go blind, for that would mean destitution. Did I turn him away? No. Because generosity is embedded in the heart of a true knight.

"Faith. The only reason I am what I am, is because God chooses it. A sober life of prayer and study is the least I can do to repay Him, for being an eye surgeon is a calling, and I am as much a warrior-monk as a knight-surgeon.

"But soaring high above all the other virtues, is Hope. For that is why I have returned to London: to give hope. My country called, my king sent messengers far and wide across Europe, and I answered that call without hesitation. Our beloved Handel lives in hope of a miracle, and I swear before God that I shall devote myself to providing just that.

"The knightly virtues are within me, and it is the knightly virtues that have enabled me to surpass all eye surgeons who have lived before. Many have cut, few have healed; the chevalier does both."

At which point he would give a humble bow and soak up the warm applause. He spoke with such conviction, everyone in the room was convinced. Even I wanted to believe him, despite knowing how easily the lies fell from his lips. It was as if we all shared a collective delusion. And yet, there was the occasional dissenter.

Reverend Ramsden had been loitering for some time, trying to introduce himself to the chevalier while other, more effusive guests continually eased him to the back of the queue. Finally, just as we were about to leave, the parson made his move.

"It is a pleasure to finally meet you, Chevalier."

"Charmed, charmed," he replied, edging towards to the door.

"And such an entertaining speech." Ramsden was determined to pursue us.

"Thank you, Reverend."

We were almost out now.

"You know, we nearly met a few years ago. In Norwich."

Finally he had the chevalier's attention. "Did we?"

"It was early in your career. I seem to remember you were raising funds to build an Eye Waggon. One of my friends was considering an investment."

We both studied the reverend, trying to divine his true intentions. "Do you still live there? In Norwich?" I asked.

"No, no. God forbid. Dreadful place. I was only visiting."

"And what was your friend's name?" the chevalier asked.

"Oh, well." Reverend Ramsden seemed suddenly awkward. "He didn't invest, if that's what you mean. More fool him, I say."

"Indeed."

The small talk bumbled along for a few minutes until the chevalier found a suitable exit, but even though we managed to leave the parson behind, the unease he had planted stayed with us.

This had always been a risk of returning to England, but as London is a hundred miles from Norwich, and given the rewards on offer, the chevalier had decided it was a risk worth taking. Now he had to think again, for as our fame grew, so did the chance of our past catching up with us. The blunt truth was that we were bigamists, and the Eye Waggon was built with money stolen from Roope. This left us open to scandal and ruin.

"Why wouldn't you listen to me?" I said in the privacy of our carriage.

"A rather academic question, Arabella."

"We should have turned the king down and stayed in Europe."

"You don't turn down kings!"

"He will be the first to abandon us when we're arrested. Even the most indulgent king would not dare to argue with the laws of God."

The chevalier gazed out of the window; crowds were leaving the opera and climbing into waiting carriages. "All we need to do is change how things are perceived."

"We cannot unpick the past."

"But that is the beautiful thing, Arabella: there is no such thing as the past. It is gone. There is only the present." A smile crept across the chevalier's lips. "And the present can be manipulated with a subtle combination of bribery and bullying."

That evening he wrote to one of his government contacts asking for an audience, and two days later we were shown into a large office in Whitehall Place, where a bewigged undersecretary listened cautiously.

"It is simply a matter of tying up some loose ends," the chevalier explained, "but it may prove inconveniently awkward."

"We take the law very seriously in this office," the undersecretary frowned. "It is not to be trifled with."

"I couldn't agree more," the chevalier said earnestly. "And yet, given the pressures on government, I assume that some cases are overlooked in favour of others?"

"It would be inadvisable to assume anything, Chevalier."

"What if there was a man, from a long time ago, who needed to be … silenced? How would that best be achieved? Could a contract prevent him from disclosing inconvenient facts?"

"A contract to deny a man his freedom of speech? Who would sign such a document? Unless he was compensated?"

"Perhaps this man." The chevalier slid a sheet of paper across the desk on which were written all the particulars about Josiah Roope. The undersecretary studied the document for a few moments.

"If he were to complain, it would be extremely helpful if his complaints fell on deaf ears," the chevalier suggested. "Perhaps that is something your department could facilitate?"

"I'm sure I don't need to remind you, Chevalier, that in England, no man is above the law."

"Of course. And yet, King George himself summoned me here, which perhaps puts a different light on matters."

The undersecretary nodded thoughtfully. "Talking of compensation, would you excuse me for a moment?" He got up and walked to the door, but as he left, he opened the lid of an enamelled cigar box on the console table.

"London," the chevalier whispered as the office door clicked shut, "where bribery is an art." He took a purse of gold coins from his pocket, placed it in the cigar box and shut the lid.

We waited in silence for quite a while, but nothing happened.

"Is he coming back?" I asked.

"Money is the grand cosmetic: it removes every blemish."

"Perhaps the undersecretary has taken offence."

"How can he know how much is there? Unless…" The chevalier's eyes darted across the walls. "Unless they have some way of spying upon us?"

"Surely not."

But a sudden paranoia had taken hold of the chevalier, and he refused to say another word.

Finally the official returned, briefly lifted the lid of the cigar box, was evidently content, and sat back behind his desk.

"This man, Roope. A colleague in the Treasury informs me that he has been declared bankrupt, which means he should be malleable."

"That is good news," the chevalier smiled. "And I assume that such a bankrupt, a man who pays no taxes, a man who owes money to the Treasury, would not be a man taken seriously by the courts should he choose to complain?"

"This time, Chevalier, you assume correctly."

TWENTY-FOUR

It was strange to return to Norwich. Once it had been my whole world, but now it seemed nothing more than a provincial backwater.

Our carriage rolled into the medieval streets, clattering over the cobbles in a triumphal entrance. We had left as felons, hurrying away under the cover of night; now we were returning dressed in the finest clothes, with powerful contacts protecting us.

Yet it didn't feel like triumph.

A new generation of urchins hurried across the road to greet our carriage, offering to help with the luggage and find us lodgings, but the chevalier swung his cane at them impatiently, chasing them back into the shadows. He had no intention of remaining a moment longer than was absolutely necessary.

We found the house on the corner of Princes Street and Tombland; I was surprised at how badly it had fallen into disrepair. The windowpanes were cracked, great folds of peeling paint hung from the walls, and water dripped from a length of guttering that had broken away from the roofline. This was not how I remembered Josiah Roope; he had always been meticulously house-proud.

The chevalier hammered on the flaking door with his fist. No answer. He tried again. "Don't tell me we've come all this way for nothing." He wiped some grime from the window and peered into the gloom.

"I still have this." I loosened the clasp on my reticule and fished out a single key. "If the lock hasn't been changed." It was stiff from lack of use, but finally we managed to turn the bolt and push the door open.

"Josiah?" I called into the gloom.

Silence.

Slowly we walked down the hallway, peering into the rooms. There was barely a piece of furniture left in the house — no pictures or carpets, no curtains or plate. Except for layers of grime, the place had been stripped. Just as we were about to turn and leave, I heard a faint scratching sound coming from the scullery.

I pushed open the door and saw a man dressed in a dusty morning gown, hunched over a bowl of broth that was perched on the kitchen table. "Be gone," he muttered without even turning round. "There's nothing left to take."

It was pitiful to see him like this, a once dignified man living like a recluse in the ruins of his townhouse.

"Hello, Josiah," I said.

He raised his eyes. For a moment, he struggled to comprehend what he was seeing, then fury creased his face. "You … YOU!" He lunged towards the chevalier. "You bastard!" But as he raised his fist, the chevalier prodded him away with his cane. Roope lost his balance and toppled over.

"Please. Let me talk to him." I helped Josiah back to his feet.

"My wife," Josiah said bitterly, "my darling wife deigns to speak with me."

"What happened, Josiah?"

"He happened!" Josiah pointed furiously at the chevalier. "That monstrous fraud."

"You are deluded, sir," the chevalier sniffed.

"I disliked him from the moment I first set eyes on him. And I was right!" Josiah's watery eyes fastened on me. "It is you who was blinded by his lies."

"That's not how I remember it," the chevalier said calmly. "Out of the kindness of my heart, I restored your business partner's sight and barely took a shilling for it."

"Restored?" The word was bitter on Josiah's lips. "You blinded him! He never saw a glimmer of light after you'd finished with him."

"Did you leave the bandages on *exactly* as instructed?"

"He was wracked with agonising pain and fever! In desperation he tore off the bandages…" Josiah stumbled over the horror of the memories. "His eyes had been reduced to festering wounds. You butchered him! The loss drove poor Mather mad with grief. He squandered his money trying to find a cure. Failure drove him to drink. The business slid into debt. Customers abandoned us." He pointed a filthy, crooked finger at the chevalier. "This is the destruction you leave in your wake."

"I am sorry if you feel that way, Roope, and you are entitled to your opinion." The chevalier reached into his jacket and took out a purse of coins. "But today we have come to do you a good turn." He chinked the money as if taunting an animal.

"Is that all my life is worth? A small purse of coins?"

"Well, if you don't want it…" The chevalier went to put the money away.

"Wait." Josiah's eyes were locked on the purse, considering the possibilities.

"This could get you back on your feet again. A bath and shave, a new set of clothes."

"It does not absolve you."

"Actually, it does." The chevalier took out a legal contract. "The price of the gold is an amnesty. You set Arabella and I free from the past."

Josiah took the document and studied the neat handwriting. "Even now you humiliate me."

"From what I can see," the chevalier replied, "you've done a rather good job of that yourself. The truth is, the only way out for you is this contract. Unless you've saved a few feet of rope to hang yourself."

Josiah studied the smirk on the chevalier's face. "You are the Devil."

"And you are in a tight spot, my dear Roope."

Unable to endure any more, Josiah howled like a wounded dog and flew at the chevalier, his hands reaching for his neck. The two men struggled like schoolboys wrestling each other, before the chevalier cast Josiah aside. "Mind the clothes! They are freshly cleaned."

Before Josiah could launch another attack, I stepped between the two men. "Leave us," I said to the chevalier. "Let me talk to…" I hesitated.

"Your husband," Josiah said pointedly. "I am still your husband."

"That is debatable," the chevalier quipped.

"Go. Please. Wait by the carriage."

Mercifully, the chevalier did as I asked.

"Was I so unbearable that you preferred a monster like him?" There was genuine bewilderment in Josiah's question.

"I was a girl. A foolish girl. What did I know?"

"Even a child knows right from wrong."

"I'm sorry, Josiah. Please, forgive me."

"Forgive…" He held his head in his hands, trying to ease the torment. "I would have forgiven you anything. But you destroyed my heart. And now I can feel nothing."

"I never wanted you to suffer." I reached out to touch him, but he recoiled.

"What did I do to deserve such cruel treatment? Tell me. I was an honest, Christian man. I prayed every day. I followed His Commandments. And now He has abandoned me."

"You are not the only virtuous man God has turned his back on."

"That is of little comfort."

"Then take the money. Perhaps that can be some small consolation."

"I deserve better."

"I know."

I emerged from the house to find the chevalier waiting in the carriage, practising a new card shuffle.

"Did you get it?"

I handed him the document.

"Good girl." He checked the signature then called out to the driver, "Let's go! Get me out of this city of cloak-twitchers!"

I watched him casually flick the cards from hand to hand. "How can you be so unmoved?"

"There is no room for pity. This is business."

"Josiah plucked me from poverty and treated me kindly. He was an honest man."

"He was a liability, Arabella. The damage he could have done to us was incalculable. He would have dragged us both down."

There was no point discussing it further. For the whole journey back to London I was haunted by Josiah's ghost, but the chevalier remained utterly indifferent, shuffling his cards contentedly.

Despite all the piety he had shown at my hospital bedside, and the extravagant promises to reform, I realised that this was a man who would never change. This is who the chevalier really was: a man devoted only to himself.

TWENTY-FIVE

It wasn't just Handel's music that people loved, it was the man himself.

Our meeting took place at the Foundling Hospital, where the composer was a governor; when he wasn't creating beautiful music, Handel devoted his time to the most helpless and forgotten.

He had arranged to meet us at the hospital entrance, and I expected a man of such wealth and influence to be accompanied by a retinue of staff fluttering obsequiously in his wake. But I was wrong; he stood at the gates with just a single child who held his hand. Handel had a serious, heavy face, but as soon as the boy told him we were approaching, he broke into such a welcoming smile it was as if light radiated from the man's heart.

"Chevalier Taylor! It is an honour."

"No, no. The honour is all mine, sir."

They shook hands. "Allow me to introduce my wife, Lady Arabella."

"Charmed! And in turn, allow me to introduce Jacob, who has kindly agreed to be my eyes today."

The boy bowed politely.

"Nice to meet you, Jacob. How old are you?" I asked.

"Eight and a quarter, miss."

"Excellent. The quarter makes all the difference."

"Come. We shall walk to the main building and take in the sunshine." Handel turned to lead the way.

A set of formal gardens stretched from the gates to the hospital. Jacob took his duties very seriously, carefully guiding

Handel along winding paths and around flowerbeds, ensuring that his charge didn't stumble or trip.

"This institution does incredible work," Handel explained. "Foundlings from across the country end up in our care. God knows what would happen to them if we weren't here."

"It is admirable that you find time to lend your support," I said.

"It is my duty. Those who have been downtrodden must be picked up by those who have been fortunate enough to prosper."

"My philosophy exactly." The chevalier nodded. "Humility in all things. It is my unofficial motto."

"You should make it official."

"An excellent idea, Herr Handel. From the very start of my career, I have insisted that at least a third of my surgery is *pro bono*. It breaks my heart to turn away the less fortunate."

"I can see that we are going to get along famously, Chevalier."

Keen to move the conversation on, the chevalier used the gardens as an impromptu eye test, asking which plants and flowers Handel could discern, which colours were vivid or faint. It was clear that his eyesight was poor, yet despite this, he seemed determined not to give in to despair. Most touching of all was the patience and concern Jacob showed, celebrating every right answer with a joyous laugh, consoling mistakes with encouraging words.

I witnessed the young guiding the old, while the old protected the young, and it filled my heart with longing. My own childhood had been about nothing more than utility; love was not a factor in the harsh poverty of the tannery.

As we climbed the steps to the entrance hall a drum started to beat time, then the doors opened to reveal a choir of children arranged in two rows, who immediately broke into 'He Shall Purify' from *The Messiah*.

"Wonderful! I didn't know anything about this!" Handel exclaimed.

We stood and listened to the choir; it sounded delightful to me, yet Handel listened with intense concentration, studying each voice and how it worked with the whole. As soon as they finished, we applauded politely, while Handel roared with pleasure.

"Bravo! An excellent performance! Especially the articulation of the sixteenths. I can tell you've been working on those."

As the children dispersed, laughing and chatting, Handel reached out to pat heads and shoulders, sharing in their youthful energy. Only once we were in the privacy of his office did he confess to the deep melancholy he was struggling against.

"Every time I see something, I wonder if it will be for the last time. Each face, every building and cloud … sometimes I just stand and stare at a tree, trying to memorise every leaf in case it has to last me for the rest of my life."

"One cannot live at such a pitch," the chevalier said gravely.

"It is my fault!"

"No. You must not blame yourself."

"Why was I in such a hurry to make that journey? It could have waited until the storm had passed. The carriage was going too fast. I could feel it slipping on the road. I should have told the driver to slow down. I should have told him!" Handel fell silent, trying to contain his emotions. He drew a breath. "One moment I was sitting there, the next we were upside down in the ditch. Here…" He pointed to a scar on the side of his head. "This is where the axle struck. It was such a blow. I could see blooms of light in my eyes, like fireworks. It is the last thing I remember before passing out."

"Then we need to correct the damage that has been done," the chevalier said firmly.

"Music comes through sight. I can only compose because the world enters my soul through my eyes: beauty and sorrow, fear and love. In a world gone dark, I fear my music will wither."

It was tragic to see a great man so desperate. Yet it was more terrifying to think that he was putting his trust in my husband.

"I have heard about your surgical genius, Chevalier. I have prayed for a miracle, and now that miracle is standing before me."

"And yet," the chevalier sniffed, "I understand I was not your first choice?"

Handel hung his head, embarrassed by the observation. "Last year I was persuaded to see a surgeon in Tonbridge Wells, Samuel Sharp. You know of him, perhaps?"

"Vaguely. And not in favourable terms."

"Indeed. At the time, I was losing the sight in my right eye, but shortly after Sharp's surgery, the affliction spread to both eyes."

"These inferior butchers have much to answer for," the chevalier lamented.

"I pray to God that you can unpick his negligence."

"Let me take a look." The chevalier opened his case of surgical instruments.

I helped Handel onto the couch, where he lay propped on some cushions. Gently the chevalier started to clamp open the composer's eyes.

"You are admirably calm. Most patients recoil from this."

"My father was a barber-surgeon. In Halle. He never operated on eyes. But I know that when patients struggle, it makes everything worse."

"Indeed it does."

The chevalier took out a magnifying glass and studied the composer's eyes. I held a mirror to reflect light from the window so that he could see in greater detail. After some minutes of close examination, the chevalier removed the clamps and sat back in his chair. "I believe I can restore your sight."

"I knew it!" Handel's face burst into a joyous smile again. "There is hope!"

"The motions of the pupils and the reactions to light are all promising."

"I knew you would not let me down, Chevalier. Some of my friends tried to deter me, but they don't understand. Prayer alone is not enough; one needs a great surgeon."

"Which would make another fine motto," the chevalier quipped.

Handel roared with laughter. "If ever music abandons me, I shall make a new career as a writer of mottos!" He called his assistant into the room to find the earliest date in his diary for the operation.

I studied Handel as he asked about different aspects of the surgical procedure.

How I longed to meet those friends who had tried to deter him; perhaps they had heard rumours about the chevalier that gave cause for concern.

I had failed to protect one great composer; I would not make the same mistake again.

We arrived back at the house in St James to discover that a large wooden box had been delivered from Parry's Medical Instruments.

"Finally! My design has arrived." Eagerly the chevalier carried the box into the front parlour, where he unscrewed the lid and lifted out a huge, polished brass eye. He gazed at it in wonder. "Did you ever see anything quite so beautiful?"

The anatomical model was eighteen inches in diameter and represented all the parts of a human eye. It had been so perfectly constructed, that each element slid apart from the others like a three-dimensional puzzle: the cornea swung down to reveal the iris, which was hinged so that it could expand and contract; behind that was the lens which could be slid out to reveal the vitreous chamber and the retinal wall.

"And look at these." The chevalier opened a special drawer revealing extra attachments. "These represent ailments of the eye that can be slid into place to illustrate different conditions."

"It's beautiful."

"It is quite possibly the most important surgical instrument ever made. Not only is it a shining bauble to dazzle prospective clients, but it enables me to rehearse operations before I perform them." He slid some attachments into place. "This is why Handel is going blind: the lens has become dislodged and sits at a tangent to the cornea, you see? Now I can study it at my leisure while planning the surgery."

He was in such a good mood playing with his brass eye, that I decided now was the moment. "Could I ask for one favour?"

"At this moment, London will give us whatever we desire."

"Decline the operation."

He looked up from the model and blinked in confusion. "What?"

"Say that it cannot be done. That Handel's eyes are too damaged to repair."

"Out of the question."

"Please. Do this for me."

"It is nothing to do with you. The reason we are here, the very reason we are the toast of the town, is precisely because I am to restore Handel's sight."

"If you love me, you will grant me this."

"No! What's got into you?"

"I have an uneasy feeling."

"You would seriously turn triumph into failure? For a mere 'feeling'? This operation will be the making of me. It will secure my reputation and my wealth."

"You said that about Leipzig."

"Forget Leipzig! Europe is nothing to me! Bastardly gullions, the lot of them! What happens in London is all that matters. This city is the world." He turned his attention back to the brass eye, like a child with a toy.

"And what if the operation goes wrong?"

"It won't. I told you: I am a reformed man. No drinking before surgery. And now I have this magnificent anatomical model on which to practise."

"I forbid you to operate on Handel," I said quietly.

"Forbid?" He stared at me. "What on earth do you mean, forbid?"

"Exactly that."

"My dear Arabella, I think you need to go upstairs and have a lie down. You are not in a position to forbid me anything."

"As your wife —"

"Exactly so! *My* wife." He pushed the brass eye away. "Who owes me everything. Including obedience."

"If it wasn't for me, there would be no Eye Waggon, and you would be nothing."

"How dare you insult me?"

"It was my money that built the thing."

"That is not how I remember it."

"By rights, half of your wealth should be mine."

"You are deluded, woman!"

"Do not force me. I warn you."

"Or what? What will the little urchin from the tannery do?" He poured a brandy and slugged it back. "The poor never really shake off the dirt of the gutter, and you would do well to remember that, 'Lady' Arabella."

"I know that your precious Book of Testimonials is fake. Every single one was written by you, and I can prove it."

The chevalier looked at me in silence, his eyes cold with anger. "What did you say?"

"You are a fraud who butchers innocent people. I have written a full and honest account of how you murdered Bach, just one of your many victims. And unless you decline to operate on Handel, I will publish it and ruin you."

The clock ticked heavily in the room.

We stared at each other in deathly silence as he tried to formulate a response.

Finally, he scoffed. "What an absurd woman you are. Utterly deranged."

"Then what is this?" I held up one of the fake seals that he had used to create his testimonials. "I have the whole box of them, stored safely with the confession."

He tried to take it from me, but I was too quick. "So you see, dearest husband, your reputation is in my hands."

"Seriously? You would ruin us both? Destroy everything that we have built? Strip all the fine clothes off your own back? Are you so vindictive? So stupid?"

"All I ask is that you spare Handel. Operate on all the others, the lords and ladies, and all the sycophants at court. But spare Handel."

He gave a long, mournful sigh, then sank into a chair. I had been braced for rage, but now he put his head in his hands in a great show of despair. "To think that you could turn against me so cruelly … after all the love and care I have shown."

"You don't understand; I am doing this to protect you. To protect both of us."

"I could have walked away. When you were sick in Cologne, I could have abandoned you. But I didn't. And my reward is to be stabbed in the back?"

"If you really love me, do this one thing for me."

His shoulders started to shudder, and he sobbed into his hands like a broken child. Instinctively I went to him, but he pushed me away.

"Judas! Such disloyalty! Such wanton betrayal." He stood up, left the room, and slowly climbed the stairs like a broken man.

I didn't know what to do. Should I go to him? Should I leave the house?

I sat down at the table and gazed at the half-deconstructed brass eye. I had not expected triumph to feel quite so empty.

And then I heard it — footsteps thundering down the stairs. I looked up to see him storming into the room like an ogre, fist raised, his face contorted with rage.

"Stop!" I flinched, but there was no time. He punched me across the face, sending me reeling backwards. I stumbled over a footstool and fell to the floor. The room was spinning, my vision blurred.

I felt his hands grip my shoulders and haul me back to me feet. "Please! No!"

He held me by the hair and punched my face with his other fist. Again and again. Venting his fury.

I felt blood explode across my lips, and pain seared through my eyes. I tried to hold him off, arms flailing, but I couldn't even reach him.

"Help!" I managed to scream. "Help!"

I heard footsteps. A servant rushed into the room.

"GET OUT!" the chevalier bellowed, and the terrified servant scurried away.

He threw me to the floor, and blood splashed onto the polished wooden tiles. Desperately I tried to claw my way across the room, away from the monster.

"Wrong way!" he taunted, and grabbed me by the hair, dragging me around until I could see the door.

Safety. If I could just make it out of this room.

But as I crawled, more blows rained down on me as the chevalier lashed out with his boots. He kicked my legs, my buttocks, my back, over and over again, until I just curled up into a ball, arms wrapped around my head, praying for the agonising assault to stop.

A moment of silence. Was it over? I could see my hands trembling with shock, hear the sobs choking from my mouth.

"Don't give up now, dearest. You want to go? Go!" the chevalier taunted.

I felt his hand grip my hair, then he started to drag me towards the hall.

Screaming in pain, I tried to scramble into a crawl so that he wouldn't tear my hair out. He bundled me past the stairs and along the hall towards a door leading to the cellar.

"I think perhaps you'll feel more at home down there." He opened the door and pushed me down the wooden steps.

A falling blur, then my head cracked on something hard.

It was cold and filthy and pitch black.

The only warmth down here was from my own blood, pooling on the stone floor.

TWENTY-SIX

I must have passed out. For how long, I do not know.

The next thing I remember is being dragged to my feet by strangers who tied leather restraints around my arms and legs, then lifted me out of the blackness of that cellar. The chevalier was waiting at the top of the steps, directing the men, who I now saw were medical orderlies.

"A fever has rendered her temporarily insane. She needs to be confined for her own safety," the chevalier instructed in his most authoritative medical voice.

"Bastard!" I gasped. "You can't do this!"

"I beg to differ. You are my wife, which gives me the absolute right to dispose of you as I wish."

Rage welled up inside me, but my mind was still confused and my face throbbed with pain. Unable to find the words to express my loathing for this man, I screamed and spat a globule of bloody phlegm, which landed on his face. It was a brief moment of satisfaction, but retaliation was swift as the orderlies bound a gag tightly and painfully across my mouth.

Calmly the chevalier wiped the blood from his cheek. "You see what I have to deal with, gentlemen?"

"Don't worry, sir," one of the orderlies replied. "We get far worse."

"I'll give you a few weeks to calm her down, then I will call on the master physician to see what can be done."

"Very good, sir."

The chevalier turned his back on me, and the orderlies dragged me towards the front door. I tried to struggle, but it was useless. Bound tightly, I couldn't kick or scream, and my writing was no match for their strength. In a few moments I was bundled into the back of a secure cart and locked inside.

Pressing my face to the small, barred window, I caught snatches of London drifting by. The streets were busy with carriages and people carrying on with their lives, oblivious and indifferent to my abduction. We headed up Long Acre and along High Holborn; when we passed through Smithfield, I realised where they were taking me: Bedlam.

I glimpsed the grim, reclining statues of Melancholia and Raving Madness as we passed through the gates of the hospital. The formal gardens and monumental architecture of the place belied the true nature of what went on behind these high walls.

The cart doors were opened. Hands reached inside, pulled me out and strapped me into an invalid chair. Without any words of explanation or comfort, I was wheeled into hell.

Those inmates who were not considered dangerous were allowed to roam along the wide corridors, presenting a grotesque tableau of shrieking and fretting, of rattling manacles and trembling tics, of deluded agitation and utter despair. The violent ones, like myself, were dragged into cells and chained to the wall. I kicked and screamed and tried to fight back, but it was useless.

"The more you fight, the longer you stay in chains," one of the orderlies said. "If I were you, I'd be a good girl."

It was the longest night of my life. Crouched in the filthy straw that crawled with lice and fleas, I listened to the cacophony raging around those brutal halls of insanity; it was as if a grotesque and terrifying play was being performed in an endless cycle of sadness. I heard the ravings of the deluded, the moans of the insomniacs, the fearful chatter of the paranoid, and the diabolical threats of the violent. Worst of all was the weeping: tears of self-pity, of sorrow, of guilt, of despair.

After a thousand years, dawn finally broke.

Somehow, a narrow beam of sunlight forced its way through the impenetrable grey walls to form a tiny patch on the wall. I shuffled my chains through the filth and stretched out a hand, until my fingers could touch the light. I let the warmth soak into my skin, and slowly my composure started to return.

If life had taught me one lesson, it was resilience. That was the only thing my parents had given me, albeit unwittingly, but I knew it was the key to surviving Bedlam. I was not mad, but if I didn't fight, this place would surely turn me to madness.

But how can the weak and vulnerable resist? What weapons can a woman use when she is chained in a cell?

When I was a child, marooned in the torment of the tannery, I would look at the trees to find solace. They are the great survivors, the great stoics among us. Trees do not fight what they cannot change, but let the forces that would harm them run through their branches. The storm seeks to fell the tree, but the tree flexes and bends, eluding the wind's grasp. And as it flexes, the tree becomes stronger. So must I be to survive Bedlam.

Yet it tested me to my limits.

The humiliation and neglect I could endure; but the 'curative treatments' were barbaric. They strapped me into a chair suspended from the ceiling and spun me at great speed until I vomited bile. They forced me to take laxatives to purge my body, hoping to take the melancholia with it. They blistered me and covered my body in leeches, drawing blood until I was too weak to stand.

The only treatments that gave me strength were the cold baths. Other inmates screamed and fought to avoid being plunged into the great stone tanks in the basement, fearing that cleanliness and water would make them sick. But I embraced it. I let the cold eat through my flesh until my very bones felt numb. Through sheer willpower, I forced that bitterly cold touch to drive every last drop of compassion from my heart.

With strength came calmness.

After a few days I was unchained from my cell and allowed to roam. Despite its imposing design, the building was crumbling. Huge cracks were growing across the façade as if it had foundations of sand; the outer walls were buckling, creating gaps in the roof, so that whenever it rained water poured down the inside walls and pooled in the cells.

More worrying than the state of the building, was the state of the patients. As I wandered the corridors, peering through the barred doors, I became immune to much of the suffering. Yet one man's plight still managed to move me. He had been a sea captain who had fallen on hard times and lost his mind through drink. Now he was held in a metal contraption that secured him to the wall whilst allowing him to sit or stand, but that was the limit of his movement. He had been caged like this for twenty years.

His utter powerlessness terrified me.

Visiting the freakshow in Bedlam was a highlight of the week for many respectable Londoners. Every Sunday the wealthy and the educated would stroll casually along the wide corridors of the asylum, staring at the lunatics, mocking their strange mannerisms and pitying their lamentable sorrows. It was a ritual encouraged by the hospital governors, who hoped to excite the compassion of visitors in order to elicit donations. It did indeed provide a valuable income, even though much of the charity was diverted into the pockets of the guards and orderlies.

Though such voyeurism may seem callous, the general consensus was that exposure to madness served as a warning to the sane to keep their baser instincts in check. The terrors of Bedlam awaited anyone who allowed their passions and appetites to dethrone reason; so a day in the asylum was both a school of misery, and a lively entertainment.

For the inmates, the advantages were more elusive. All but the most passive were secured to the walls, and had to endure being taunted, ridiculed, and poked with sticks. God forbid we should try to resist; that was the surest way to guarantee seven days of corrective treatments.

Most degrading of all was the humiliation of having our genitals groped by these voyeur-visitors. Many of the patients had been forced to endure the excesses of men's sexual desire on the path to Bedlam: rape, incest, abuse and abortion. It had pushed some women into prostitution, others into madness, and the dank corridors were full of chatter about the perversions and appetites of 'respectable' men. Yet for all the worldly knowledge that was shared by the inmates, not once did I hear anyone describe the particular sexual practices the chevalier had taught me on our travels across Europe. Even in a place like this, he had found new ways of making me feel shame.

The one consolation of the public visitations was that the hospital chaplain had to put his liquor aside for a few hours and pretend to do his job.

In Bedlam, a great pageant was always made of Christian mercy, and on freakshow days any inmate could request spiritual time alone with the chaplain. Here was a lifeline;

perhaps this man could help me regain my freedom. He may have been a drunk, but he was still a man of God, which surely meant he would have some compassion as well as credibility.

I woke early on that Sunday and immediately set to making myself look as normal as possible: I combed my hair straight with my fingers, then set to rubbing the worst stains off my clothes. As I approached the small chapel where the chaplain sat, I tried to look suitably humble. "Father, do you have a few moments for a lost soul?"

Aware that we were being observed by a wealthy sugar trader and his family, the chaplain gave a benign smile. "Come in, child. Let me console your pain with the Holy Spirit."

As I entered, he touched my head in a gentle benediction, then helped me into a seat. "What is it that troubles you?"

Suddenly, a loud scream echoed down the corridor, followed by sounds of fighting. The sugar trader and his family hurried away to get a closer look, anxious not to miss a moment of high drama. As soon as they were out of sight, the chaplain's eyes glazed over. He picked up a large sandglass, turned it upside down and watched the stream of grains start to fall. "That's as long as you've got."

"Father, I am keen to repent my sins and make amends for the ills I have done, in the hope that God will let me out of this asylum."

"We cannot know the mysteries of His mind," the chaplain replied mechanically.

"I feel as if I'm getting stronger with each passing day. I really do."

"Good, good."

"Perhaps, Father, you could discuss my case with the governors?"

The chaplain gave a weary sigh. "Child, I am here to minister to your soul, not to interfere with the healing of your mind. That is for the physicians."

It was clear that I would have to raise the stakes. "I have information. Scandalous information about a man who is the toast of London."

"Is that so?"

"Chevalier Taylor, the eye surgeon — you have heard of him?"

"Of course."

"He is a fraud. His botched surgery has left a trail of maimed patients in his wake. He claims to have treated the great and good of Europe, but the testimonials he boasts are fraudulent. He has written them himself."

I waited for a stunned reaction, for outrage, for more questions. But the chaplain just yawned. "Well, I shall remember him in my prayers. Is that all?"

"Didn't you hear what I said?"

"You must not let these things upset you."

"Listen to me!"

"Calm, child. Be calm."

"These things I'm telling you are not the rantings of a lunatic. Chevalier Taylor murdered Bach! I have proof!"

"Ah, proof, I see. And you have this proof *here*?"

"No, of course not. But I can get it as soon as I am released."

A knowing smile crept across the chaplain's face. "The proof is never to hand, is it?"

"Please, you must listen to me! The chevalier is my husband."

"That's nice for you."

"No! It isn't. It is horrendous! I tried to restrain him by threatening to expose the truth, and that was when he had me locked up in here."

"Do not torment yourself with these thoughts, my child."

"He murdered Bach! And now he is going to turn his knife on Handel!"

"You must not fret about what you cannot control. Such thoughts will only drive you to distraction."

"Listen to me!"

The door creaked open and an orderly appeared. "Everything all right, Father?" The orderly glared at me, and I lowered my head to appear chastened.

"Nothing to worry about," the chaplain smiled, and the orderly withdrew.

The priest had protected me. That was a good sign. He may have been incompetent, but he didn't have a malicious heart. I decided to try again, calmly telling him the truth about the chevalier, the whole story, with specific details to prove this was not some deluded fabrication.

The chaplain gave the impression of listening attentively, but when I had finished, he just shook his head. "It seems to me that your husband was trying to help this Bach fellow."

"Help? Is that what you call performing an operation when drunk, with shaking hands? Then fleeing into the night?"

"I am not a surgeon. I don't know about medical details."

"The chevalier killed Bach as surely as if he'd plunged a scalpel into his heart. He murdered a genius. He murdered music!"

The chaplain gave a long, weary sigh. "Well, Bach is with God now, so he is at peace."

"That is not peace!"

"God's justice is the great guiding light in our lives. It may not come in this life, but we can be assured of it in the next."

"And what if God has abandoned us?"

Finally, the chaplain started to pay attention. "Be careful what you say, child."

"What if He doesn't care? Or doesn't even exist? Who will fight for justice then?"

"Words like that convince me that you have a long way to go in your healing," the chaplain said firmly. "A very long way." He glanced at the timer as the last few grains of sand slithered into the bottom of the glass. "I shall pray for you." He rang a little bell and the orderly returned. "Take her back to her cell."

"But I haven't finished."

"Come along, now." The orderly reached out to grab my arm.

I pulled away. "Leave me alone! I don't belong in here!"

"The times I've heard that." The orderly unclipped a baton from his belt. "Don't make this more difficult than it has to be."

"It is the chevalier! He is the one who should be locked up!"

"Enough!" The orderly lashed out with his baton. I dodged backwards to avoid the blow, but the chaplain extended his foot and tripped me up.

As I stumbled they pounced on me, pinning me down so that the orderly could clamp manacles around my hands.

I screamed and writhed, kicking out wildly with my legs, but I was no match for the orderly's brute strength. As he dragged me from the room, I saw the chaplain's vacant face staring at me with contempt. Overwhelmed with rage, my feet lashed out again and hit the hourglass. It flew off the table and smashed onto the stone floor, spilling glass and sand across the room.

"You imbecile!" the chaplain screamed. "You will be punished for this!"

It was the only time I had seen him get angry. I had told him of shocking crimes and brutal malpractice. I had told him of lies and betrayal, and he had calmly refused to believe it; but now that I had smashed his pathetic bauble, he was swearing revenge.

How would I ever escape from this madness?

TWENTY-SEVEN

The rain which brought such misery to Bedlam, brought only minor inconvenience to Mayfair, where crowds were gathering outside Handel's house in Brook Street. Had the celebrity-chasing socialites been possessed of any idea about the reality of eye surgery, they would have stayed far away; there was nothing to be witnessed here except pain and fear. But as always, ignorance and jollity made fine bedfellows. Some enterprising hawkers were doing a brisk trade selling umbrellas and brandy shots, and a clergyman led others in an impromptu rendition of a famous chorus from *The Messiah*. I am told that on the fringes of the crowd, some shadier characters had opened a book on whether or not the operation would be a success.

Handel watched the whole circus from one of the music room windows on the first floor of his house. His closest servant, Peter LeBlond had not left Handel's side all morning, and had been steadily plying his master with brandy to get him as drunk as possible.

"We should have sold tickets, Peter," said Handel, trying not to slur his words. "Is nothing deemed beyond the pale in London, as long as it draws a crowd?"

"It is a measure of their love for you, George."

"Even the bookmakers?"

"Perhaps it's best to focus on the choir."

Because of Handel's fame, the chevalier had agreed to carry out the surgery in the composer's own home. Over the previous days, equipment had been moved from the Eye Waggon into Handel's composition room in the middle of the house; the special chair, the delivery arm, and all the instruments and lenses had been set up according to the chevalier's precise instructions. Handel's closest friends, a group of six men, now waited in the impromptu operating theatre for the grim procedure to begin.

An excited roar went up in the street outside. Handel and LeBlond peered out and saw a convoy of three carriages pull up.

A small troop of soldiers emerged from the first carriage and cleared a path in the crowd. The door to the second carriage opened and four uniformed nurses made their way solemnly into the house; they had no function, and I doubt if they even had medical training, but the chevalier had hired them for the occasion to add a sense of drama.

A moment of hushed anticipation, then the door to the final carriage swung open and the chevalier appeared, wearing a long black gown and a distinguished grey wig. The crowd burst into a spontaneous cheer, and the chevalier took time to bask in their adulation, doffing his hat, bowing modestly, and even signing his autograph on copies of the *Daily Gazetteer* that were thrust at him by eligible young women.

It was somewhat unclear whether the true celebrity was the patient or the surgeon.

With great solemnity, the chevalier tested Handel's level of inebriation by asking him to read a passage in Latin; having declared him fit for surgery, he secured him in the chair then turned to Handel's friends.

"Gentlemen, I would ask that you all take a few steps back. I need space to perform this most delicate of operations."

They obeyed immediately.

"I must also insist on complete silence during the procedure. The slightest murmur could break my concentration. So if you feel the need to faint or vomit, kindly leave the room. Have I made myself clear?"

They all nodded silently.

"Good." The chevalier turned back to Handel and checked that the straps were secure and the eye clamps in place. Then he got to work.

Even though the spectators had been warned, nothing could have prepared them for the scream that echoed through Handel's house on the first incision. Even though the composer had longed for this moment, and even though everyone knew the cut was designed to heal and not harm, nothing could allay the terror.

Imagine seeing a sharp blade moving towards your precious eyes. You cannot turn away, you cannot blink, all you can do is feel the agony of the incision and see the world turn red with your own blood.

At least two of Handel's friends fainted before they could reach the door and had to be dragged out.

And yet, I am told by witnesses who were there, the more difficult the surgery became, the more the chevalier thrived. I had seen him operate many times, and too often he had been hasty, cavalier, impatient; but now he was transformed by the great challenge he had taken on. According to Peter LeBlond, it was like watching a man enter a trance-like state; his breathing became as regular as clockwork, his hands as cool and steady as marble. All the showmanship and theatrics of his entrance were discarded like a cheap coat; now the chevalier was focussed on just one thing: conquering the composer's blindness.

Perhaps he saw this as his magnum opus, a chance to prove to the world that he really had been touched by greatness. Perhaps he felt that God was watching him, and that now he could find redemption for all the mistakes of his life. Perhaps.

For two hours Peter LeBlond sat next to the chair, clasping Handel's hand, while the chevalier worked in absolute silence.

Finally, the surgeon stood back and declared, "It is done."

As the chevalier secured the bandages around Handel's head, binding his eyes tightly, spontaneous applause erupted in the house.

"Bravo, Chevalier! Bravo!"

He stood up and took an extravagant bow, drinking in the adulation. Then he turned to the nurses. "Accompany Herr Handel up to his bedchamber and make sure he is comfortable." They leapt into action, leaving the chevalier free to work the room, shaking the hands of each spectator in turn.

When he reached the window of the music room, he flung it wide open to look down on the rain-soaked crowd. "The operation is done! It is a triumph!" A euphoric roar went up; the whole of Brook Street was alive with joy. "Handel's future is bright, and he will prosper mightily!"

To the crowd's delight, the chevalier plucked some carnations from a vase on a nearby table and started tossing them down to the most attractive women. He drank in the love of the mob for a full quarter of an hour, and only then did it occur to him to go and check on the patient, who lay on his four-poster bed, terrified and exhausted. Handel's lips mumbled some words, but they made no sense, not even to his closest manservant. Perhaps he was praying, or perhaps he was in shock.

"Is this normal?" Peter LeBlond asked anxiously.

"Absolutely," the chevalier smiled. "You have my word, Peter: there is nothing to worry about." Then he took a sealed letter from his jacket and put it on the bedside dresser. "I will leave the invoice here. For your kind attention."

Yet this patient was different.

Until now, the chevalier's *modus operandi* had been to leave town while the patient's bandages were still in place. But in London, a strange delusion had taken root in his mind, a delusion of greatness. He had decided that Handel was to be everlasting proof that he was indeed a brilliant surgeon. By restoring sight to the most famous composer in Europe, the chevalier intended to wipe the slate clean of all his previous failures.

In the history of medicine, there was never a patient who received such assiduous aftercare as George Frederic Handel. The chevalier visited him three times a day without fail; he administered the finest tinctures, supervised curative bloodlettings, and arranged every aspect of the composer's diet. There was considerable patient anxiety to be managed, but nothing that a little laudanum couldn't deal with, and a perfectly normal part of the healing process. Sleepless nights were also a problem, so the chevalier got into the habit of sitting in the window seat and reading to Handel, or sharing the latest gossip from elite social circles, until the composer's mind was at ease.

Perhaps for the very first time, the chevalier felt that deep sense of satisfaction that comes from seeing a patient heal. Day by day, the composer's strength grew, colour flushed his cheeks, his appetite returned to its former glory, and his mind turned to planning his next great work. "It shall be an oratorio about light," he declared. "Light in all its forms, from the first moment of its creation in Genesis, through to the last terrible moments in Revelation when the sun and the moon grow dark and the stars no longer shine. And in between will be all the glories of dawn and dusk, of sunlight warming a new-born's skin, of first love in the moonlight, of light dancing in the green leaves of summer."

"It sounds magnificent, George."

"I can already hear themes rippling in my mind — it will be unlike anything I have written before. Music to glorify light."

Even the chevalier found it impossible to listen to Handel speak and not feel elevated. Deep in his soul, I suspect he had always known the truth about his own failings, which is perhaps why he kept moving with such restless energy. Now, finally, the chevalier could see an end, a place of peace. His journey to it may have been flawed, but he had arrived.

No wonder he was anxious when the day finally came to remove the bandages.

He wheeled Handel's chair to the great window so that the patient's face was bathed in light, raised his hands to the dressings, and hesitated. To his surprise, the chevalier realised that he wasn't sure where to begin, as had so little experience in taking bandages off; under normal circumstances he would be fifty miles away.

"Are you nervous?" Handel asked.

"Not at all, maestro. I just want to make sure this causes you no discomfort." Carefully he untied the knot at the back, then gently started to unwind the bandages. With each turn, the chevalier's anticipation grew, but as the dressing eased away from Handel's eyes, there was a pungent whiff of decay. Very slowly the chevalier unwound another turn and lifted the cotton pads away, to reveal two eye sockets that were black and fetid, marbled with angry yellow puss.

"How do they look?" Handel asked eagerly. "Are they good?"

"They are … beautiful," the chevalier said as he stared at the wounded mess of Handel's eyes. "Quite beautiful."

In truth, all the chevalier's great work lay in ruins: the neat stitches he'd used to close the incisions around the composer's lenses had caused a haemorrhage in the sclera, and the surrounding tissue was swollen with infection.

"Tell me when I can open my eyes!"

"Wait! Wait!" the chevalier said hastily. Quickly he pushed the pads back onto Handel's eyes and started to wind the bandages into place.

"What's wrong?"

"I think they just need a few more days."

"Why? What has happened?" There was panic in Handel's voice.

"A miracle, is what has happened, maestro." Quickly the chevalier fished a clean bandage from his bag and started to apply it. "Your eyes are healing to perfection."

"Then why they delay? You said ten days."

"That was for one eye. As I have operated on both at the same time, nature needs more time to heal."

"I … I don't understand."

"Just as you need twice as long to boil two eggs, so the body needs longer to heal two eyes."

"So, my eyes are like eggs?"

"Indeed. Just so, George."

"But everything is good, yes?"

"I have never felt more confident." The chevalier laid a reassuring hand on the patient's shoulder. "Just a little more time."

TWENTY-EIGHT

According to the driver, the chevalier used my incarceration to indulge all his hedonistic appetites. There is a reason they call London the City of Whores, and my husband seemed determined to sample every alley and street.

Reeling from his disappointment at the failure of the surgery, he found drunken solace in the arms of three young admirers who were experts in pandering to a man's ego and emptying his purse. In the morning, the women had gone, and their pleasures were just memories, but the chevalier's problems remained: how could he hide his catastrophic failure? His triumphant return to London had been predicated on his ability to restore Handel's sight. The finest salons in the city were buzzing with talk of his genius, and King George himself had taken a personal interest in the case; so how could the great surgeon now survive the truth?

For two days the chevalier didn't get dressed or leave his room; he just sat there, mired in self-pity, searching for a way out. Slowly, as he later confessed to me, a plan started to form in his mind: he would have to 're-present' the facts. He would have to change the meaning of what had occurred, so that *he* would become the innocent party, and all the blame would settle on Handel's shoulders.

Galvanised with excitement, the chevalier summoned his servants and got dressed.

He arrived at Handel's house as normal to conduct the routine checks and administer all the medications the composer had come to expect. But instead of leaving straight away, the chevalier told Peter LeBlond that he needed to spend some time in the composer's front parlour to draw up a new treatment schedule. Left alone, he slipped out of the room and started to wander around the house, snooping in various rooms, gathering as much evidence as he could about Handel's lifestyle.

In the huge basement pantries he noted a prodigious love of port wine, a mountain of sugarloaves, and cheeses such as most men only dream of. These were quantities of food more suited to a large family than a bachelor.

In the music room the chevalier was intrigued by the sheer number of candles stacked in boxes, and conversations with servants confirmed that Handel frequently spent many hours composing through the night. Observations in the bedroom revealed that the four-poster had been positioned so that sunlight would flood onto the pillows in the morning.

Having gathered threads of information, the chevalier set about knitting them into a compelling fabric, which he then aired in fashionable social circles. Every casual enquiry about the composer's health became an opportunity to alter the narrative.

"It is a most complex case," the chevalier would say with a frown. "Changes have occurred in Handel's eyes, over many years, which make his current predicament difficult."

"Changes? What manner of changes?" the mark would reply.

"Unnatural ones."

"You refer to the dreadful accident in The Hague?"

"I fear it is violence committed by his own hand, and quite inadvertently. For many years, the maestro has lived against the Natural Order, working through the night, straining his eyes over manuscripts lit only by candles."

"Such is the price of genius."

"Indeed. And he could have thrived had he allowed himself time to recuperate during the day. But his bedroom is flooded with sunlight, which is the worst possible condition for eyes to heal themselves."

"Is that so?"

"Eyes need darkness just as much as they need light. And then we cannot ignore the issue of his diet."

This was a subject that London Society knew all about, thanks in part to a savage etching that had been circulated by Joseph Goupy when his friendship with Handel had ended acrimoniously. It depicted the composer as a fat boar, sitting on a barrel of wine, surrounded by oyster shells and game.

"I regret to confirm that the rumours of excess are true," the chevalier would sigh. "And in this, Herr Handel has once again loaded the dice against himself. His body is so out of balance that healing has become most challenging."

In a matter of days, London's energetic gossips became experts in matters of health and diet, each adding their own spicy anecdote about Handel's dissolute lifestyle.

When the journals and news sheets got hold of the rumour, the momentum of the lie became unstoppable.

Now the chevalier turned his attention to the composer himself; it was one thing to have convinced the chattering classes, but to walk away from this truly unscathed, he needed to convince Handel as well.

Through a deceitful contact, the chevalier arranged for a generous hamper, packed with marzipan sweets to be sent to the composer. 'From an anonymous well-wisher,' was all it said on the card. The offering was as decadent and tempting as it was expensive. Many of the delicacies were dressed with sugared almonds, some with candied fruits and cocoa powder, others with flower petals made from icing. The colours of the rainbow were vibrantly depicted, and I am told the delightful fragrance filled all five floors of the house in Brook Street.

Two days after the delivery was made, the chevalier turned up for a routine examination of Handel's bandages, when suddenly he hesitated. "Strange," he murmured to himself.

"Is everything all right?" Handel asked nervously.

"The bandages are stained. Have you experienced any pain?"

"Yes. As a matter of fact, I have," he whispered.

"You should have summoned me."

"I thought it was nothing. I hoped … I hoped it would pass."

"Denial is of no use to us, George. Only the truth will heal you."

"It's been getting worse. At first it was discomfort, but now it is pain, all the time."

"Did you use the laudanum?"

"It didn't help."

The chevalier studied the bandages closely. "And you have followed my instructions precisely?"

"Yes."

"You have rested every afternoon?"

"Yes."

"You have taken all the tinctures?"

"Yes."

"At the precise times?"

"I swear."

"What about food and drink?"

A guilty silence.

"George, have you followed the diet I prescribed?"

"Yes … well, nearly."

"Tell me, what does 'nearly' mean?"

"I can't remember."

"For the sake of your eyes, tell me the truth, George."

"There were some delicacies, sent by an admirer."

"What sort of delicacies?"

"It was to lift my spirits."

"What delicacies?"

"Marzipan."

"Oh, dear God." The chevalier's voice was loaded with fear.

"I thought the surgery had worked." Sweat broke across the composer's brow. "You said everything was healed."

"Healing. Not healed. Do you not realise what you have done?"

"But marzipan … when did marzipan ever harm anyone?"

"Almonds, George. There is a toxic species of bitter almond that contains cyanide."

"What? No! It cannot be possible."

"Extract of bitter almond is lethal. Even in small doses. And it is particularly damaging for the nervous system. For eyes."

"But this was sweet marzipan."

"There must have been some contamination. Not enough to taste, but enough to do harm. Oh, George … this is why I gave strict orders not to deviate from the diet I prescribed."

"I'm sorry! Please, forgive me," the composer whimpered.

"Which of your servants is to blame?"

"None! It is me. It was my choice…" Overwhelmed with remorse, Handel started to sob. "It is my fault."

"Come now, try to stay calm."

"Throw them away! Tell Peter to throw them away."

"I will, I promise. But … I fear the damage may have been done."

"No, no, no. Say it is not so. It cannot be!"

The chevalier clasped Handel's shoulders, trying to comfort him.

"There must be something you can do?" Handel sobbed.

"Let me apply some ointments. Bind the dressings again. But we are in God's hands now."

The chevalier went through the motions for a few days, making a great show of diligence. He even spent several nights sleeping on the couch in Handel's room, so that he could administer treatment without delay.

But hour by hour, the pain got worse as the composer's eyes rotted and his heart broke. And hour by hour, the chevalier was on hand to deflect the blame onto Handel's own recklessness.

And then the terrible day came; it could not be put off any longer. The chevalier invited a number of Handel's closest friends and patrons to witness the removal of the bandages; he was so confident in his re-presentation of the truth that he felt he had nothing to hide.

Everyone gathered in the music room as Handel was led in by Peter LeBlond and made comfortable in a chair next to the window.

"Shall we see what God has decided?" the chevalier announced solemnly.

Handel's fingers tightened round a silver crucifix he clasped in his hands. With great tenderness the chevalier cut through the outer bandages, then started to unwind them. He tried to cling onto the last vestiges of hope, even as he saw the dreadful staining of blood and puss; finally, as he removed the last dressing and looked grimly at the devastated eyes, he had to accept reality.

"Why have you stopped?" Handel asked. "Remove the dressings. There is still hope."

There was an uncomfortable moment in the room as everyone realised that Handel was the last to understand the truth.

"George, I'm afraid I already have. The bandages are off."

"But … it is still dark." The composer raised his fingers to his eyes and winced as they touched his blood-encrusted lids. "No…" He slumped forward, his body trembling with grief. "No, no!" Tears flooded his eyes and immediately brought fresh agony.

"You should rest, George."

"No. No. No. This cannot be. It cannot be!"

The chevalier nodded to LeBlond. "Escort him to his bedchamber. He must rest."

Gently LeBlond and the chevalier lifted Handel from the chair and supported his weight. "Come now, George."

"No, no, no."

They guided him from the music room, up the stairs, and laid him on the great four-poster in his bedroom. "Rest. And sleep. I will come back this evening."

As the chevalier closed the door and walked away, all he could hear was the haunting sound of the composer's sobbing.

When he reached the music room doors, the chevalier paused. The guests had been drip-fed the alternative truth, so it was vital that his own reactions should be appropriate. He hunched his shoulders, drew a breath, and entered the room. Everyone stopped talking and turned to stare.

"I tried my best," he said in a voice apparently hoarse with grief. "I used all my skill, all my experience to try and save the maestro. But if God has decided that Handel must be blind, there is nothing a mortal man can do."

"Come, now. Enough." The earl of Burlington strode over and put an arm around the chevalier. "You must not blame yourself. We all know what has happened."

"But he put such faith in me."

"As we all do. Yet I fear the die was cast long before you arrived in London."

The chevalier glanced up and saw nods of agreement amongst the company.

"Even you cannot turn back time," Burlington said firmly. "You can only work with what you are given." Then he put his hands together and started to applaud. "Bravo for trying, sir. You battled bravely."

One by one, Handel's friends joined in, until the whole room was applauding the chevalier's failure.

As none of the guests seemed inclined to leave, Peter LeBlond arranged for refreshments to be served, and it was not long before the music room was alive with conversation. Keen to depart while the atmosphere was so forgiving, the chevalier made his excuses and headed down the stairs.

"Here, let me accompany you," Burlington said as he caught the chevalier's arm. "There is something I've been meaning to ask."

"Of course, of course."

"My aunt, who lives in Kew, has been struggling with her eyesight since this winter past. Would you consider treating her?"

The chevalier hesitated, trying to hide his incredulity.

Thinking a refusal was coming, Burlington pressed his aunt's case. "Although she is older, she has taken care of herself, and has not indulged in any of the excesses of Handel's life."

"That is good."

"And she promises to follow instructions to the letter, so she will not be working against you."

"Let me consult my diary," the chevalier replied. "I'll see if there are any spaces."

"She will pay handsomely for your expertise, chevalier. Perhaps money can make the waiting list more accommodating?"

"Indeed."

TWENTY-NINE

"He loves me, he loves me not. He loves me, he loves me not." The newest girl couldn't have been more than sixteen when she was hurled into Bedlam. That first day she was so overwhelmed and scared, I persuaded the guard to let her stay in my cell for a few days, thinking I could offer some protection. What a mistake that turned out to be.

"He loves me, he loves me not. He loves me, he loves me not." She repeated the phrase over and over again, day after day, as if trying to exorcise a demon, for the love she had experienced was not the enriching power that poets describe; it was entirely destructive. The poor girl had been delivering food to a set of chambers in Lincoln's Inn when she caught the attention of an eminent barrister. He became obsessed with her. When his letters went unanswered (she couldn't even read), he began stalking her. All his learning and experience counted for nothing against the lust that had taken hold of him. It ended as it always ends: with assault and rape. As soon as the lawyer was done, he cast her aside.

Nothing I said could console the girl, who now muttered her desperate chorus all through the long hours of the night.

"He loves me, he loves me not."

Occasionally she would stop, and I would dare to hope that she had fallen asleep, only to be disappointed when the mumbling started again. It was unrelenting.

As dawn glimmered through the barred window, I realised that with each chant, she now pinched the flesh on her arms until she drew blood, then moved her dirty fingernails to find a

238

fresh piece of skin. By morning both her arms were glistening red.

A bell echoed in the corridor outside to wake the inmates for breakfast; a few minutes later there was a rattle of keys outside my cell and the door swung open.

"She needs a doctor," I appealed to the guard. "Look at her."

"It's you I've come for."

"You can't just leave her like this!"

The guard shrugged, hauled me to my feet and marched me away.

In all the long months of my incarceration in that Hell, I had never been allowed out of my prison cell so early in the morning, and the asylum looked surprisingly different. Instead of deranged inmates lurching down the corridor, there was a small army of cleaners with buckets of water, swilling away the excrement from the previous day. They performed a vital, if unpleasant job, for madness is not the romantic distraction of a gothic poem, it is the smell of shit and vomit.

"Where are you taking me?" I asked.

"Quiet."

"Is it because of the new girl? I was only trying to help."

"I said quiet!" He swung his cane sharply across my back; inflicting pain was their answer to everything.

When we reached the end of the corridor, instead of turning right towards the kitchens, I was pushed up the steps and bundled into one of the small offices. "Behave yourself," the guard warned as he locked the door behind me.

"Well, well."

I turned and saw the chevalier standing in the middle of the office, holding a handkerchief to his nose to filter out the stench.

For a few moments I stared at him in disbelief. He could have been an angel, descended from Heaven: he wore freshly laundered clothes, a beautifully powdered wig, polished shoes, and immaculate stockings, unblemished by the world.

He looked me up and down, then burst out laughing.

"What?" I demanded.

"Look at you!" he chuckled. "An absurd spectacle!"

Under his metropolitan gaze, I suddenly felt ashamed. I glanced down and saw my own filthy clothes and bare feet, the black grime under my fingernails, the matted hair that hung around my shoulders. In here I was normal, but to the normal world I was deranged.

"Is that it? Did you come here just to humiliate me?"

"My dear Arabella, despite your fallen state, I have not abandoned you. I have merely tried to educate you. As a good husband should."

I hammered on the door with my fists. "Guard! Let me out! We're finished."

"Save your breath. They won't come until I tell them."

Reluctantly I turned to face him again. "Let me guess … this is what you've really come for." I lifted my clothes to reveal my nakedness.

He winced. "Please, woman. Put it away."

Keeping my dress raised, I locked eyes with the chevalier, then slowly pissed over the floor. "Have you missed me?" I whispered.

I listened to his breathing as he gazed at the warm pool growing on the stone slabs; for a few moments it was as if he was in a trance.

"Doesn't that feel better?" I finished and slowly readjusted my clothes.

He gazed at the steaming piss; we both knew that it was the promise of perversion that had brought him back to me.

"There is no-one quite like me, is there, Chevalier?"

"You know, Arabella," he said, his tone softening, "it would be the easiest thing in the world to leave you here to rot. But you are my wife, and I am a Christian man. Although in your current state you look abhorrent, I know that in truth you are a beautiful woman. A few months ago you had a life. We had a life together. Out of the generosity of my soul, I am prepared to forgive you, and restore to you what you once had. My only condition is that you put aside your ludicrous paranoia and return to being my obedient wife."

"You want my silence."

"Not especially. I quite like hearing your voice. But you must stop making baseless and deluded accusations. Do that, and I can lift you out of horror this very morning."

"Have you done the surgery on Handel?"

"I have."

"And? Is he alive?"

"Have a little faith, Arabella. Of course he is alive."

"Can he see?"

"It seems God had other plans."

"So you blinded him."

"Herr Handel proved to be his own worst enemy. Not only had he spent many years abusing his body, at a critical phase of the healing he disobeyed my orders. It is not my fault that he is now blind."

"But he is alive?"

"Very much so. Sitting in his bed, no doubt composing a merry little tune as we speak."

What was I to feel? Relief that he wasn't dead? Grateful that he was only blind? There was little comfort in that.

"So, Arabella, what is your response?"

We looked at each other in that strange moment, the piss pooling between us. I think we both knew that no-one would ever believe the truth, not from my lips. My voice was now utterly discredited, and if I didn't go along with the lie, it was clear I would never leave the walls of Bedlam. This is where I would die.

"Very well," I murmured.

"A wise choice, Arabella. And not that I don't trust you, but…" He took a legal document from his jacket and laid it on the table. Next to it he placed a quill and a small pot of ink.

I looked at the contract. "Seriously?"

"If you talk out of turn, you will end up back in this prison of shit and lunacy." He dipped the quill in the ink and offered it to me.

One signature, and my life changed in an instant.

Now I was treated like a guest rather than an inmate. Kind hands helped me bathe in hot water and wash myself clean of the filth of that place. My hair was combed and dressed. I was given fresh clothes and shoes, then escorted with utmost courtesy to a carriage outside.

A nod to the driver, and I was transported through the gates and into a different world: a world of liberty and rights, a world where I would not have to live in perpetual fear of beatings and brutality … unlike the wretched souls I left behind.

Picking up the threads of my old life was not so easy; the eternity in Bedlam had scarred my soul.

When I was safely back in the house in St James, I took off the clothes they had given me in the asylum and burned them, for I felt an overwhelming urge to obliterate all trace of that godforsaken hospital. Then I spent several weeks alone in my rooms, trying on every dress and corset, every bonnet and pair of silk gloves, every pair of shoes. I would stand and gaze at my reflection for hours, trying to fix this image of my identity in my mind and erase the ragged madwoman. At one point I put on every piece of jewellery and gold that I owned until I looked like a knight in strange, glittering chainmail.

In the end, I settled on black as my colour of choice; in black I felt untouchable, and I instructed my maid to take all my finest dresses to the dyer's so that he could turn their vibrant reds and greens and yellows into monolithic black.

I gradually returned to the social scene through a series of elegant receptions and lavish dinners, where everyone greeted me like an old friend and happily went along with the respectable lies.

"Wonderful to see you looking so well, Arabella. How were your travels?"

"Fascinating, thank you. And most enlightening," I would reply to this typical enquiry.

"We have missed you on the circuit, but travel is good for the mind."

"Quite so. I feel like a new woman."

"Some wondered whether you would ever make it back."

"No, no. It is good to travel, but better to return."

No-one said what they were really thinking, least of all when they were enjoying the chevalier's champagne, but I had developed some sharp skills in Bedlam. Within those grey walls, survival depended on knowing what was occurring behind your back, which lunatic was about to tip into a violent rage, or which guard was wielding the whip. Now I discovered that those skills were perfectly suited to society gatherings, where I could sense people gossiping behind their hands or studying me from the shadows. Speculation was rife about my madness, but I had more pressing problems than worrying about reputation.

Sleep remained difficult. When I closed my eyes, images of the harrowing sadness of that place seeped back into my mind. Sounds of suffering echoed in my ears, and the air around me seemed to fill with the stench of insanity.

There were some nights I found it easier to walk the corridors of the silent house until I was so exhausted, I would collapse into a stupor.

At breakfast one morning, the chevalier deigned to pass comment. "Perhaps it would be better to have the eggs served in your rooms? Having breakfast with a dark-eyed ghost is really rather unpleasant."

I stared at him in disbelief. "Do you have any conception of what you put me through?"

He just studied the announcements columns in the *Chronicle*. "Don't look back, Arabella. It is time to move on."

"That is easier said than done."

"Come now, you have everything one could possibly want. You live a life of luxury and ease. You are waited on hand and foot, and you bask in my reflected glory."

The chevalier really had turned 'moving on' into an art, and it amazed me how untroubled he was by his legacy.

The earl of Burlington's aunt opened the door to a new sphere of society patients, and as the chevalier's career reached ever-greater heights, he commissioned a special set of surgical tools made from gold. Then he turned one of the reception rooms in the house into a 'Room of Celebrity' and commissioned a painter to create frescos depicting himself as a philosopher in ancient Greece, discussing medicine with the Gods.

It enraged me, but I had to applaud along with all the other sycophants; it was that or be sent back to Bedlam. Yet with every humiliation, my heart cooled, and my mind became more calculating.

Yes, I despised him. But I discovered there are many types of abhorrence. There is the hot passion of anger, the turmoil and frustration of resentment, and the cold acid of pure hate, which is far more deadly. In time, I discovered that my mind could find peace by meditating on the revulsion I felt for my husband.

And when you sleep with hatred in your heart, unimaginable things become possible.

It was with some difficulty that I persuaded the chevalier to attend concerts, as he bored quickly of any activity that involved keeping his mouth shut for extended periods. Yet a carefully choreographed display of wifely affection finally secured his agreement to attend a performance of *Dixit Dominus* at St Martin-in-the-Fields.

It wasn't just the music that drew me there; I had heard rumours that Handel himself would attend, and I was desperate to see that he had made at least a partial recovery from my husband's butchering hands.

The music was sublime, imbued with such beauty and grace that it was like listening to the mind of a god. As the majestic chords filled the church, I looked up at the balcony where Handel sat alone, hunched over, a black band wrapped around his forehead just above his eyes, signifying his condition. His face was bathed in a soft, flickering candlelight that he would never see, and he listened with intense concentration to this music that he had written as a twenty-two-year-old man.

What was he thinking now?

Was he listening with envy to the optimism and energy of his youth?

Was he remembering what it felt like to be so fully immersed in life?

Or was he simply filled with despair at the darkness that had now enveloped him?

I glanced at the chevalier, head lolling forward on his chest as he dozed through the concert, utterly indifferent to the music. And as I studied him, I saw my own parents in their tyrannical bigotry, refusing to travel more than a few miles from their home, oblivious to everything except their own brutish needs. And I saw Josiah Roope slurping his soup with self-satisfied relish, so full of smug contentment, and so happy to lecture his young wife.

All my life I had been fighting to escape from ignorance, but it had followed me like a spectre, disguising itself in ever finer clothes, but never wavering in its determination to drag me back down to the underworld.

As the concert ended and everyone hurried to waiting carriages, I saw Handel escorted from the church by his loyal servant, Peter LeBlond. With infinite patience and kind words, he guided the composer down the steps and made him comfortable in a carriage. I found it impossible to reconcile the haunting apparition of this broken man with the soaring music I had just heard.

A few days later I arrived at Handel's house unannounced, cradling a large bouquet of flowers, and introduced myself only as a well-wisher from the concert.

"I'm afraid the maestro is not receiving visitors at the moment, ma'am."

"Please. I won't take up much of his time."

"There are no exceptions."

"Perhaps if you give him these, he might change his mind?" I offered Peter the flowers.

"He prefers not to have flowers in the house anymore. It torments him that he cannot see their beauty."

"But I have chosen them for their scent, not their colours. Please. I beg you, ask him."

Reluctantly Peter showed me into the house and offered me a seat in the front parlour. He took the flowers and disappeared up the stairs.

As my eyes wandered over the space, the finality of Handel's condition was brought home to me. Rails had been fixed to the walls to help him move safely around his home; the staircase now had double bannisters; all the ornaments and casual furniture had been removed so that the floors were clear; large, embossed letters had been fixed to every door so that touch alone could identify the rooms. It was clear that Handel would never see again.

I heard the floorboards creak, footsteps approaching … but it was just Peter LeBlond. "I'm afraid he will not see you, ma'am."

"Is he composing? Please tell me that he is hard at work."

"I wish it were so. But he has written nothing since the operation."

"He will write again, though. Won't he?"

Peter said nothing.

"There must be something I can do to help. I have money."

"Money cannot buy what he has lost," Peter replied. "The maestro cannot face the world anymore. It has died for him."

"Surely his friends can save him from this despair?"

"I'm afraid even they are powerless."

"But they visit him?"

"For conversation. That is all the maestro can endure."

"That is a start. I could not bear the thought of him being alone when his music continues to give so much pleasure. Perhaps friendship will rekindle inspiration."

"This house was once full of inspiration. A whirl of musicians and singers rehearsing new compositions." He pointed up to the ceiling. "In those rooms above us, themes from *The Messiah* were sung for the very first time. But now … it has turned into a house of silence."

"He must not give up hope. Inspiration will return. It must."

"Perhaps if you pray for the maestro, it might help."

There was nothing more to be said. Peter ushered me to the front door and showed me out.

And that was when I made my decision. A world without justice is no world at all, yet God refused to humble the chevalier. High society adored him and the law was beyond reach, for when I tried to speak out, I was deprived of my liberty and very nearly my life. If there was to be justice, it would have to be at my hands. The world would only be protected from this charlatan if he suffered in the same way that his patients had suffered.

The chevalier had to lose his sight.

He must be blinded.

And I must be the person to perform the dreadful act.

The only question that remained was how to execute the deed without destroying myself.

THIRTY

As the chevalier's reputation soared, he took to collecting books; not that he had any interest in reading, of course, but he loved to stand in front of the huge library shelves when interviewing clients, basking in the reflected glory of all that bound wisdom.

Fortunately, the demands of being a celebrity-surgeon meant that he had to travel frequently across London, which left me free to enjoy the books instead.

I soon realised that the library was as corrupted as the chevalier's mind, for the thousands of volumes had been arranged without any regard to their content; rather they had been shelved according to the colour and size of their spines. Some shelves were dedicated to fat books, others to thin books, and yet more would run from fat to thin and back again, creating a visual wave. He liked to cluster blue volumes together but preferred to alternate red and black spines to create a chessboard effect. Although the aesthetic was pleasing, it made it almost impossible to find anything.

For countless hours I scoured the shelves, my neck strained at an awkward angle, searching for a treatise on chemistry, until finally I stumbled upon *Materials Liquid & Solid, their Definitions and Unique Properties*. The book was as dry as it sounds, but it was mercifully slim, and I persevered until I found the word that was to set me free: methanol.

The author, Nicasius le Febure, set out in great detail how methanol, (or wood alcohol), had a long and noble history in science, and had been used by the ancient Egyptians for embalming Pharaohs. Crucially, it was also a poison. Just a teaspoon of methanol when drunk causes permanent blindness by destruction of the optic nerve.

Here was the answer to my prayers.

Naturally, I could not walk into a shop to buy this elixir, as suspicion would immediately fall on me when the chevalier became sick, but further study revealed it was not difficult to make if one had a simple still.

The house in St James had a large cellar that was partitioned into different areas to store coal, wine, salt and what have you, but behind these functional areas was a honeycomb of chambers that were cluttered with domestic debris. I selected one that had a rickety door and set about clearing it; this was to become my alchemical laboratory, where I could transmute wood shavings into vengeance.

It would have been far simpler to buy a pot still, but that risked laying a trail of evidence, so I decided to make one myself. I acquired an innocent copper kettle from Leather Lane Market and vandalised the suspension system on the Eye Waggon to secure a three-foot length of small-bore pipe — by this time, the chevalier was far too grand for peripatetic surgery. After some experimentation, I managed to secure the pipework into the kettle spout and seal the gap with cork putty. Then I arranged some old bricks into an improvised hearth big enough to light a fire.

The testing had to be carefully timed in case anything went wrong, but the chevalier had recently started treating a wealthy dowager in the newly fashionable Terrace at Barnes, which meant he was out of the house most afternoons. I dispatched the servants on domestic errands and went down to the cellar, locking the door behind me. There was no shortage of firewood down there, and I set about two logs with an axe until they were reduced to a pile of chippings. These I placed into the copper kettle with some water, then lit the fire.

I waited patiently, taking care to fan the smoke towards a small, barred window so that I didn't suffocate. It seemed to take an eternity for the still to heat up.

Had I put in too much water? Was the cork seal leaking?

After what seemed like an age, there was a gentle simmering sound, and clear liquid started to drip from the end of the copper pipe.

I caught a tiny drop on my finger and dabbed it on my tongue: a bitter, pungent taste, just as the books described. Methanol.

Immediately I chopped up more wood, for I needed to distil as much as I could before anyone returned; by the end of the week, I had almost a pint of poison.

Administering it required some careful thought.

Somehow, I had to get it into the chevalier's food and drink, but too big a dose and the strong taste would arouse suspicion. Even if I could overcome this, a large dose risked causing death, and that was not the point of the exercise. On the other hand, the book explained that too small a dose and the poison would pass through his system, causing only minor discomfort. I needed to keep a constant flow of doses into his body to create a build-up of toxin, and to this end I decanted the methanol into a small phial, which I carried with me at all times.

By staying alert and spending as much time as possible with my husband, I found that I was able to drop tiny amounts of the liquid into his food and drink throughout the day. One drop in his morning tea, one drop in each glass of sherry and brandy, two drops in his game soup, three drops in his nightly syllabub where the sugar masked the bitterness.

All this necessitated a performance of loving diligence on my part, ensuring that we always ate together and dismissed the servants early in the evening. The chevalier, believing that I craved intimacy with him, was happy to oblige.

Gradually the methanol built up in his body, and one by one the symptoms started to appear.

The headaches were first, and I would urge him to lie quietly with his head on my lap, so that I could soothe his brow with my fingers. Not long after, he was afflicted with dizziness, at which point I insisted that he was working too hard and should cancel some of his appointments.

Blurred vision came next. Not all the time, but in waves, like a migraine. This was harder for me to explain away, but his profound ignorance of biology proved for once to be my ally. A surgeon with even a modicum of talent would have realised what all the symptoms had in common, but the chevalier was happy to accept my explanation of stress from overwork. Like a loving wife, I scolded him for putting his patients' health above his own and shooed him to his bedchamber, where I could personally supervise his recovery.

The following week he started to stumble and fall. Admittedly it was over obstacles that I had discreetly placed in his way as a test, but the fact that he didn't see them gave me reason to hope that the damage was now irreversible. Inside I felt a deep satisfaction, while on the surface, I played the role of concerned wife to perfection, fretting and sobbing, and insisting that we consult a specialist.

Only now did it occur to me that such a physician might identify the true cause of the chevalier's growing blindness ... which could prove very awkward for me.

"Look up. Look down." The only sound in the consulting room was a little whistle every time Dr Ensore breathed. "To the left. And to the right."

The chevalier remained silent as he underwent the eye examination, but I knew what he was thinking: Ensore was an old-school surgeon who had not kept up with the times and should not be trusted. The problem was, we didn't have much choice; the chevalier's reputation had swept all before it, and as a result most of his rival oculists had left London to find business elsewhere.

I sat next to my husband and offered reassurance by holding his hand. Ensore lowered the magnifying lens and sat back in his chair.

"Well?" The chevalier looked at him searchingly.

"There is damage to the eyes. Both of them."

"Obviously. But that is not why we came here." The chevalier did not even try to conceal his irritation. "What can be done about it?"

Dr Ensore scratched his forehead. "The symptoms you describe, the other symptoms … if they are connected, it could be that you have consumed something poisonous."

"What?" I exclaimed. "How on earth could that happen?"

"Ridiculous," the chevalier scoffed.

"But, but … have you changed your chef recently?" the doctor asked.

"I have no idea who is in the kitchens!" the chevalier snapped. "It is of no interest to me."

"What about your eating habits?"

"We both eat the same food," I intervened. "If something was poisonous, then we would both be afflicted, not just my husband."

"You must be mistaken, Ensore. Where did you train?"

"In Paris."

"I rest my case." The chevalier shook his head contemptuously. "What do the French know about eyes?"

"But, but … there was, I remember, a rogue wine merchant in Paris. When I was a student there, it was quite the scandal. He had corrupted a batch of wine to make a bigger profit. Ten people lost their sight as a result."

"Fascinating though your reminiscences may be, they are irrelevant," the chevalier said sharply. "What is the best treatment to restore my eyesight?"

Dr Ensore cleared his throat, shuffled in his chair, and finally looked down at his shiny shoes. "I'm afraid there is nothing I can do."

"You can operate!"

"It would be of no use."

"No, no, no. You are mistaken."

"Chevalier, it is not the lenses that are failing, but the retinas."

"Look again."

"I'm afraid it would change nothing. The damage is clear. There is no cure, no treatment, nothing you can do except prepare for blindness."

Shock hit the chevalier like a physical force. The blood drained from his face, giving him a ghastly pallor. He moved his lips as if trying to speak, but no sound came out.

In the deathly silence, all we could hear was the little whistle from Dr Ensore's breathing.

This was my moment. "Dear God," I whispered in shock. "The brandy."

Dr Ensore looked at me. "I beg your pardon?"

"It is the one thing my husband loves that I don't touch. Brandy."

"What?" The chevalier looked at me in a daze. "What are you saying?"

"Could the brandy be tainted? Just like in Paris?"

"No. No… It is vintage brandy. From Barrington's."

"I must say it seems unlikely," Ensore agreed. "Barrington's is the most reputable merchant in London."

"Did you not see that article in the *Chronicle*?" The lies flowed so effortlessly from my lips. "Just last month a spirit importer disappeared owing a small fortune. Barrington's was one of the creditors."

"I haven't heard of it," Ensore frowned.

"They are trying to keep it quiet, to avoid a scandal. Now we know why." I clasped the chevalier's hand tightly. "I fear you have been wronged, my darling. We can do something about this."

"So he can heal me? He can restore my sight?"

"Er … that's not…"

"No." Ensore was emphatic. "I'm afraid that is lost."

"But we can seek legal redress in the courts," I urged, trying to sound excited. "If we can find this man, this importer, we can sue for compensation."

"Compensation?" The chevalier gazed at me through hazy eyes. "What possible compensation can there be for blindness?"

The starkness of his question silenced me. There was no answer. There was just the little whistle from Ensore's nose.

The chevalier's grief broke when we returned to St James. Howls of anguish echoed round the house as he wept for his misfortune. Tears smudged his powdered face and his arms flailed in fury. He pulled paintings off the walls and smashed vases onto the floor.

"What did I do to deserve such cruelty?" he wailed. "All I have ever sought is to help people!"

The servants tried to contain him, but that only made the situation worse. He had to witness his anger by destroying anything he could lay his hands on.

Finally, after rampaging through the house for an hour, the chevalier slumped on the floor, broken and exhausted.

"Come, my love," I said gently. "Let me take you to your rooms. Rest awhile."

He whimpered like a hurt animal as I helped him to his feet. "Oh God, oh God, oh God. What will become of me?"

But as I guided him up the stairs, step by step his grief turned to cold hate. "Promise me you will find this rogue merchant, Arabella."

"I swear."

"Track the villain down. Lift whatever stone he is hiding under so that his crimes are exposed."

"He shall have no mercy from me."

"I will sue him in the courts. I will bankrupt him and his family. His children's children will curse his name and his memory."

"He will suffer, my love."

"I will sue him into the Dark Ages!" the chevalier thundered. "For I am the victim of a monstrous fraud. The injustice of it. The terrible injustice."

"Do not torment yourself further. I will take care of everything."

"It is a scandal that any man should be allowed to get away with such an atrocity. A scandal."

For the next fortnight I made a great display of working tirelessly to track down the 'rogue trader'. Every evening over dinner, I would give a detailed account of my labours to the chevalier.

I told him that I had interviewed Barrington's and every other wine merchant in London.

I told him that I had visited the now vacant premises of the crooked importer in Bankside and questioned the landlord in great detail.

I told him that I had spent long hours combing through customs documents at Wool Quay, trying to piece together the movements of the charlatan.

In truth, all I had done was sit under a tree in Hyde Park and feed the ducks, and as the weather was unseasonably warm, it really was a most pleasant few days.

When I finally broke the news to him that all my enquiries had come to nought, the chevalier flew into another violent rage. I watched calmly as he smashed his way through the drawing room, tearing curtains from their poles and throwing vases at the mirrors; it was dispiriting to see such wanton vandalism. When his passion was finally spent, he slumped to the floor, tears pouring from his bloodshot eyes.

I went to him and cradled him in my arms. "It's all right. I am here for you. I am here."

"Everything is just shadows," he whimpered. "The world has vanished. I have fallen into darkness."

"Can you see my face?"

He looked up at me and shook his head. "You are just a blur. A grey blur."

"What about now?" I took his fingers and touched them to my face. "Can you see me now?"

His fingers ran gently over my cheeks. "So beautiful," he whispered. "Always so beautiful."

"And I am still yours."

"Even like this? In my wretched state?"

"I will never abandon you, so there is nothing to fear. I will help you and support you always, my love."

"Do you promise?"

"You have my word."

He clung to me like a baby. "That means the world to me, Arabella. You are a fine woman. I am so fortunate to have you."

"Quiet, now. You're making me blush."

"If I have ever done anything to hurt you, I apologise with all my heart. I have always loved you. Everything I have done has been in your best interests, even if sometimes it might not have felt like that. You do understand?"

"I think so."

"And you forgive me?"

I hesitated. Even though this was part of the trap, I still could not form the word in my mouth. All the grace I had received from the music of Bach and Handel was still not enough to make me forgive this monster. So I deflected. "In sickness and in health, to love and to cherish. I take my vows seriously."

"Thank you, Arabella. Thank you."

Now I could really get to work.

The very next day I closed his medical practice, wrote to all his pending clients to cancel their appointments, and put a small announcement in the *General Advertiser*: *It is with heavy regret that the famous oculist, the chevalier Taylor, announces his retirement on grounds of ill health. He has been honoured to serve so many patients, gifting them with his surgical genius to restore God's light to their blighted eyes. He trusts that his reputation is secure in the living proof they afford.*

All the equipment from the consulting room was packed into crates and put into storage in a warehouse on Shad Thames. I sold the Eye Waggon to a goldsmith in Hatton Garden who wanted to adapt it into a secure transport for shipping his goods to the Continent.

Isolating the chevalier from his wide social circle proved surprisingly easy, as I now controlled all the information that flowed into his ears. In those first few weeks, there were many callers at the house who came to offer their support; I turned them all away. When the chevalier asked why none of his friends had enquired after his health, I feigned sorrow as I described how my letters to them had gone unanswered. "I fear they have turned their back on you, my love."

This news provoked another outburst of indignant fury. "How they fawned over me when I was favoured by the court! The sycophants! The spineless social climbers! And now that I need their friendship, they treat me like a leper! Was ever a man as cruelly treated as me?"

Naturally, I soothed his troubled brow and calmed him with wifely love. And in truth, at this point it was not my aim to torment him, but to isolate him. I needed him to be utterly dependent on me, to trust me, to give himself over completely into my caring embrace.

THIRTY-ONE

Having been a 'man about town' for so long, the chevalier struggled at first with a life of domestic confinement. His sleep became restless, he was troubled by strange dreams, he started to drink to excess, and he developed an uncouth habit of lounging around the house in his night clothes until lunchtime.

He certainly tested my patience.

Hoping to impose some structure on these listless days, I insisted that every afternoon I should read to him. He would make himself comfortable in the upper drawing room, a decanter of port at his side, while I would try to enlighten him. It proved to be quite a challenge. Novels bored him; even the lively *Tom Jones*, which was then all the rage in London, proved too much for his limited attention span. Society news stirred his envy and filled him with resentment at what he could no longer enjoy. Shakespeare, or indeed any poetry, was the quickest way to send him to sleep.

Mercifully, he stumbled upon the joys of gambling on horses, and this soon became his primary obsession. I spent many hours reading the names of runners and riders to him, describing conditions of the turf at Epsom Downs, Ascot, and Newmarket, and he would listen quietly, drawing up mental lists of which horses were going to win. He would then dictate precise details of which bets were to be placed where, and at what odds. One of the servants would be dispatched to Garraway's Coffee House in Change Alley, where a number of bookmakers ran their firms.

It was curious to watch the chevalier become obsessed with such a mindless pastime. Perhaps it made him feel powerful to wrestle with chance; perhaps it brought some excitement back into his shell of a life. When he won, he would spend the rest of the day boasting about his 'deep insight' into the world of horses and stride around the house as if he was a Master of Destiny. On his losses, which were far more frequent, he remained silent.

It was of little consequence; what really mattered was that his only contact with the outside world was through me, and if reading mindless lists of silly names was the price I had to pay, so be it. However, I must confess, there was a certain cosy domesticity in sitting together every afternoon. Perhaps if we had done this years earlier, the catastrophic breakdown of our marriage could have been avoided.

It was on one of his winning days, when the chevalier was feeling like a clever peacock, that I slipped him the lie about an encounter with Peter LeBlond. "He was most excited and made a point of asking about your health."

"Must we discuss this?" the chevalier said moodily. "I don't want to rake all that up again."

"One of Handel's nieces in Germany has sent him a learned paper that sets out the curative effects of spa waters on failing eyesight."

"The waters? Don't be absurd."

"Apparently he is a surgeon at the University of Heidelberg, and highly regarded." I picked up a book and affected nonchalance. "But what do the Germans know about eyes?"

"Exactly."

Yet as we sat in silence, I could hear the chevalier's mind working, turning the idea over, until his curiosity was too much to contain. "What does this Heine say should be done with the waters? Should one drink them? Bathe in them?"

"I really couldn't say. It was only a fleeting conversation I had."

"Maybe you should call on LeBlond and find out some more."

"Would you really give the time of day to such old wives' tales?"

"I read one or two interesting things from Heidelberg University a long time ago. I would be curious."

"If you insist, I will call on him next week and ask to borrow the learned paper."

"Tomorrow, Arabella. Why not do it tomorrow? What have I got to lose?"

"A wager on the Queen Anne Stakes, if you don't stop talking and let me read you the field."

The next day I went for a pleasant stroll through Whitehall Gardens, then up the Charing Cross Road, where I bought a medical journal in Cecil Court. I cannot recall what it was about — congestive fever, I think — but what did it matter? After I had mangled the contents through a German dictionary it became a *Learned Treatise on the Radical Improvement of Eyesight Using Restorative Waters.*

I read to the chevalier that afternoon as he sat quietly in his chair by the fire. Although the journal was perched on my lap, the contents poured out of my own mind. "The author conducted tests on two hundred and thirty-five patients over a period of fourteen months… Experiments used the spa waters at Baden-Baden, Aix-la-Chapelle, and Oberstaufen… Significant improvement was noted in three quarters of the patients, both in their ability to discern shape and colour, and in retinal clarity."

Every now and then I would garnish the literary confection with some specialist terms: "Diätetische Einschränkungen … optischer Sehnerv … Ursachen für Blindheit…" I also produced some obscure mathematical calculations about "light density" and "retinal obfuscation".

The chevalier nodded sagely, making out that he was following the argument closely, even asking me to repeat one or two passages. When I finished, I tossed the treatise onto the side table. "Thank goodness that's over. I think the racing odds made more sense."

"No, no," the chevalier said. "Don't you see what this means? We must go to Bath immediately."

"Bath?"

"To take the waters. I believe this professor is onto something."

"But he said you had to do the treatment for ninety days."

"Then we shall go for a hundred."

"And the cost, my love. Remember, you have no clients now. And this house is not cheap."

"Get rid of it. Close the house down and let us move to Bath."

"Are you serious?"

"Who needs London? It is cheaper in the provinces. We can maintain our lifestyle. We shall befriend others who are undergoing cures. There will be none of this cruel snobbery of the court gossips. And I can take the waters every day."

"You really think it could work?"

"Those Romans knew a thing or two, Arabella. There's a reason they built the baths there. Once my sight is restored, I can find new clients and resume my practice. You must make all the arrangements immediately."

It was in this flurry of enthusiasm that I took control of his finances. For how could I make all the necessary arrangements unless I could write cheques and hire solicitors and settle bills? How could I draw up a new household budget unless I had full knowledge of the chevalier's bank accountants? There were documents to be signed, old leases, new leases, quitclaims, deeds, codicils, options and waivers, and I would diligently read out the legal contracts before the chevalier signed them.

But occasionally I would 'forget' to read out an obscure clause that transferred property and money into my name. Accidents happen; I am only human, after all, and the most important thing, the thought that occupied my whole mind, was my husband's health. If there was a chance of restoring his sight, what else mattered?

I chose the house in Bath primarily for the great privacy it afforded, as I did not want curious neighbours prying into the execution of justice.

It was arranged that the chevalier would take the waters every afternoon with a designated spa-doctor, so that I could devote my time to ensuring our possessions were safely shipped down from London. As well as all the normal domestic alterations (curtains, wallpapers, and rugs), I had to supervise the special modifications in the attic. For this I engaged workmen from Gloucester, some fifty miles away, as I didn't want anyone in Bath to be aware of what I was doing; there is nothing quite as irritating as a gossiping workman. They spent a week pulling up floorboards and packing the cavities with wool and cloth to deaden the sound, then another three weeks partitioning rooms and installing special locks, chains and bars. Finally they set about hiding the staircase to the attic behind a false wall on the upper landing.

The builders asked no awkward questions, and when the work was finished, I dismissed all the domestic staff and hired a fresh team on whom I imposed a strict new routine: they were not, under any circumstances, to venture to the upper floors of the house; and, no matter what, they had to ignore the deluded ramblings of the unfortunate and tragically stricken chevalier.

Now I had to test the facility.

That afternoon, orderlies from the spa brought the chevalier to the front door and offered to help him to his bedroom. I gave them a generous tip but declined the offer.

"How were the waters?" I hugged my husband affectionately as I guided him to the stairs. "You look well."

"I do feel better. It really is quite relaxing in the steam."

"And your eyes? Is there a change?"

"I know it is early days, but there was a flicker of light, which I have not seen before."

"Excellent!"

"Where are you taking me, Arabella?"

By now we were on the upper landing.

"It's a surprise."

"Oh? How intriguing." He smiled.

"I've been planning it for a while." I clicked open the false wall and guided my husband up towards the attic.

"This was a good change for us, Arabella. I am starting to feel hope for the future."

As we reached the top landing, I kissed him tenderly. "This has brought us closer together, hasn't it?"

"You are a remarkable woman."

I swung open the door to the attic room. "Now, hold my hand, and say nothing."

The chevalier giggled like an excited child as I led him to the far wall. "Hold very still." I picked up the steel collar, opened the clasp, then clamped it round his neck and snapped the padlock shut.

"What on earth…?"

"Hush, now."

His arms reached up and felt the heavy collar. "I don't understand." He groped along the chain towards the wall where it was securely fixed.

"There are three bowls within your reach."

"What are you doing?"

"One contains water. One food. The third is for your shit."

"Arabella!"

"Try not to get them confused."

"Is this a jest? If so, I do not like it!"

"It certainly amuses me," I said, and walked back towards the door.

"Arabella! Where are you going?" Now there was panic in his voice. "Are you leaving me?"

"How could I exact revenge if I left you?"

"What is the meaning of this? Revenge for what?"

"Calm, now."

"Remove this wretched collar and chain! Explain yourself, woman!"

"Finally, Chevalier Taylor, you will get what you so richly deserve."

"Damn you! Damn you to Hell! You have lost your mind!"

"Perhaps."

"You cannot deprive me of my liberty! It is illegal and immoral!"

"Dearest husband, you did not complain when you deprived me of my liberty. You showed no remorse when you destroyed genius and butchered patients. You have given the world nothing but pain and misery. Now you must pay the price. The world must be protected … from you." I closed the door and locked it securely.

At first, I was alarmed by his screaming and cursing, for it was so loud I wondered if my plan would work. But as I walked down the stairs it became less and less noticeable, and once I clicked the false wall shut and entered the sitting room, I couldn't hear a thing. The Gloucester workmen had done their job well.

Before I went to bed, I checked on my husband. Immediately the door opened, he flew at me with uncontrolled rage, only to be jerked back by the chain-collar around his neck.

"Witch! Devil! Monstrous whore! You blinded me, didn't you? This is you! Admit it! You evil bitch!"

The ranting and raving went on for a while.

"I will have you arrested! For kidnap and torture and abuse! You will hang for this! I swear to God, you will hang!"

"Why do you shit on the floor?" I asked calmly. "I have provided a pot. Use it."

Furious, he bent down, scooped up some excrement and tried to hurl it at me, but it is not difficult to dodge a blind man's missiles.

"Clean it up," I instructed.

"You are the gaoler. You clean it up!"

"Oh no, husband. That is not how this works."

He spat at me but fell a long way short.

"Once a week I will bring you a bucket of water and a scrubbing brush."

"Go to hell! Lickspittle!"

"If you wish to roll around in your own excrement, that is your choice. But you will not leave this room if you stink of shit."

"What of my treatments? You cannot deprive me of those!"

"Once you are clean, I will take you for your treatments."

He fell silent, thinking about how that would work, but he was too obvious. Did he really think I would give him the chance to speak to someone, after all the trouble I had gone to? Now he was under my control, I was determined to keep it that way. I placed a clean bowl of drinking water on the floor. "If you knock it over, there will be no more until morning."

I watched as he lowered his face to the bowl and slurped like a dog.

"This is stale!" he bellowed.

"Oh dear. Never mind."

What I didn't tell him was that the water was heavily laced with laudanum, so that when I came to fetch him in the morning, he was drooling and incoherent. The drug made it impossible for the chevalier to reach out for help or raise the alarm.

Half-stumbling, half-walking, I got him down the stairs and into a wheelchair, then opened the door wide to let in the glorious summer morning.

I must confess I was a little tense on that first walk. Did we look suspicious? Was the chevalier really semi-conscious, or was he just waiting for his moment to betray me? As it turned out, I needn't have worried, for Bath is a city full of wrecks being wheeled by their unfortunate relatives; here the chevalier was just another broken man.

And so the Great Lie began.

Every Sunday morning we would emerge from the house to parade ourselves around the elegant streets of Bath. You may well have seen me, dressed in my finest silks, dutifully pushing the chevalier in his creaking invalid chair, his broken eyes hidden by dark glasses, his trembling fingers clutching the wrought iron handles, his head lolling onto his chest in a stupor. No-one ever suspected that he was a prisoner in plain sight. And the more broken he was, the more virtuous I appeared, the dutiful young wife tending her husband with Christian stoicism.

I was happy to exchange polite greetings with passing acquaintances, but made sure I never stopped to talk, just in case the chevalier found a way of betraying our little secret.

In the perfect elegance of the Assembly Rooms, I patiently fed my husband tea and scones, dabbing away his oozing chin-dribbles without complaint.

While the city's finest promenaded around the beautiful question mark of the Royal Crescent, I would park my burden in the shade of the ha-ha and read aloud from the classics that I knew my husband loathed.

'What a saintly wife!' the chattering classes would whisper as they glimpsed the touching tableau. 'What forbearance!'

Without fail, we would take our places in the abbey along with the upright and elegant citizens of Bath. It was always such a bore to listen to the pompous sermons, but I endured them for the music. When the deep harmonies of the organ and the soaring voices of the choir filled the abbey, I was transported to the only place I have ever found true enlightenment.

It is frighteningly easy to break a man's will. He adapts to his terrible surroundings and accepts the unacceptable because the alternatives are death or madness. What makes Purgatory so painful is that it is endless; and so it was to be for the chevalier.

Locked up, abused, alone, knowing that I was using his money to pay for concerts by the very men he had destroyed... While the music of Bach and Handel lives on, the chevalier has vanished, and I have spent many evenings burning his letters and notebooks to erase all trace of that fraudulent man from history.

So should ignorance die, wretched and forgotten.

PART SEVEN: DOCTOR HARVEY

THIRTY-TWO

It astonishes me how calm Arabella is. No-one who has made a confession so saturated in horror should be sitting this comfortably in her prison cell.

"There you have it, Dr Harvey, the truth. All of it."

Her fine features shimmer between beauty and dread ugliness. There is not a flicker of remorse on her face, no hint of self-doubt. She is like granite: polished, hard, impenetrable. Perhaps this is the true face of evil.

"Do not weep for him," she warns as if reading my mind. "Do not pity a man whose life and career have been so entirely destructive."

"He is still a man. A human being."

"I would dispute that. He has abused the innate trust humans have for each other, and that has put him beyond the bounds of pity."

"Christ died on the cross so that men could reach up, not down."

"You want to talk about God?" Arabella replies. "As I recall, Lucifer was once the most beautiful of all the angels, but when his pride and arrogance stirred him to rebellion, did God turn the other cheek? Did He forgive the sinner? No. He cast him out of Heaven and plunged him into the eternal torture of Hell. He punished Lucifer. Pitilessly He watched His beloved angel suffer. God did that."

"If you are deaf to religion, then look to the law," I counter. "That is a higher principle we must all respect. Even kings are subject to the law."

"That same law which decrees a man must be hanged for stealing twelve pennies, but which allows a lying, fraudulent aristocrat to destroy genius and butcher his patients with impunity?"

"The law is not perfect."

"It is doing nothing to help *your* people, Dr Harvey, condemned to slavery in their thousands."

"One day the law will act, and in the meantime, it protects the freedom that was granted to me."

"A very selfish attitude."

"What you have done, Arabella — cold-blooded, sadistic revenge … that is not the way."

"Some enemies you can reason with. Some you must destroy."

"However you try to disguise it, I fear God will judge you harshly."

"Bach devoted his life to God." Arabella's voice crackles with defiance. "Every note he put on the stave was to celebrate the divine. And look how God repaid him."

"It is not for us to question God."

"But I do." An enigmatic smile crosses her face. "And I want to know, is He on the side of justice? Or of ignorance?"

I look down to avoid her gaze. "You will find out soon enough."

"But where do you stand, Dr Harvey? Or are you so obsessed with being accepted by this society of hypocrites, that you have lost your courage?"

"It is irrelevant. If I do as I've been instructed, you will vanish into an asylum. If I fight for you to have a trial, you will most likely be hanged. What difference does it make?"

"There is an alternative… You could set me free."

I look at her in bewilderment. "That is not in my gift."

"But you *could* do it. I have money. You have the trust of the authorities. Between us, there is a way for me to walk out of that prison door."

"No!"

"You need to choose. We all need to choose. Whose side are you on?"

"You have put me in an impossible position, Arabella! Do I understand why you blinded him? Yes, of course. What the chevalier did was monstrous. But what you did to him…"

"Show some courage, Dr Harvey."

"I am just a city doctor, trying to get on with my life."

"But it's not easy, is it, when you don't quite belong?" She reaches out a hand and gently touches my face. "Those delicately carved features, the deep brown eyes … how many generations has it been?"

I push her fingers away. "My practice flourishes. I have plenty of clients."

"And yet I am quite possibly the only woman in this city who sees who you really are." Slowly she walks around me. "Those beautiful women in the elegant ballrooms … so unreachable in their perfection… How you long for them. And though you fascinate them with your exotic looks, they would never touch you."

"Stop this." I try to move away, but she takes my face in her hands.

"Whereas I see a man of integrity. And compassion. A man who respects his professional vows. A humanitarian. A true doctor, unlike the wretched man to whom I'm married."

I look down, trying to stop her peering any deeper into my soul. "You are asking too much of me," I whisper.

"You and I, Dr Harvey. It is down to people like you and I to act. The outsiders. Without us, there will never be justice in the world."

I step back from her, finally breaking the spell. "I'm afraid you have missed the point, Arabella. You see, for my entire life, I have tried *not* to be an outsider. I cannot throw all that away."

"Look in the mirror, Dr Harvey. You will never truly belong. And you know it."

The walk home doesn't clear my head — quite the opposite. Every footstep sharpens my predicament and deepens the conflicting thoughts pulling at my mind.

As I enter the hallway, I hear a woman's laughter coming from the drawing room. I check my watch; it's too late for patients. As I glance up, I see Joseph standing on the stairs. He mouths the word 'Sorry.'

I take off my hat and push open the drawing room door. The chevalier is sitting in a chair by the fire, cooing with pleasure as a young woman snuggles on his lap, stroking his hair. She has too much rouge, too much cleavage, and is clearly one of the professional women who no-one mentions, but who make Bath such an attractive leisure destination for men with money.

"I think it's time you went," I say sharply.

Startled, she turns to look at me. "What's it to you?"

"This is my house."

"Oh." She pauses as she tries to understand, then turns to the chevalier. "But you said —"

"Best you run along, my dear," the chevalier interrupts. "We'll pick this up another time."

"Will we now?" she says coquettishly, and gives him a long, lingering kiss.

I clear my throat, indicating my annoyance, but she takes her time. Reluctantly she uncurls herself from his lap, picks up the money he's left on the side table, then walks out of the room.

"Can someone call me a carriage?" she demands from the hall.

"Get out!" I can't hide my anger any longer.

"Charming," she mutters, and slams the front door behind her.

"Quite the prig, aren't you?" the chevalier says as he buttons up his breeches.

"Can you think of nothing except your own sordid desires?"

"You're very emotional tonight, Dr Harvey. I thought you'd be pleased to see me on the road to recovery."

"I have just come from your wife, languishing in prison. Her life is in ruins because of you."

"Quite the reverse, I'd say. *She* is the problem."

"Her confession has left me wondering how true that is."

"Really?"

I watch the reflection of the fire in his dark glasses. "I have grave doubts about you, Chevalier."

"Try and keep a sense of reason. You're only there to establish the facts."

"Oh, I have plenty of facts. More than you would like. Far more."

"So, when will she be carted off to the asylum?"

I remain silent, and for the first time I see doubt on the chevalier's face.

"There is nothing to agonise over," he declares. "Banish her into oblivion!"

"It's more complicated than that."

"You are mistaken, sir! There is nothing complicated about wantonly blinding your husband, imprisoning him, and torturing him for your own pleasure." He reaches a hand towards me. "Come here!"

"No."

"She's got to you, hasn't she? Admit it."

"Her confession is persuasive."

"You are a fool, Harvey."

"Coming from you, I'll take that as a compliment."

"What fantastic story has she concocted this time? What self-pitying nonsense has she dreamt up to dodge her fate?"

"It did not seem like nonsense to me."

"You do know she had a breakdown in Cologne, and another in London? There is a deluded side to that woman. Beneath all those fine clothes, she is utterly mad."

"You fear her, don't you?"

He turns away from me, letting the warmth of the fire play on his face. "I have nothing to fear. I am the victim of a terrible crime, and no matter what she says, Arabella will be destroyed. One way or another."

"Yet if this went to trial —"

"That will never happen. I have been given assurances."

"If the truth does come out, your fall from grace will be savage."

"Have you heard of the Moon Paradox, Dr Harvey? It is one of the oldest optical illusions in history, and one of the first things they teach you when you train to become an oculist. It asks, *Why is the moon so much larger on the horizon than when it is high in the sky?* Of course, it is nonsense. The moon does not change in size over the course of the night. It's impossible, but people will swear blind that it does change. Why? Because people do not care about facts or mathematics or geometry;

they only care for what they can see with their own stupid eyes. Whatever confession Arabella makes will vanish as if it was written on water, because her truth counts for nothing. She will always be a felon. And who believes a felon? History will remember my story, because I will write it. I have control over how it will be handed down. And as every optical illusion reminds us, deception is real; the truth is not."

I can feel anger grinding inside me. "If that is all you have learnt as an oculist, then you are a disgrace to your profession."

The chevalier scoffs. "You are just a provincial quack, whereas I am a well-travelled surgeon of international repute. Who do you think the world will listen to?"

"A fool who travels, remains a fool."

The chevalier shakes his head. "I should have known better than to expect someone like you to understand. After all, that is why England has conquered the world, while deep down, you people will never be more than chee-chees in dirty rags."

The slur punches me in the gut. "You are blind. How can you possibly know what I am?"

He senses my disgust, and smirks. "I can smell it on you, Dr Harvey. We all can."

Stunned by the insult, I am unable to move.

He grabs my arm and pulls me close. "Commit my wife to the asylum by tomorrow night," he whispers, "or I will inform the marquess of Lansdowne that you have abused your position of trust to obtain sexual favours from her. A sordid act which has fatally compromised your judgement."

I jerk my arm free from his grip.

"That would soon put an end to your charade of playing the white man."

There is nothing more I can say to this man. He has condemned himself with his own mouth. Any doubts I may have had are finally blown away like a cobweb in the breeze.

"Wake up, Harvey. Those in power will always favour me over you," he smirks.

He's right. No matter what I say, the Birds of Prey will never let this scandal get to a court of law. They would rather have Arabella murdered in her cell.

THIRTY-THREE

I arrive at the prison early; I need to do this now before fear clouds my thinking. The gaoler closes the cell door leaving me alone with Arabella, but I wait until I hear the key turn in the lock before I speak.

"You must vanish. Get out of Bath, get out of England. Disappear and never return."

She looks at me warily. "The authorities have agreed to this?"

"No."

"So there will be a fat bribe to pay."

"I don't want your money. I don't want anything from you, except that you disappear."

"I wish it was that simple." Arabella puts her fingers to her temples as she tries to think through the ramifications. "You cannot let me escape unless you deal with the chevalier as well. He will surely hire assassins to hunt me down."

"I fear he will be too busy trying to destroy *me*."

Arabella looks at me searchingly. "What if *you* were to silence him, Dr Harvey? With some judicious medication?"

"I am not a murderer."

"Just a thought." She shrugs.

"Is life really so cheap to you?"

"Apologies. I was thinking aloud."

She says it as lightly as if she had just stepped on my toes at a dance; it is unnerving. "What the chevalier did, how you punished him … that is a world of darkness I never want to witness again."

"You think I wanted any part of it?" Her voice rises in agitation. "All my life I have reached for enlightenment, only to be dragged down by ignorance. When I was suffocating in darkness, I did what I had to, or I would have been destroyed."

"Why do you pick a fight with me? I am trying to give you another chance."

A clanking sound in the corridor outside — other inmates are slopping out, and we fall silent until the guard's footsteps pass.

"The only solution is that the chevalier and I must both vanish." Arabella regains her composure as she focuses on what needs to be done.

"I am a doctor, not a magician."

"Fortunately, Dr Harvey, we live in a country where the ruling class has perfected the art of making inconvenient obstacles disappear. Idiot sons and mad daughters are whisked away in the middle of the night. They vanish into convents and monasteries, which are generously rewarded for their discretion."

"Now you really do sound like the Keeper of the Beehives."

"It's common knowledge in the circles of power, but no-one dares speak of it. How could the royal blood that rules over an empire produce weakness and infirmity? It is unthinkable, so it cannot be allowed. There is a well-oiled mechanism for dealing with such wrinkles, and that is how we shall dispose of the chevalier."

Secretly I am impressed by Arabella's ingenuity. I imagine a world with the chevalier gone; a world that no longer has to fear his threats and ignorance and entitlement. "Do you know someone who could arrange such a thing?"

"Give me pen and paper. I will write to a lawyer in London to set things in motion."

"You'll need to be quick. Be ready to leave here tomorrow night."

"It's too soon."

"That's as long as we have, or the chevalier will…" I hesitate. Should I tell her of his threat? Or would that make me more vulnerable? "It's tomorrow or never."

"In which case, tomorrow will be perfect." She looks at me with genuine gratitude.

For a few moments her defences are down, and I glimpse a softness in her face.

"Where will you go?" I ask. "Once the chevalier is taken care of?"

"I will effectively be widowed. A free woman." She steps towards me, holding my gaze. "Perhaps I can finally start to live."

"Alone?"

Her eyes flutter over my face as if she is assessing me. "Why do you ask?"

We look at each other in silence.

What man could possibly be up to the task of making this woman happy? She seems to exist in a world of her own, to follow rules that only she understands.

Slowly she leans closer and gently kisses me.

"Don't be afraid," she whispers.

Suddenly, a key clatters in the door. Immediately Arabella backs away.

"Slops and shit!" the guard yells. "Slops and shit!"

Obediently, Arabella reaches for her bucket.

The long hours drag. I find it impossible to focus on work. Patients come and go. I hear them talk, I nod and smile, I offer sympathy and prescribe tinctures, but everything now seems anaemic. My life as a respectable doctor feels precarious and fragile, like an intricate model of someone else's life.

Arabella terrifies me, and yet a part of me envies her. She has lived with such full-throated passion it makes me question every choice I've made.

And now she is inviting me in.

All I have to do is find the courage to throw away what I have so meticulously built.

Finally dusk falls, and the plan is set in motion. I drug the chevalier's wine with a dose of laudanum which quickly renders him compliant, then Joseph and I lift him into the carriage and secure his hands with manacles.

We park in the shadows outside the prison, away from prying eyes; I enter alone and present a formal letter to the constable.

He reads it slowly, then reads it again. "Released into your custody, Dr Harvey?" He scratches his beard. "This is most irregular."

"She is not a regular felon."

"And at this time of night?" He shakes his heavy head. "I'm sorry, sir. This needs to wait until morning." He thrusts the letter back at me, but I refuse to take it.

"Write your objection on the letter, Constable. Sign it with your name, and I will personally deliver it to the marquess of Lansdowne."

The constable hesitates. "I'm only doing my job."

"As am I."

"A man can't be punished for doing his job."

"If only that were true. But performing your duties and following orders are not always the same thing."

"What do you mean?" He looks anxious.

"I'm sure the marquess will explain it to you in person when you are summoned to account for your insubordination."

"Insubord…" He blinks.

I have put this honest, plodding man, who has spent his whole life being obedient, in an impossible position. That a part of me enjoys it is a warning: perhaps I have already spent too long with Arabella.

"Of course," I add, lowering my voice and taking the poor man into my confidence, "if you think of this as a chance to prove your personal loyalty to the marquess, then I am sure he will find a way of showing his gratitude."

It works.

The constable isn't happy, but he unlocks the cell door and lets me walk out of the prison with Arabella in my charge.

I guide her through the shadows. She opens the carriage door and sees the chevalier, drooling, his hands manacled.

"You're sure he's drugged enough?" she says warily.

I show her the bottle of laudanum. "It's all I have, but it should be enough to keep him quiet until you're on the ship."

"You're not coming with me?" Her vulnerability catches me off guard.

"Arabella, how can I rest until I know for sure the monster has left the country?" I offer my hand to help her up.

The carriage jolts and sways as we speed towards London along the recently turnpiked roads. We make swift progress, and manage to pass through the various toll booths without arousing suspicion. As long as the chevalier appears to be sleeping, we will get away with this.

Little is said on the journey. What can you say to a woman who has made such a terrible confession? And yet for all that, there is still so much that is unknowable about Arabella.

I sleep fitfully, grabbing as much rest as the lurching carriage allows, but she never gives in to tiredness. Her eyes are fixed on the sweeping darkness outside. It is just as the prison guards said: she defies sleep.

THIRTY-FOUR

"Let's get to work, Dr Harvey."

I wake with a start and struggle to find my bearings. We are in London, in the heart of the legal district.

"Stay with him." Arabella gestures towards the semi-conscious chevalier. "Just in case."

"Where are you going?"

"To get everything finalised." She is sharp and crisp, unruffled by the bruising coach journey. Her resilience is astonishing.

She disappears into a sombre building in Stonecutter Street, but as I watch the bewigged lawyers walking to their chambers, I become acutely aware that I am in the company of a fugitive from justice and an abducted aristocrat. Quickly I pull the blinds across the carriage windows, hoping that everyone is too busy to pay attention.

After what seems like an age, Arabella returns, carrying a small portfolio of documents. "Here is our new life."

"And you really trust this lawyer?"

"He knows better than to ask questions that would result in him not getting paid." She opens the flap in the roof canopy and instructs the driver to take us to Hatton Garden.

As we bump through the streets, she studies the documents: identity papers, sterling bonds, stock certificates, a letter of introduction to Berenberg Bank in Nuremberg.

"We will be well provided for, Dr Harvey," she says with quiet satisfaction. "Never underestimate the greed of a charlatan."

In the jewellery quarter we track down the goldsmith who bought the Eye Waggon all those months ago. He has converted it into a high security vehicle for shipping valuables; what used to be the operating room is now a large strongbox reinforced with iron bars and multiple padlocks.

"This is perfect." Arabella's eyes glint when she sees it. She makes a generous offer to the goldsmith, who puts on a great show of hardship as the prelude to a negotiation. Within the hour, Arabella has secured not just the waggon, but the driver to go with it, and we make our way in convoy to the Pool of London.

In an alley off Shad Thames, we transfer our load: the chevalier is imprisoned in what used to be his operating theatre, drugged and chained inside his own creation.

"But you and I can sleep in here." Arabella opens the door to the living quarters behind the driver's perch. "The lawyer has arranged a passage to Calais for both of us, leaving on the high tide."

She beckons for me to climb into the carriage, but I hesitate.

"It's more comfortable than it looks," she reassures. "We travelled across Europe in this."

I gaze at the dark, plush interior that promises so much. Temptation is drawing me into her world, where all the rules that have held me in check will be swept away, where every dark desire can find a home without shame.

"Make the leap," she whispers. "I will catch you."

And suddenly I realise that Arabella is a woman who has obtained everything she ever wanted, while in her wake she has left a trail of broken husbands. Is she the victim? Or the true villain?

I take the bottle from my pocket and hand it to her. "When the laudanum wears off, he may have a violent reaction."

"But you will be with me."

"No. He is your problem now."

"So you've decided."

I cannot put myself at the mercy of her unknowable nature. I cannot.

For a moment she looks hurt. "You are so wrong, Dr Harvey." She lifts a hand to my face; her fingers are warm on my skin. "It is not me you need to fear."

Arabella leans forward to kiss me, but this time I recoil. I don't trust myself. I am one kiss away from abandoning everything I have built. And for what? Who knows if she will ever find happiness; maybe her destiny is to be defined by revenge.

"I wish I had your courage, Arabella."

"You've made your choice. And I respect you for that." She retreats behind her polished veneer, out of reach once again. "But please, spare me the sentimental goodbyes."

"I hope you find forgiveness. Maybe even salvation."

"I'll take my chances with God." She shrugs. "But perhaps I can still find peace."

"I hope so."

"Who knows?" she says breezily. "I am still young enough to become a mother. Maybe I could start a family of my own."

I wonder at the thought; imagine having Arabella as your mother.

"You are a good man, Dr Harvey."

"I'm not so sure."

Then she turns, climbs into the carriage and is gone.

THIRTY-FIVE

It feels like a lifetime since I last sat in the bookless East Library of Lansdowne Hall, facing the three Birds of Prey. The marquess stares at me over his spectacles.

"Vanished?"

"Indeed, my lord. The problem has vanished," I reply.

"What exactly do you mean?"

"Both parties have gone, never to be seen again. Neither in this city, nor in England."

"That is not what we instructed."

Lansdowne glances at Viscount Melville, who is not so indulgent. "You have overstepped the mark, Harvey."

"You wanted to protect the reputation of this city —"

"That does not make you judge and jury."

"My lords, there was no way of resolving this case without doing considerable damage."

"Damage to whom?"

"To every aristocrat in the country. To the reputation of the medical profession. And to King George himself."

"That is precisely why we wanted the woman locked away in an asylum," Melville insists. "Silenced."

"The chevalier may have been the victim, but he wasn't innocent," I say in my defence. "If anything, his crimes were worse than hers."

"But we had no intention of pursuing the chevalier," Lansdowne says pointedly. "So that is not an issue."

"Unless *you* intended to make trouble." Melville looks at me with his small, hard eyes.

"My lords, I had hoped it would not be necessary to mention this, but the chevalier was planning to blackmail you."

"Us? For what?"

I feign reluctance.

"Come on, Harvey. Spit it out."

"The chevalier claimed to have met a man while he was taking the waters, a notorious cardsharp, who boasted that he had taught one of your lordships how to cheat at whist." I watch them shuffle in their chairs, and I wonder if my lie has inadvertently hit home. "And he said that ever since, one of you has been cheating the other two." Furtive glances flit between them as mistrust takes root. "Thankfully, with the chevalier gone, no such slanders will ever surface." I smile.

"*We* are not the point!" Lansdowne says with a firm voice, trying to regain the moral high ground.

"Quite." Stratford chimes in. "Dreadful crimes have been committed, yet no-one has been hanged, or publicly humiliated, or fallen into disgrace. That is unacceptable!"

I remain silent, waiting for their anger to subside. "Trust me, gentlemen," I say finally, "it is better this way. The chevalier and his wife were as bad as each other. Now that both have vanished into thin air, we don't have to worry about either."

"That is no longer the point," Lansdowne frowns. "We gave you specific instructions, and you have disobeyed us."

"I thought it was for the better, my lord."

"We don't care what you think. Only what you do. It is most disappointing."

"You will suffer for this, Harvey. Mark my words." The earl of Stratford relishes passing judgement on me.

I have had enough of their games. "Are you really going to throw a respected doctor in gaol? How would that look in the elegant salons of Bath? Punish me, and you will only escalate this scandal."

Lansdowne allows himself a small, patronising chuckle. "You have got the wrong end of the stick entirely, Dr Harvey. We have far more effective ways of punishing you than gaol." He waves his hand to indicate that the audience is over. A servant opens the library door. I have no choice but to leave.

Over the coming weeks I discover precisely what the marquess meant. One by one, my wealthier patients start to fall away, invitations to dinner parties dry up, and I find myself excluded from the guest lists to galleries and concerts. It is a slow death. I can survive with fewer patients as I have modest tastes, but it's clear I will no longer thrive in this city.

How different it would have been had I tugged my forelock and done as I was instructed. Instead I chose to follow the truth. But men like Lansdowne will never understand that, because the truth is irrelevant when you own half the country.

I regret the waning of my practice, but I do not regret helping Arabella escape. She acted without flinching; she may be the cruellest woman I have ever met, but a part of me cannot help admiring her.

So I shall lower my gaze and focus on those patients who remain loyal, one ailment at a time. I shall embrace the minutiae of the day-to-day and remain grateful for the mediocrity of existence.

Yet just beneath the surface, Arabella still haunts my heart. When I wake in the small hours, my mind circles back to her, like a planet drawn into the orbit of a dark sun.

Where is she now?

What if I had stepped into that carriage with her?

Would I have finally discovered what it means to live a life with passion?

Or would I have woken one morning to find myself the victim of some biblical vengeance for an injustice I had unwittingly inflicted upon her?

Tonight I find myself wandering up the hill to her old house. It is stuck in time, exactly as she left it, for it cannot be sold without Arabella's legal instruction, and she has vanished. A light is burning in the kitchen window — a scullery maid visits once a week to make sure the rats have not found a way into the larders. She lets me in without question.

I wander from room to room, marvelling at the cold sterility of the façade Arabella created, until I find myself in the library. As I read the titles on the spines, once again I can feel the passion that drove her to rise above ignorance, and the haunting loneliness she found on her quest.

I pick up a musical score containing a collection of Bach partitas. At some point she must have tried to learn them, for the first few pages are heavily marked with fingering and phrase lines. The effortless complexity of the music must have defeated her, for she barely got beyond the first piece.

Yet on the very final page, written in a neat hand beneath the staves, are two simple words: *The Longing*.

POSTSCRIPT

It is a year since I finished writing this account and stowed it safely in my desk. But this morning a letter arrived. Once again my peace of mind has been thrown into turmoil.

It is from her.

Dear Dr Harvey,

I had forgotten how cold Prague is in the winter. After the longest journey, we arrived in the city at twilight just as the wind was turning, barrelling up from the Vltava in biting blasts. The snowfall was so heavy and silent, it was hypnotic. Perhaps that's why the residents are always so quick to retreat behind their ancient stone walls.

Correspondence with various Church authorities, together with a generous bequest to the Vatican Treasury, finally secured a 'permanent facility' for the chevalier at the Carmelite Convent in Prague.

The convent sits in the shadow of the castle walls, and the approach to it is reassuringly forbidding; our carriage wheels slipped dangerously on icy cobbles as we struggled up an impossibly steep hill to reach it.

Finally, we came to rest outside the gates just as the bell tolled for compline. One of the nuns who was closing the shutters saw us arrive, and immediately called for help. A small group of sisters emerged and battled through the snow towards us.

I unlocked the padlocks on the waggon and slid the bolts. "You may want to stand back," I warned the sisters.

Then I swung open the door and a nauseous smell punched out into the cold air. When the laudanum was finished, the chevalier went into a lengthy period of toxic withdrawal, throwing himself against the walls of the strongbox, clawing at his own flesh, slamming his head onto the floor.

Now his wounds were infected, and he had sunk into a fever. The stench was so bad, it tested even these devoted Sisters of the Lord.

But they had been given their instructions from the cardinal, and they obediently lifted the stricken chevalier onto a stretcher and took him down to a secure room in the cellars.

I handed the Letter & Warrant to the abbess, who checked them carefully. "He is weak and poorly," she said disapprovingly. "But we can heal him."

"That's good," I replied. "It has been a difficult journey."

"He'll find a good home here."

"With all due respect, that is not the intention." I pointed to a specific clause in the warrant. "Under no circumstances is he to be let out. No matter how long he lives."

"I do understand the concept of obedience," the abbess replied coldly. "We have done this sort of thing before."

"Your reputation is second to none," I smiled.

"You can leave now. Or you can stay for a few days as our guest, until you are ready to resume your journey." The abbess turned her attention back to the warrant. "It makes no difference to me."

A novice arrived to take me to my room, but as she led me past the chapel, I heard the most haunting voice echoing along the stone corridor. It was an aria, the same one that I had first heard in Leipzig.

It was the music of Bach.

I stopped at the open doors and gazed in; a solitary nun was standing by the altar, her eyes closed, singing from the depths of her soul.

It was the moment I understood that I had finally come to rest. Why should I ever leave this place? What was there outside these walls that could possibly be more beautiful than Bach?

At first the abbess was wary of me, but after a suitable display of devotion I was accepted into their order. It is a relief to finally be liberated from the tyranny of material possessions. All my life I have struggled to *find security, only to now discover that true strength comes from having nothing at all.*

To be honest, the religion is a chore. The routine is dull. The constant prayer tests my knees, and my conviction that God is at best cruel and vindictive, at worst non-existent, has not changed.

But the music…

The music within these walls is all the salvation I require, and I would live any number of lies to remain immersed in such sublime beauty.

There is no sound that nourishes my soul as much as Bach.

Actually, perhaps that is not quite true…

For when I wake in the small hours, occasionally I hear a distant wail of pain and anger drifting up from the cellars. It is the chevalier, howling like a dying dog, bemoaning his tragic lot.

And then I smile, close my eyes, and fall into a deep sleep, listening to the music of his misery.

A NOTE TO THE READER

Stay away from eyes!

This was one of the first pieces of advice given to me when I became a full-time writer. People get very anxious about eyes, they make a terrible subject for jokes, and any hint that eyes may be harmed often causes people to recoil.

This was clearly going to be a problem writing *Requiem of Revenge*, but the reason I pressed on is that fourteen years ago I had extensive retinal surgery on my right eye, and felt I could write about this from the heart. I vividly remember going through the gamut of emotions, from fear of the dark curtain drawing across my vision, to the sense of dread on learning what is involved in eye surgery.

Perhaps this is one of the reasons I was so fascinated when I stumbled on the story of Chevalier John Taylor lurking in the footnotes of history. I always listen to music when I write, and Bach and Handel are two of my favourite composers, so to discover that they met a similar fate at the hands of the same man was shocking and compelling. The more I researched the fraudulent eye surgeon, the more resonances I found with the modern world: the obsession with spin, the triumph of deception, the casual disregard for truth, and the amount of havoc that is caused by charlatans who always manage to slip through the fingers of justice.

Although this is a fictionalised account, the most shocking elements of this story are all true. For economy and dramatic effect, some characters have been combined and some fictional bridges have been constructed to tie elements together. But the shameless, destructive charlatan at the centre of this story is completely authentic. Dr Johnson, who knew the chevalier personally, said of him, "Taylor was the most ignorant man I ever knew … he was an instance of how far impudence will carry ignorance." The chevalier's utter lack of self-awareness is recorded in his own memoirs when he declares, "To a genius, nothing is impossible. What statues, sirs, what columns shall be reared to me!"

Nothing, however, had prepared me for a very strange twist of fate…

When I was deep in the middle of revisions for this manuscript, my right eye suddenly became sore and bloodshot. It turns out that some fragments of lens tissue left behind after the original operation have managed to break free and journey through the pupil, and are now trapped between the cornea and the iris.

Brilliant, highly trained surgeons have stepped in to sort the problem out, and writing this book has made me appreciate their immense skill more than ever. But the timing of all this has triggered a battle in my mind: while the Human Me is anxious, Author Me is celebrating the opportunity to witness eye surgery from a patient's point of view, incision by incision (the first operation was performed under a general anaesthetic). This detail could then be put straight into the final draft of the manuscript — how much more authentic can you get?

But the crucial question throws me:

Surgeon: *Would you prefer a local anaesthetic or a general?*

Author Me: *Local! I want to experience every moment!*

Human Me: *Hang on a second… How complicated is it going to be?*

Surgeon: *Well, the anterior chamber is straightforward, but there is also some lens material in the posterior chamber, and we won't really know how tricky that will be until we get in there.*

Author Me: *Ooh. This is gold dust. What a thing to experience. This is True Research!*

Human Me: *Wait, wait. 'Tricky' in a medical context might not be such a good thing. Will there be just the one incision?*

Surgeon: *Actually, we'll need to make three incisions; two in the cornea, one in the sclera.*

I know what this means. My mind goes back to the retinal surgery, when the eyeball was punctured in three places to facilitate the operation. This is not trivial… Do I really want to be conscious through the whole thing? Or do I want to embrace the miracle of general anaesthetic and let the procedure pass in a moment?

As I write this, I am just a few days away from the operation, still wondering whether I should listen to Author Me or Human Me…

Either way, thank you for coming on this journey. I hope you've enjoyed reading the novel as much as I've enjoyed writing it, and I would love to hear your thoughts. If you have time to post a review on **Amazon** or **Goodreads**, that would be great, or if you'd rather give me feedback through social media, here are the links.

Website: www.RichardKurti.com
Instagram: RichardKurtiWriter
X (Twitter): @Richard_Kurti

Sapere Books is an exciting new publisher of brilliant fiction and popular history.

To find out more about our latest releases and our monthly bargain books visit our website:
saperebooks.com

Printed in Great Britain
by Amazon

49074015R00165